G000123762

BARRACUDA SWARM

A NOVEL BY EDWARD J. MCFADDEN III

SEVERED PRESS
HOBART TASMANIA

BARRACUDA SWARM

"Time is a thief. It steals our memory, our hopes, and our strength, leaving only the sense there's never enough of it." — Clive Cussler, The Solomon Curse

(RIP Clive Cussler - July 15, 1931 – February 24, 2020)

1

The twelve-foot wood skiff pushed through the calm Caribbean Sea, its old ten horsepower outboard clawing at the still water, the beater puffing and farting, the sound like machinegun fire in the deep of night. Shards of moonlight cast long finger-like shadows across the inky sea, and stars blinked through gaps in the cloud cover. A gentle breeze brought the scent of hibiscus, rotten fish, and salt. To the east, the lights of Tetu Island sparkled like an oasis in the blackness, the faint tinkle of reggae music floating on the wind like a siren's song.

Scar smiled. The party never ended on Tetu.

He sat on the skiff's gunnel, holding on with one hand, the other working the outboard's control arm. The old Johnson wheezed and popped as he eased up on the throttle, the whine of the motor fading, the vibration running through the old boat dying away. The boat skipped and hopped as it cut through a band of whitewater, and Scar turned the boat to starboard, away from Boot Tip shoals. Every five seconds the sea bloomed with light as the lighthouse marked Boot Tip Point, and the eyes of stunned sea creatures stared up through the clear water. His long gray hair was pulled back in a ponytail, but rebellious strands blew across his face, tickling his nose, and wind-tears dripped from his eyes as he peered into the darkness. The white beach poppies on his faded Hawaiian shirt glowed in the moonlight, green clouds of pale light leaking from the scopes of the night vision binoculars hanging around his neck.

He put the motor in neutral, and the skiff rocked to a stop, the boat's wake slapping the transom, lifting and pushing the craft forward on the tiny swell. Scar looked through the binoculars, scanning the horizon to the southwest.

Kraken Island, as named by the locals, was a dark mound to the west. Not a single light shone in the blackness, but Scar knew the place was churning like a swarm of bees. He let the binoculars fall to his chest, the plastic lanyard digging into his neck. The private unnamed island was owned by Sir Javier

Ratson, a billionaire whose shipping and fishing empire stretched across the globe, touching every ocean and bay. Scar believed Ratson and his various businesses were responsible for the wave of pollution that had infected the waters around Tetu, but because the man was connected in the British and American governments, all Scar's warnings and accusations had fallen on deaf ears.

It was time to get proof. Then the authorities wouldn't be able to ignore him.

Scar put the motor in gear, twisted the throttle control, and the boat pushed through the ocean like a brick. He changed course, pointing the bow of the skiff at Kraken Island. The wind swirled and sea spray arced over the gunnel. Scar ducked to avoid being doused in the face and caught a whiff of his own body odor. He crinkled his nose. It had been a few days since he'd taken a shower, but it was his clothes that smelled. There was nothing that couldn't be washed off his body with sand and a simple skinny-dip in the bath-like Caribbean Sea, but getting laundry soap, going to the laundromat, it all took so much time.

The current picked-up, tugging on the boat and pulling it south. Scar killed the motor, but left it down so he could steer. He slid from the gunnel and pressed his back to the side of the boat, watching two seagulls as they wheeled overhead in the starlight.

The strait between Tetu and Kraken Islands was deep; the current swift, and Scar's skiff slid along at five knots, silent as a seagull fart and just as invisible.

Kraken Island took shape as Scar peered through the binoculars, the green hazy glow revealing nothing. The Caribbean Sea popped and snapped against the boat, and the skiff listed slightly as it was dragged along. He yawned, his face tight with dried seawater, eyes stinging with weariness and rum, his back reminding him he was too old to be playing spy like a kid. He was sixty-one. This wasn't his world anymore, yet here he was, trying to save it from a bunch of rich, entitled shitbirds that used his home like a toilet and left a mess behind when they jetted back to their posh pads in New York and London.

Scar rolled his shoulders, Drake's voice echoing in his head. "Without tourists, how would we make money? The island wouldn't survive. You'd be living in a cardboard box," his boss would often say.

Tetu Island sits between the US Virgin Islands and the British Virgin Islands, at 18.057 degrees north by -64.609 degrees west. The tropical paradise was discovered by Frenchman, Pierre Belain, who named the twelve square mile island Tetu, which means 'stubborn' in French, because he and his crew couldn't agree about whether they should stop at the island. The French had been unable to hold the island, and after it passed through a short period of self-rule, the 'bastard' Virgin Island was jointly taken by the US and the British, and the border split the island right down its center, though people moved freely between both regions as though ruled by one democracy.

Kraken Island was a mile to the west, a large dark stain on the horizon. Scar worked the motor's control arm, the silent engine squeaking as it spun on its mount. The skiff floated north and slowed as it eased out of the current.

The rattle of chain flowing over wood, the splash of the anchor hitting the water, and the squeak and buzz of the anchor line as it ran over the gunnel brought Scar familiar comfort. The small claw anchor bit into the sandy bottom, and the boat jerked to a stop, ripples of whitewater bubbling around the boat's waterline.

A school of fish zipped through a window of moonlight, their scales glistening like diamonds in the churning water. The sea gurgled and snapped as the school rushed past, and Scar thought the fish were grunts because they had blue stripes, but he couldn't be sure. Whatever the creatures were, they were moving fast, as if fleeing.

The faint sound of surf rolling onto the beach, the rattle and scrape as shells were dragged over sand and stones, and the faint whistle of the wind lulled Scar toward sleep. He stretched, brought the binoculars to his eyes, and focused on the cove notched in the leeward side of Kraken Island where most of the island's activity took place. The island was only a mile long from the shoals on its northern tip, to its southern end, and half that distance from its windward side to its sullen and serine western shore. The cove was still, no lights split the darkness, but as Scar scanned the shoreline, he saw guards walking on the dark beaches that gave way to mangroves, and then to a forest of candlewood mixed with Caribbean pines.

For appearances, Scar put out a line, his small red and white bobber floating away from the boat with the current, disappearing and reappearing in the sea ripples. He positioned his black camera case next to him for easy access, took the final pull of water, and settled in to wait for sunup.

Scar was startled from a thin veil of half-sleep, and he bumped his elbow on the gunnel, his back going rigid. He squeaked in pain as he lifted the binoculars. Kraken Island was still silent. In the east, a bruised horizon marked the coming of day. He rolled his shoulders, and shook himself, chasing away sleep.

Something surged through the sea to the west, a thunderous roar echoing over the ocean. A fist of whitewater rolled toward the skiff like rapids, thousands of small whitecaps shifting and undulating.

Scar realized it wasn't a single beast, but a school of fish. Maybe dolphins? What else swam in schools and were big enough to make such a ruckus?

The stench of rotting flesh filled the air as the field of whitewater approached, thousands of tiny black eyes and white teeth glinting in the turbulent water. The beasts climbed and mounded on each other like a tightly wound ball of twine, all the slender blade-like predators biting and pulling, trying to lead the swarm. Knife-like snouts filled with teeth appeared in the mass of fish and were turned under an instant later as the horde writhed and twisted.

"Barracuda," Scar muttered to himself. "What the hell?" Barracuda were antisocial beasts that rarely traveled together.

The school of slender predators surged and slithered over one another, creating a churning sea of teeth that rolled over the surface. Fish upon fish, scales shining in the pale light, their eyes aglow with hatred and hunger. Thousands of the large, predatory, ray-finned fish swelled over the surface, jumping from the water, jaws snapping.

The swarm broke on the bow of the skiff like a wave, Barracuda slamming into the boat and bubbling over the gunnel.

Scar kicked and stomped at fish as they flopped in the bottom of the skiff, jaws biting, black, red-rimmed eyes shining in the moonlight. He punted one off the boat, but another almost got him, Scar knocking it away at the last instant. The fish hit the gunnel and landed on the deck, the Barracuda spasming in its death throes, jaws closing on his foot which only had a flipflop for protection. He stifled a scream, grabbed the fish by the tail, and tossed it overboard. Tiny red dots of blood blossomed on the top of Scar's foot, puncture marks from the Barracuda's needle-like teeth. If the beast hadn't been sucking for air, half his foot would be gone.

The last fish was running out of air, and it flopped and tossed around the deck. Scar went to kick it overboard, but paused.

Barracuda eyes usually looked glassy black with a white ring, but this creature had red stripes running around the outside of its eyes. The creature's chest rose and fell, its wet eyes bulging and going wide as it took its final breaths.

The Caribbean Sea erupted all around the skiff, Barracuda driving themselves into the wood boat, climbing over each other like ants, and launching from the water like guided missiles with teeth and powerful jaws.

The Barracuda in the skiff went still. The roar of the swarm was like a massive wave, the hiss and snap of a thousand biting jaws echoing over the sea. An ache settled in Scar's back and cold dread seeped through his extremities.

The school of Barracuda circled the boat, the current caused by the beasts spinning the skiff in a circle as the creatures attacked and bit at the boat.

Scar's head jerked frantically as he tried to watch all sides. Fish launched through the air and slithered over each other, all hammering at the boat with one purpose as if controlled by one mind.

The pop and crack of wood splintering echoed over the sea, and a thin stream of water ran into the boat.

The ravenous swarm took turns making strafing runs at the skiff. Scar dodged and avoided fish as they launched from the sea and climbed over each other like maggots eager to get an entire corpse for themselves. The creatures came on with an intensity and fury Scar had never seen. Barracuda were known for their ferocious behavior, but he'd never seen them work together to take down prey. Adults of most species are basically solitary, but young and half-grown Barracuda do frequently congregate. But full-sized adults? Cooperating?

A board snapped and popped free, the thin stream of seawater spraying into the boat becoming a torrent. Scar pressed his hands to the hole, willing the leak to stop, but clear water ran through his fingers, filling the boat.

A gray dawn inched over the clear Caribbean Sea, bringing the light of day.

The thunder of the pounding swarm lessoned, and the turbulent sea flattened as the school of Barracuda disappeared into the depths.

Scar sat, his heart running at 4000RPM, pain splitting his head, mouth dry as flour.

It was then he heard the faint buzz of an outboard, and the slap and rumble of a boat coming in his direction. Ratson's men were a nuisance, but judging by the amount of water pouring into the skiff, he needed them tonight. Scar threw a towel over his camera case and picked up his fishing pole. The lure was bitten off, but he held the pole anyway, gazing north, his back to the approaching boat.

The rumble of the outboard grew, and Scar glanced over a shoulder.

A boat emerged from the gloom, its NAV light sending red and green daggers across the still sea, the white all-around light atop the cabin illuminating the deck around the pilothouse.

"Ahoy." Two figures stood veiled in shadow beside the pilothouse.

Scar felt exposed. He was still shaken from the Barracuda, but he'd been runoff by Ratson's men so many times he knew several of them by sight.

The skiff was half-full of seawater.

"Anyone there?" a raspy voice said.

Scar said nothing as he got low, hiding behind the skiff's gunnel.

Gunshots rang out. Three fast taps followed by three plunks and splintering wood.

"Shit, O.K.," Scar said as he put up his hands and sat on the gunnel.

The boat's engine purred, then stopped. The twenty-one-foot Grady White jolted to a stop, wake crashing against the boat's transom as it rocked in the water.

A spotlight came on and Scar was blinded. He covered his eyes with his arm, and yelled, "Who the f—"

Thwap.

Scar felt the slug catch him in the right shoulder, and he stared at his attackers, a surprised indignance spreading over his face. They'd shot him. Who the hell did the assholes think they were?

Pain radiated from the bullet wound, and he fell forward, the steady stream of water rushing through the hole in the boat showering him. He rolled over so he could breathe, sucking in saltwater, coughing and spitting. He pulled for air, an explosion of pain blossoming through him.

An outboard sparked to life, and Scar heard the knock and tap as the boat's pilot put the motor in gear. Bubbles popped and gurgled, and he felt himself fading, a deep cold wrapping him in an embrace. It reminded him of the time he'd almost drowned. He'd been so cold. So at peace.

The sun inched over the rim of the world, the cloud cover replaced by white strands of cotton candy, the red-orange of daybreak painting the sky. Scar felt heat on his face, sweet sunlight, and he smiled as all his worries fled.

2

Headlight beams arced through the mangroves, casting spider-like shadows over Heel Rock and the Caribbean Sea. A gentle breeze brought the scent of smoke and salt, the beach grass rustling like a million crabs crawling from the sea, their hard underbellies tapping and tinkling on crushed shells and pebbles. Stars blinked through tattered clouds, the remains of the prior day's storm drifting over the star-filled sky like pulled cotton. A cable tapped against the flagpole, and tiny waves snapped and popped as they broke on the rocky beach in the darkness.

Vader rose from where he lay by Drake's side, sticking his black nose in the air and sniffing, head bouncing. The black Newfoundland-lab mutt looked up at Drake and Louise with red eyes before plopping back onto the deck and resting his head on his paws.

"Damn," Louise said. "I thought you said tonight was for us?"

Drake and his girl sat on his back patio, the ocean lapping on the rocky shore, the gentle sound of stones scraping over stones drowned out by the approaching car. He had no idea who was coming up the drive, or why, but as Louise had concluded, it was most likely the barflys. He shrugged and said nothing.

Louise took a long pull on her wine, her dark brown eyes staring at him above the rim of her glass.

Drake took a pull off his beer, but it soured his stomach as tension built there like a twister gathering strength. Who would be coming to his house at ten o'clock at night? His friends and crew knew better than to bother him at home. He considered getting up and finding his cellphone, digging out the Remington, but decided he didn't want to spook Louise.

Haley Right's Toyota minivan emerged from the gloom, moonlight glinting off the pile of fishing poles and equipment strapped to the cargo basket on the roof.

Louise sighed loud and hard. "Why do they always come to you?"

Drake's neck cramped and a nervous ripple of anger washed over him, but he beat it back. "Must be something important, otherwise they wouldn't have come."

She raised an eyebrow.

Louise wasn't a fan of the crew Drake hung out with at Dugan's Oasis, which she liked to call DO-nothings. He understood. The bar was like the small echo tour company he ran, another life he kept separate from her. He liked Louise, and someday might love her, but her obsessiveness led to the need for boundaries. She understood this, which was what pissed her off. That he might want time away from her, that fun was to be had without her in attendance, ruffled her feathers in a way that made Drake question their long-term future as a couple.

The hum of the minivan's engine grew, headlight beams illuminating Drake's bungalow, gravel popping and cracking as the car rolled up the driveway.

Vader whimpered and lifted his head.

Louise stared at Drake, her eyes asking questions, her pursed lips and narrow eyes telling Drake he better come up with something fast.

"I wanted nothing more than to spend a quiet night with you," he said. That was true.

"If it's some stupid emergency about a guy who told them about a guy who might want to snorkel off the reef tomorrow, you're going to send them away?" she said.

"Yes," Drake said. That wasn't true, but what relationship of any type survived without a few white lies? He trusted Haley Right. Liked her. More than liked her, and at times he thought she felt the same. But group dynamics being what they were, neither of them had been brave enough to take the first step. A step that would most likely break the group apart, regardless of the success or failure of Drake and Haley's relationship.

Louise rolled her lips like she tasted something foul, her eyes narrowing further as a smile spread over her face. "It's just I hardly know anything about you," she said. "You're so… secretive."

"Private," he said. He'd told her how he'd been a chief mate in the US Merchant Marine, and how he forfeited his position and rank because he'd had enough of the sea. Louise had known that was ten kinds of bullshit, but so far, she hadn't pressed him in their six months of casual dating.

"That shell you maintain around yourself, you mean?" she said.

Drake said nothing. He knew these types of questions were traps designed to lure him into conversations he didn't want to have. He knew making that assumption wasn't fair, but there it was.

"They look up to you like you're a god," Louise said. "What the hell did you tell them? More than me, apparently."

The relationship train they were on was coming to a sharp curve in the track and Drake worried they were about to go off the rails. "Sea stories. Boring stuff. Last time I tried to tell you a fish story you almost gaffed me."

She chuckled.

Drake lowered his defenses to DEFCON three, and said, "Kidding aside, I think it's because I've spent most of my life off island. I'm like an exotic animal."

Her eyes narrowed again. "You'll tell me when you're ready?" The question hung out there like a toxic cloud.

"There's really nothing to tell," he said.

"I know, nothing happened the first forty-six years of your life."

He said nothing.

The robot-like bleats of a nighthawk tooted in the dark mangroves, and a faint burp-bark escaped Vader.

"I think I'm starting to have real feelings for you, Drake. I need to know there's more to us than steak, beer, and sex. I mean, that's fun and all, but where is this all going if we can't have one night just to ourselves?"

"Come on. Give me a break, at least until we know why they're here." It sounded reasonable coming out of his mouth, but the words didn't have the desired effect.

"How about I just leave? Walk the beach home by myself. Maybe I'll meet someone on the way that finds me more attractive than five barflys."

"You're more attractive than all of them," he said with a straight face. Haley was just as pretty.

She deflated as she smiled, all bluster gone. "It's just... It's not only our relationship I'm talking about. I worry about Marley. He's young and impressionable. He's a smart kid that could have a future."

"Look, I know. He's my top guy," Drake said.

"That's not what I mean, and you know it. He should be hanging around with people his own age, not a bunch of has-beens, never-weres and never-will-bes."

"Shit, white zinfandel turns you cold," Drake said, but this time he couldn't keep the smile from spreading over his face.

She punched him on the shoulder. "I'm serious. Helen can take care of herself, and so can Haley," she said, waving at the minivan as it came to a stop on the gray gravel driveway with a crunch. The headlights went out and car doors clicked and popped as they were opened.

Drake pulled his gaze from the van and pecked her on the cheek. "What about Julian and Jillian?" The twins worked for Drake on and off.

Louise crossed her arms over her chest. "Those two wouldn't know how to go to the bathroom without you telling them how. How did they live before you got here?"

The house was dark, and Drake leaned over and blew out the candle on the table before them. "Maybe if they think we're not here they'll go away." Drake knew they wouldn't, and so did Louise.

"They'll see your car in the drive," Louise said.

The crunching footsteps stopped, and a woman yelled, "Drake? You here? Sorry to… um, intrude, but it's important."

Drake said nothing as he lifted his eyebrows and peered through the darkness at Louise, who still had her arms crossed over her chest in the perpetual 'I'm waiting for you to handle this' pose. Drake said nothing.

"It's Scar," the woman said. "He's missing."

Ten minutes later, Judge's porch picnic table was packed, his friends sipping beers as Louise looked on with contempt carved on her freckled face. Vader shifted position so he could see the table, but hadn't moved.

Brother and sister pair, Julian and Jillian, sat next to Judge, their short blonde hair and blue eyes leaving no mystery as to their Scandinavian descent. Marley, a young Jamaican orphan who'd come to Tetu for job opportunities, sat in a deck chair at one end of the table, and fishing charter captain Haley Right sat at the opposite end. Across from Drake sat Helen, a sixty-one-year-old retired crossing guard who was just as tough as some of the battle worn soldiers Drake had met, and Louise.

"Do you ever answer your phone, mate?" Marley said. The young man's brown face was slick with sweat, his red t-shirt stained dark under the arms, his surf shorts torn, the stash pocket ripped and hanging. His dark eyes gleamed in the candlelight, a tight haircut making him look bald in the darkness.

Drake lifted his eyebrows and said nothing, the candles at the center of the table spitting and puffing.

"Marley is right. What if someone wanted to book an outing for tomorrow?" Jillian said. "You might have funds from dubious sources, but we need to work to eat."

"And drink," Julian said.

"So get jobs. They always need dishwashers at the resorts," Drake said. He stared at them, making a show of it. "You know, rake the beach and haul away the seaweed."

"I was just—"

"What? You're concerned about my business now? Paying bills?"

The twins said nothing.

"What? Mom coming to town?" he pushed.

Julian looked down at his beer.

Helen said, "We've been trying to call you. Scar didn't show at Dugan's tonight."

Drake's head jerked and his eyes went wide. There were very few things on Tetu that one could rely on; the sun rising and falling, the Earth rotating around the sun, the stupidity of tourists, and Scar making a daily appearance at Dugan's. "When was the last time you saw him?" Drake asked.

"He was in last night, like always. Where were you?" Julian said.

"He's got other things to keep him busy," Louise said.

"Did you check down at Teapot Cove? Maybe he fell asleep, or he was too tired to drink," Drake said. If that was what had happened, it would be a first.

Helen said, "We checked everywhere, Drake. Searched the whole damn island, and… his skiff is gone."

"You sure?" Drake said. "He leaves that thing all over the island."

"True," Marley said. "But most of the time, like almost always, it's beached down at the pot."

"Drake, the line his keel made in the sand is still there," Haley said.

"How do you know it's his?" Drake said.

"It was fresh when I checked the area. The tide would've washed it away, and he always pulls his boat up on the northern edge. If it wasn't him, it was someone doing the same thing he always does," Marley said. "I've sat down there with him a million times. His boat was there last night, I'm sure of it."

"He say anything unusual last night?" Drake asked. "Act weird?"

The entire group laughed, including Louise.

"You serious, man?" Marley said.

Scar was the local environmentalist and conspiracy investigator. Drake knew very little about him, other than he'd hinted at being a law enforcement officer when he was younger. Scar was homeless by choice, and because he knew every nook and cranny of Tetu, he had no problem finding places to put up his Army tent and avoiding the police, who had no real interest in finding him.

"You know what I mean," Drake said. "He tell you anything specific? His plans for the night?"

The Caribbean Sea lapped on the rocky beach, the gurgle and snap of stones being pulled over stones in rhythm with the rattling mangrove leaves.

"He said he was going to watch Kraken Island," Helen said.

Drake rolled his eyes and his mouth fell open a crack.

"I know. I know. What else is new? But this time sounded different," Helen said.

"She's right," Jillian said.

Nodding heads and murmurs of approval from the others.

"He said he'd overheard two of Ratson's people talking down at The Deck. Saying something about a special experiment that was supposed to happen last night."

Drake waited for her to continue, and when she didn't, he said, "That it?"

"You know him, man," Marley said. "When he started talking scientific formulas, the salinization rate of water, how it affects the oceans, pollution—" Marley tossed up his hands.

"We tuned out," Haley said. "You know how he can be."

Drake did. The old man was sharp as a blade, but sometimes his thoughts moved faster than his mouth, and when he got excited, he skipped words and entire sentences.

"So you guys don't really know anything?" Louise said. "He could be passed out on a beach somewhere, or in someone's backyard hammock."

Helen looked at the crew, and when nobody challenged Louise, she said, "I know he didn't come to Dugan's. I know if he was able to come, he would have."

"So you say. How well do you know him?" Louise said.

Drake considered putting a stop to the bickering, but given the combatants, he figured it was best for him to shut his piehole.

"I wouldn't expect you to understand. Getting together at Dugan's is important… to some of us," Haley said. Her eyes flicked quickly to Drake, then to the floor.

Louise shifted her smoldering gaze to Drake. "Did any of you go to the police?" she said as she stared at Drake, ignoring Haley, the 'aren't you going to do something' eyes knifing Drake like a blade.

Helen shook her head no. "You know, the twenty-four hours thing. And you're not wrong, what facts do we have?"

"Did you ask around? Anybody seen him since last night?" Drake said.

Marley nodded. "Checked all his usual stops. His schedule is as regular as you and number two. Nobody saw him all day."

"He wasn't seen at any of his usual haunts tonight or after he left us last night," Helen said. "That's why we came here. We didn't know what else to do."

"I'm worried about him," Jillian and Julian said at the same time.

Drake got up and stared out to sea, his black and gray-streaked hair blowing in the gentle breeze. "It's dark. We don't know shit, and Scar is a loose cannon and loner. I say we give it until first light, and if he doesn't turn up, we go to the police."

Drake turned back to the group and they all stared at the picnic table like he'd just asked for a loan.

"We don't have anything in the morning, right boss?" Marley said.

Drake shook his head no. His tour company, Tetu Echo Adventures, took tourists and butterflies—what islanders called people who had vacation homes on Tetu—on kayak, snorkeling, and hiking tours all around the island. He didn't advertise because he didn't really care if he got business. It was a hobby, something to keep him busy that brought in a little cash and gave him a loss for his tax return.

"We'll meet you at the station in the morning," Helen said.

"No," Drake said.

Twelve eyes stared at him in the candlelight and Vader ripped a snore.

"Large groups make things difficult. Confuse the issue. Plus, it will be easier for me to get in to see someone if it's just me, and maybe one other person."

"Who?" Helen said.

"I know most of the cops from the harbor station," Haley said. "I'll go with you."

"Of course you will," Louise said. She got up, collected her empty wine glass, and headed for the house. "Anyone need anything?"

A chorus of 'no thank you' and 'not for me'.

"Night then," she said. "See you inside, Drake."

He smiled at her back, but said nothing.

"You better go take care of that," Jillian said.

"We did intrude," Haley said. "I hope I... we haven't caused you a problem."

Drake met Haley's eye and said, "Pick me up at sunup."

3

The next day dawned overcast and rainy. Drake smiled. Answer his phone, his ass. If he'd gone through the effort to get a tour booked, he would've had to postpone because the tourists always insist on going early. They've got a schedule and adjusting the schedule—that they set—in any way usually meant a cancel because people on vacation had zero patience and a limited window of time on Tetu.

Drake looked up at the clouds as they rolled past at warp speed. Sauron's Eye would burn off what remained before Helen rolled out of bed. You'd think the tourists could read the monthly weather calendar on the chamber of commerce website, but that would take thought, and rum wasn't a thought inducing free radical, especially when consumed at vacation levels.

Squalls of fog and rain swirled over the sea like thin cyclones, tiny whitecaps breaking in every direction. The beach grass whistled and sang, the familiar scent of salt and rotten eggs assailing Drake. He stood on Heel Rock, a giant precipice of stone behind his house. Tetu Island was shaped like an upside-down boot, and the cliff was in the northeasterly corner.

"Morning," Louise said.

He smiled over the rim of his mug as she approached.

She took a sip of tea. Always tea, Earl Grey, never coffee. "What are you up to today when you're done getting laughed at?" she said.

Drake lifted an eyebrow, but said nothing.

"So...." She turned to leave.

"What do you want me to say? You're right? We're probably wasting our time? Fine. You're right. Now what?" Drake said, with a little more anger than he'd intended.

Louise's face hardened, then her eyes shifted to the ground. "What is it about you that draws you to every hard luck case? Every charity?"

"Scar is no charity case, and you know it." Drake's anger was building, and he heard Ester's voice in his head. His psychologist would tell him to take a breath, don't respond. He breathed, but it didn't help.

"I know. I know. It's just sometimes I feel like I'm dating you, plus your five siblings. You know what I mean?"

The sea breeze brought the rank scent of dead fish and Drake crinkled his nose as he took a final pull on his coffee. He went to Louise and wrapped his arms around her, his empty mug dangling from a finger. "I know last night... ruined the mood. I'll make it up to you."

She cradled her mug and kissed him on the cheek.

"Promise," Drake said.

Louise chuckled.

"What?"

"Well, don't promise."

"Why?"

"Something might come up," she said.

Drake pulled her in close and tried to kiss her, but she pushed him away. "Hot tea here," she said, but she was smiling. She placed her mug on Heel Rock and threw her arms around him. They kissed hard, the Caribbean Sea rolling onto the rocky beach, tumbleweeds of dried seaweed skipping across the shore, surging for the mangroves, only to get hung-up in the beach grass.

"Uh, um," said a voice from behind them.

Drake and Louise turned to find Haley. Her short blonde hair blew in the breeze, and Drake thought she'd applied makeup. She looked good.

"Sorry, Louise. Seems I'm like a bad penny," Haley said.

"Seems so," Louise said. She pecked Drake on the cheek. "See you later?"

He nodded.

"Bye, Haley," Louise said as she retrieved her mug.

Drake and Haley stood in silence on Heel Rock, watching Louise disappear into the beach grass.

"That woman doesn't like me," Haley said.

True that, he thought. Drake said, "Naw, she likes you. You know women get competitive with each other, especially when a Prime A chunk of beef like me is on display."

She punched him on the shoulder. "Let's go."

They held each other's gaze until Haley broke it off.

In the minivan, threading down Drake's gravel driveway through the mangroves, she said, "Anything special I need to know?"

The car crunched to a stop when they reached Rock Hill Road, and she made a left and headed for Fredericksville, the capital of the American side of the island.

"Naw," Drake said. "We'll tell Feddi what we know, but it's barely been twenty-four hours, and though we know Scar's schedule is like clockwork, I doubt Feddi will care."

Haley nodded. "Do you think the others are pissed they were told not to come?"

Drake threw up his hands. "They're adults, they can do whatever they want."

Haley pulled her eyes from the road, a smile spreading across her face. "You know they all look up to you."

He sighed. "What about you?"

Haley gripped the steering wheel, her eyes locked on the road. Her right cheek turned a shade of pink. She made a left on Loop Road, the only double lane paved road on Tetu. It ran around the outer edge of the island and passed through both capitals and ports. The lighthouse on Boot Tip Point stuck from the mangroves, its light dark. Black clouds pushed in from the ocean, pockets of fog and heavy rain slowing their progress.

The town of Fredericksville sat at the edge of Simpson Bay on the leeward side of Tetu. There was only one road that led from Loop Road down into the village, and it was packed solid with cars twenty-four hours a day, seven days a week. Haley got in line, inching forward every few moments, the tinkle of steel drums, car radios, and the rumble of the town floating through the open car windows.

Fifteen minutes later they'd gone half a mile, but the old municipal courthouse where the police had their offices could be seen on the corner of Main Street. Cars were parked everywhere; on sidewalks, in alleys, double parked along the roads. There was barely enough space for Haley to squeeze the minivan through, and when she reached the front of the courthouse, she said, "You want to go in and I'll try and find a spot?"

Drake looked around sarcastically. He considered telling her to pull the van up the curb and onto the sidewalk before the

Grace Allen Memorial Court Complex, but decided against it. The cops didn't even push things that far. The scent of charred meat and bacon made Drake's stomach gurgle. His morning coffee had done just enough to wake his body up, and it was screaming for fuel.

Drake got out of the car. "Do your best, but if you—"

Haley sped off, tires chirping. A spot had freed-up down the street.

A crowd streamed down the sidewalk, most of the women dressed in this year's newest fashions, wearing fancy floral sunhats, designer jewelry, and gold strapless heels. The men looked straight out of GQ; hair plastered back, five hundred-dollar shades, and the required pastel colored shirt with cargo shorts.

Drake looked down at himself and sniffed. He could smell his Old Spice, so that was good, but his flip-flops had seen better days, his gym shorts were torn, and the 2018 Super Bowl shirt showing the New England Patriots as champs had a tear on its shoulder, and several permanent stains. He loved the shirt because the Patriots hadn't won the Super Bowl that year. They lost to the Eagles, and he'd been able to snag one of the unneeded t-shirts when the container ship carrying the incorrect apparel stopped at Grand Cayman for fuel, and an old Merchant Marine friend snagged him one.

"Ready," Haley said. She strode up the stone steps of the three-story brick building that was one of the oldest structures on Tetu. She held the door open for Drake and he made a show of slipping through. A guard stood at a podium inside the entrance and he directed the pair to the office of Trevor Feddi, Deputy Chief of Tetu Island Police. The island's police department was small, and dealt mostly with petty thefts, and tourist fights and complaints. Drake knew that if Scar was really missing, or in serious trouble, the locals weren't equipped to deal with it or any sizable emergency. Standard protocol involved calling on the U.S. and U.K. Virgin Islands for assistance.

That was the challenge. Getting Feddi and his boss to stick their necks out for a non-citizen who they considered a homeless person at best, a bum at worst.

Feddi greeted Drake with a handshake and a smile. "And Ms. Right, how have you been? Caught anything lately?"

Drake noticed Haley restraining her frustration. Every person she ran into asked her that question. "You know how it is," she said through tightened lips. "Tetu giveth, and Tetu taketh away."

Feddi chuckled and extended his arm, directing them into his office. "Can I get you anything? Water. Coffee. You drink tea, right Haley? Care for one?"

Nobody else would notice, but Drake saw Haley's lips draw into a tighter line. Tetu was small, and everyone knew everyone's business. It was both endearing and incredibly frustrating if you enjoyed privacy.

Feddi sat and straightened a pad on his desk and took a sip from his mug. Then he lifted a pencil, made sure it was sharp, and turned his cool eyes on Drake and Haley. "So, what is it you've got?"

Drake looked at Haley, who looked at the worn tile floor. He sighed. "You know Scar, right?"

Feddi's expression shifted from one of casual merriment to a stern mask of non-emotion. "I'm familiar with the man, yes."

"I believe... we," he said as he motioned toward Haley, "we believe he's missing and in need of help."

"Missing? From where? The man has no known address. He sleeps in the mangroves out your way most nights. Why do you think he's missing?"

Drake looked to Haley for help again, but she was still staring boreholes into the mosaic tiled floor. Drake wasn't sure how much he should tell Feddi. It wasn't a trust issue, though he knew Feddi was in Ratson's pocket, as was all island law enforcement. The story sounded nuts—how Scar had heard about some experiment, and the only proof his friend was missing was him not showing up to drink his daily fill of beer. Feddi would dismiss him if he laid out the facts, so he juiced things up a little.

"He was supposed to meet me last night at Dugan's. Said he had something to tell me. Plus, we needed to go over the week's schedule," Drake said. As he said it aloud the lie sounded even worse.

Feddi's brow furrowed and he leaned back in his chair, the ensuing screech of metal on metal like fingernails being dragged over a chalkboard.

"Look, I know it isn't much. But Scar always does what he says. Never misses a charter and is never late," Drake said. It was all mostly true.

"Never late?" Feddi said. "I've seen the man. If there was a picture of a person in the dictionary next to 'late person' it would look just like Scar." He straightened his empty pad and put down his pencil.

"Well, I know him, and if he said he'd meet me, he'd meet me. Something's not right," Drake said.

"And?" Feddi said. "Do you know how many cops we have on duty right now?"

Drake rolled his eyes.

"Four. And you want me to send one on some wild goose chase to find your friend passed out under a palm tree up on Boot Tip?"

Drake said nothing.

"What do you think he wanted to talk to you about?" Feddi asked.

Drake hiked his shoulders.

Haley said, "He's been ranting more than usual about something bad going on over on Kraken Island. That there was some big experiment happening last night. He was planning on checking it out. That's probably what he wanted to talk about."

Drake sighed. So much for keeping things simple and non-crazy. They should've gotten their story straight in the minivan.

Feddi's eyes shifted to the floor at the word experiment, then he leaned in. "Drake, Haley, you seem like good people, honest people. Let this go. It will do nothing but bring you trouble and harm."

"My friend is missing out on that damn sea, and you're telling me to mind my own business?" Drake said. He understood the politics of the situation, but he also understood he'd never come to island police for help. He didn't cry wolf, and he expected them to do their job.

Feddi patted the air in a calm down gesture. "I didn't say that, but right now, you've got nothing. What would you have me do?"

"Send a boat out. Take a look around Ratson's—"

"Unless you've got more to tell me, we're done here. The desk sergeant will take a report, and I'll tell my people to keep an eye out, but that's more than enough at this time."

Heat rose from the tips of Drake's toes to his cheeks, rage building like a volcano. He got up, put his closed fists on Feddi's desk, and through gritted teeth he said, "If Scar dies out there because you delayed, we're going to have a big problem."

A smirk spread over Feddi's face. Everyone knew Drake. No way he'd get physical with Feddi. It wasn't his way.

Anger pulsed through Drake, Feddi's smug expression taunting him. He wanted to hit the man more than he'd wanted to punch someone in a long time, but that wouldn't help his friend.

"Thank you for your time," Drake said.

As promised, the desk sergeant took a report, and Drake and Haley exited into the hot mid-morning sun, the clouds already more scattered than the former Soviet Union.

"I won't ask, because I know the answer," Haley said.

"Sorry for dominating the conversation in there," he said.

"He wouldn't have listened to me anyway," she said.

"Are you going to bring the Mary Queen to the party?" Drake said. Haley and Drake had been hanging around each other for so long they'd reached marriage level on the mindreading scale, and she knew without having to be told that Drake was going to look for his friend.

"I've got an afternoon charter," she said.

"No worries. Marley can come with me. Maybe Tweedledee and Tweedledum."

"I'll go for marlin in the straits. Make a point of going slow around Kraken. Maybe float into Deep Hollow Cove," she said.

"See you out there," Drake said.

She smiled.

4

Haley dropped Drake off at home and he was met by Louise and Vader.

"So?" she said.

"As predicted. Took a report and ran us off," Drake said.

She harrumphed. "And now I suppose you and your posse are going to handle things yourselves?"

"Marley's on his way," Drake said. "But it's not like that. We're just going to take a cruise, look around, and meet Haley off Boot Tip."

"Why isn't she going with you?" Louise said, a slight hint of sarcasm buried beneath honey.

"Come on now," Drake said.

"You grab breakfast?"

"Naw. I asked Marley to stop at The Hub. You want anything? I can ring him."

She crinkled her nose like she'd smelled something rancid. "From The Hub? No thanks."

"What? The breakfast burritos are good," he said. And cheap.

"You bringing the twins, or Helen?"

Vader half barked, half snorted.

"You're coming, boy," Drake said.

Vader turned back toward the sea and rested his head on his paws, the matter settled.

"I called Helen, but she doesn't get up until 10AM most days and didn't answer, and the twins..." He threw up his hands. "Sometimes I think they're more work than help."

"You need me to come?" Louise said. She loved the beach and the ocean, but got sea sickness if she spent too much time bobbing around on the Caribbean.

"Naw," he said.

"O.K., then," she said. She kissed him on the cheek. "I'm going home to get ready for work." She stared at him.

Drake knew what she wanted. She wanted him to say that she should really keep some things at his place, maybe take a drawer in his dresser, a key, but Drake was an unmovable sperm whale. They'd only been dating six months, and he wasn't looking for commitment. His face started to cramp from lack of movement.

She tore her eyes away and headed for her car.

Drake crossed over Heel Rock and threaded his way down a thin switchback path that led to the small rock beach behind his house. There were some old folding chairs leaning against the cliff, and he pulled one free and snapped it open. The clean scent of Caribbean air pushed over him like he was opening an oven, the crackle and pop of stones rolling in the undertow more soothing than classical music.

His boat, the Sand Dollar, bobbed in the gentle surf a hundred yards from shore. The gray twenty-six-foot Zodiac Nautic was a semi-rigid open boat with a center console and dive platforms on both sides of the twin 150HP Yamaha outboards. The craft's inflatable gunnels, which had handholds all along their length, were designed for safe and easy access to the sea for all ages, even in rough water. The boat was the one thing he'd bought new when he'd started Tetu Echo Adventures, and he took care of it like it was a baby. More than one tourist had gotten their head bitten off for spilling rum punch on the forward lounge cushions, or dropping cigar ash on his pristine white plastic deck.

Drake watched the hull rise and fall, gently slapping the clear water.

Vader lifted his head and barked, but there was no fury or anger in it.

"Morning, boss." Marley emerged from the mangroves, brown paper bag in each hand.

"Top of the morning to you," Drake said in his best Irish brogue as he received one of the bags.

Marley held up the other bag. "For later. I'll put it in the cooler."

Drake nodded, and was about to bust the kid's stones about how he paid for the food, when Marley chirped like a parrot.

"I put it on your account at The Hub," the kid said.

That was their custom. "Thanks for picking it up. I need it."

"Things went as expected then, eh mate?" Marley said. He put the lunch bag down atop a large boulder, strode across the rock beach, and rinsed his hands in the Caribbean.

"Yup," Drake said as he pulled a white Styrofoam cup from the paper bag. "More coffee. I always said you were a good boy."

Marley didn't answer as he searched the shoreline, six-inch waves rolling over the pebble beach.

"It's over there," Drake pointed to the east of where Marley was searching. He pulled free his breakfast burrito and took a bite.

Marley spotted what he was looking for and waded a few feet into the water. He bent and brought up a line and followed it back to the beach. There he uncovered a claw anchor with two lines connected to it. He unclipped one of the lines and started pulling in the Sand Dollar. The rope jerked, and Marley said, "That pully must be getting rusty as shit. It's gonna stain the rope."

"Yup," Drake said. "When you've got some time, I need you to set a new line for me. That'll keep it out of the water." There was a mooring made from a fifty-gallon drum filled with concrete set a hundred yards out with a spring line attached to it, allowing the boat to be pulled in and out without resetting the anchors or getting wet. Drake picked up his customers in port, and he had friends down there that let him dock his boat during storms, or if he was going to be off island, which he hadn't been in three years.

"Sure thing. I'll take care of it," Marley said as he pulled on the rope, the Zodiac jumping and gliding over the tiny waves.

Drake had worked on many ships. Given thousands of orders, but there was only one response that made him really smile. I'll take care of it. Yes, sir. 10-4. No problems. No thousand questions. No need to spend so much time explaining and assisting that the help turns into a hinderance, which was why he was giving the JJ twins to Haley for the day.

The Sand Dollar crunched onto shore, tiny waves slapping the transom. Marley unclipped the guide rope from the bow and held the boat steady as his gaze shifted to Vader. "Hey, mon, you want me to turn this rig around for Mr. Vader?"

Marley jokingly called the dog Mr. Vader because Drake and the others teased him that the dog was treated better than he was most of the time.

"It's calm. I can lift him," Drake said. In rough seas, the rear platforms could be used to get the heavy beast onboard. The animal loved the water, but getting in and out of the boat wasn't Vader's favorite thing because it involved being bearhugged and lifted by Drake.

Sensing the upcoming humiliation, Vader got to his feet and shook himself.

Drake and Marley exchanged smiles and Drake said, "I swear he understands what we say."

"No doubts," Marley said.

Drake lifted Vader onto the boat and Marley held the bow steady as Drake climbed aboard.

"You gonna have JJ meet us at the dock?" Marley said.

It was a Thursday, and that meant the brother and sister pair would be eager to work for weekend drinking money, but Drake didn't really feel like listening to their constant bickering. Did he need their help? When he had tourists on the boat, they were incredibly helpful, swimming in the sea with the kids, getting extra close to the old men and women. The twins were his puppies, but he didn't need any cute and lovable slackers today. He said, "Not today. We're just going to look around."

Marley nodded, his eyes falling to the deck. The sixteen-year-old orphan lived in a boarding house with eight other guys, and when Drake didn't have tours, the young Jamaican didn't make money and had to hunt for odd jobs, most of which were taken by older folks. Drake had the boy over to eat regularly, but he was proud, and wanted to earn his own way. If Drake died out at sea, Marley would get the house, the Sand Dollar, Vader, everything he owned. That sure as shit would piss his sister off.

Drake said, "Listen. I've got an idea. What if I pay you to have dinner and hang out at The Deck tonight, so—"

Marley's face went rigid like he'd taken a pull of strong whiskey.

"Hear me out," Drake said. The Deck was a tourist pit, and no self-respecting islander would be caught dead hanging out there. "You eat, have a few beers out back, rustle us up a charter for tomorrow."

Marley's face brightened.

"You can have half of what we make after gas and bait because you're helping me today. Deal?"

"Deal."

Drake sat behind the center console and Vader moseyed to the bow, where he jumped and put his front paws on the gunnel, black nose into the wind.

Marley pumped the fuel bulb, putting pressure in the gas line, as Drake lowered the motors, the hydraulic whine echoing over the crystal-clear Caribbean Sea.

Metal scraped on metal as flywheels spun, and the Yamahas rumbled to life, thin streams of water pissing into the ocean from their cooling injection ports. Drake spun the wheel as Marley took a seat next to him. He pushed down the control arm and the motors grumbled, then he dropped the hammer and the boat leapt from the water, engines screaming as the vessel came up on plane. The rigid V hull cut through the still, bathtub-like sea, throwing a veil of spray as it knifed away from the shoreline.

Vader stood on the bow, curly black hair covered in a thin sheen of water, long bushy ears flying in the wind.

Drake felt the sun on his neck, the clouds tattered tissue paper, the dark rain clouds off to the west. He adjusted the GPS and SONAR fish finder mounted to the console above the steering wheel. He turned on the UHF radio and tuned it to channel thirty. "Mary Queen, this is the Sand Dollar, do you copy?" Drake said into the handset.

Static. Water popping and snapping against the hull.

He repeated the call twice, before Haley's voice crackled over the comm.

"We copy, Drake. What's your twenty?" she said.

"We're just pulling out now."

Haley said, "Saw a pod of dolphins, but they were acting strange."

"Strange?"

"Yeah. It was like… it's crazy," she said.

"What?"

"It was like they were trying to get us to follow them away from Kraken Island," she said. "Rushing away, then stopping and turning back when they discovered we weren't following."

Dolphins are smart creatures, and it wasn't unheard of for the friendly fish to attempt to help wayward people and vessels. He said, "I heard a story about a fisherman whose boat had capsized, and a dolphin brought him back to shore, the guy hanging on the fish's dorsal fin the entire time."

"Jack Sparrow, eh mate?" Marley said.

Drake lifted an eyebrow and said, "See you soon, Haley. Sand Dollar out." He set the handset back in its cradle. The engines screamed and spat fifteen-foot rooster tails as Drake arced the Zodiac around Boot Tip Point. A line of whitewater and breaking waves ran from the tip of the point, the shadow of the lighthouse falling over the shoals. Simpson Bay and Fredericksville sat under a curtain of morning mist to the east, charter boats, large catamaran party cruises, snorkel and dive boats, and jet ski tours funneling through the channel like rush hour on a major highway. Good things came to the butterflies who adjusted their precious schedules.

To the southwest, the green tangled mess of vegetation that was Kraken Island stood out like a blemish on the tranquil Caribbean, palm trees along the sand beach swaying in the gentle breeze. Fish jumped from the sea, seagulls circled overhead, and in the distance a cloud of the flying sea rats hovered and swirled.

Marley stood and got next to Drake so he could hear him over the hum of the engines. "You catch major shit last night, mate?"

Drake turned and looked at the boy. The kid… young man, was smarter and sharper than folks gave him credit for. Despite his inexperience, out on the sea Drake would rather have Marley by his side than anyone else, Haley and Helen being the possible exceptions. Marley was good with people, logical and smart, and he was tough for a guy that weighed a shade over a buck-o-five. He pursed his lips, turning Marley's question over in his mind. What about Louise? Could he count on her out here? He didn't think so. Not only did she get seasick, but she had a natural aversion to sticking her nose in other folk's business, which left her with ample time to stick her nose into business she felt justified sticking it into. Those she loved, for example.

He said, "No more than usual."

"She don't like us very much, does she?" Marley asked. "Me and the gang, I mean."

"She likes you plenty," Drake said.

The pair chuckled, but Vader barked. Not his halfhearted, kind of pay attention yelp, but a sharp, insistent bark that sounded like a tourist had just walked on Drake's small lawn of weeds and cracked seashell beds packed with yucca.

"What is it, buddy?" Marley said.

The black newfoundland-lab mix had his snout pointed to the southwest, tail stiff, body rigid.

Drake flipped the wheel, putting the Zodiac on the same course as Vader's nose.

"You think there's anything to what Scar is always raving about Ratson and Kraken Island?" Marley said.

"Many locals and tourists are in the pocket of Sir Javier Ratson. The billionaire managed to buy that island without naming it, like it doesn't exist. Myths and rumors have swirled for years about Ratson's excessive polluting of the Caribbean, plus many other nefarious activities. So do I think Scar was probably picking at a scab? Yeah, I do."

"Pisses me off how an ex-patriot Brit is untouchable on our side," Marley said, referring to the U.S. controlled side of the island.

"The police aren't interested in stirring Ratson's anger without any proof of wrongdoing, and nobody cares about Scar anyway, remember?"

The scent of rot washed over the sea, and Drake pulled back on the control arm and brought the Zodiac to a crawl.

A greenish-gray cloud the size of a football pitch filled the sea like sewage, dark black and white strands running through the cloud like snotty entrails.

"I've seen this before. It looks like shark shit, but it can't be," Marley said.

"Why's that?" asked Drake.

"You know how many sharks it would take to produce that much waste? Plus, sharks don't generally hang out together in large numbers," Marley said.

"Ever seen it anywhere else?" Drake said.

Marley stared into the sun, all traces of the morning cloud cover gone. He closed his eyes as he lifted his chin. "Yeah, actually, though, it didn't look exactly like this, and the waste cloud was much smaller. Barracuda."

Drake eased down on the throttle and powered through the field of fish crap, the outboards churning the sea, the scent of rot and shit making Marley gag. It took every non-puke breathing exercise Drake had in his arsenal to stop from hurling up the egg burrito.

This didn't add up. A school of Barracuda? The predatory fish sometimes hunted in small groups, and pairs had been known to help each other. But a school of Barracuda? Couldn't be. There had to be another explanation.

"Should I take a sample?" Marley said.

"Good idea, but with what?"

The kid held up an empty water bottle.

Drake gave him a thumbs up and Marley scooped some of the odd substance from the sea, being careful not to get any on his hands. He sniffed the open bottle before quickly twisting on its cap.

Drake dropped the throttle arm and the Zodiac leapt from the water, shrieking into the late morning sun.

5

The sun glared down like an accusing eye, and heat rolled over the Caribbean Sea in invisible waves. The trade winds were warmer than a convection oven, and Drake reached under the command console, grabbed a hat, and put it on. The green trail of waste broke up, and Drake angled the Sand Dollar southwest, the twenty-six-foot V hull cutting through the rippling sea with ease. The depth finder claimed the ocean was thirty feet deep, but with the sensor being jarred by the motion of the boat, Drake couldn't trust it. No matter. The sea bottom was speckled with plants, and along with fish they provided points of reference. Drake figured he had at least fifteen feet. As he got closer to Kraken Island, he'd need to be more careful. The fish finder showed nothing special, and he thought of Haley and searched the western horizon.

In the distance, the Mary Queen chugged through the light surf, coming around the northern tip of Kraken Island. A thin line of white smoke trailed into the blue sky from her diesel stack, two long silver outriggers bouncing and swaying off the port and starboard gunnels.

Marley sat on the bench before the command console, Vader sitting dutifully at his feet, the dog's head nodding up and down as the boat skipped over the light surf.

Drake stopped and killed the motor when they were five hundred yards off Kraken Island's northern tip. The outboards puffed and fell still, whitewater bubbling up around the vessel. The boat spun slowly in the wind as it was pushed southeast toward the strait.

"Wait here for Haley?" Marley half stated, half asked.

Drake nodded. "I want to know if she's seen anything. See if she has any recommendations about where we should look."

Marley nodded, his gaze straying south toward Kraken Island, the kid knowing their communications would most likely be monitored on the open UHF channels. He turned his dark eyes back on Drake, waiting.

"What?" Drake said. The damn kid was so respectful he didn't want to upstage Drake and was waiting for him to put together what Marley had already figured out.

The kid slipped his old iPhone from a back pocket and held it up.

Drake threw back his head. "I always forget about those damn things," he said. "You better not be calling mates back in Jamaica. I don't have no roaming money." Drake put the kid on his plan when he decided he wanted to be able to get hold of him at a moment's notice, and he got more than his money's worth.

After a brief phone conversation which revealed no new information, it was decided that the Mary Queen would float on the western side of Kraken Island, and Drake would run a search grid covering the area east of Deep Hollow Cove. Drake knew where Scar usually hid out, but with the current ripping through the strait, and high tide coming on, any evidence would've drifted south.

Drake cycled up the engines, spinning the wheel and putting the Zodiac on a southeast heading. Sea spray arced over the bow, but it felt good, the cool mist combating the stifling heat. Fishing vessels and tourist cruises dotted the southern horizon like chickenpox, the island's bread and butter making good on the island's motto, Peace in the Sun. Gulls circled and cried, and occasionally a pelican dive-bombed into the water, sucking in minnows like whales ate krill.

Vader got up, staring west. The dog jiggled and swayed as the boat skipped and hopped over the sea, and when the beast looked back at Drake, he pulled back on the throttle.

As the boat slowed, the dog put his front paws on the starboard gunnel. He barked twice, but it was the 'I have no idea why I'm barking' yowl.

Marley joined Vader, shielding his eyes as he searched the glowing surface of the Caribbean Sea. With the sun reflecting off the water, it was impossible to see anything beyond a few hundred yards in the glare.

Drake grabbed the binoculars and joined his mates. "Got something?"

"Not that I can see," Marley said. "You know how this dog is, mon. He's more perceptive than most people I know."

"Perceptive?" Drake said. The kid had stopped going to school when his mom died. He'd been seven.

Marley giggled. "That word-a-day calendar thing Louise gave me for Christmas."

Drake peered through the field glasses, fighting to see through the white sunglow that covered the surface of the sea like snow. "Here," he said as he handed Marley the binoculars. "You've got younger eyes."

"And I'm better looking," Marley said as he accepted the binoculars.

Marley took his time, slowly scanning the horizon to the south.

Drake dug out the cooler he kept in the storage compartment under the seat before the command console, and pulled free a beer. He didn't normally drink out at sea, but his nerves still hadn't stopped jumping. The tranquil peace of the Caribbean usually drove away all worry and angst, but not on this day. His stomach churned, and with each passing second, he became more certain something bad had happened to Scar.

"There!" Marley's head jerked back like someone had pushed on the binoculars.

Drake took a long pull of beer and put the can in the drink holder on the command console. "Where?"

Marley pointed southeast, and Drake spun the motors and dropped the boat in gear. He went slow, the Sand Dollar pushing through the calm sea like a children's blow-up pool. Marley steadied himself against the gunnel, still peering through the binoculars.

Alarm sounded and job done, Vader retreated to the cone of shade before the command console and plopped to the deck with a snort.

"Head east a little," Marley said.

Drake changed course; the sun glare more intense as they drove right at the sun.

"Full stop," Marley yelled.

Drake hesitated—the kid never gave orders to anyone—but he recovered and brought the Sand Dollar to a shifting and dipping stop. Drake joined Marley, who pointed at the water about ten feet away.

Floating in the gentle surf, bobbing and tumbling like a cork, was a cracked and splintered piece of wood.

"Shit," Drake said as he ran for his net.

The shredded plank was about five feet long, and there was little doubt it was from Scar's skiff. The color matched, and Drake recognized the wood grain. But could he be sure? Then he added, 'your honor' after the question, and realized he wasn't certain.

"What now? Feddi has to do something," Marley said.

"You'd think, but this isn't enough. It could be a broken part from any boat," Drake said.

"What do you mean? You know Scar's boat. The color. There's no—"

Drake held up a hand. "I'm not saying I don't think this is a piece of Scar's boat. I'm saying we have no way to prove it."

Marley sighed. "This is bullshit. I'm used to this crap. I grew up on an island with leaders that regularly ignored the law. I know that's not what it's like in the states. How do you deal here?"

"In the states it depends on where you live and the color of your skin," Drake said. He wasn't proud of that, but there it was. He turned the piece of Scar's skiff over in his hands, willing it to tell him what had happened, though Drake already had a pretty good picture.

Scar had seen something Ratson's people didn't want him to see. Things got out of hand, Scar refused to back down, and they removed him from the equation, knowing nobody would care.

Except, they hadn't factored Drake into their plans. He was no crusader, but one could argue he'd been exiled on Tetu for doing the right thing. For not allowing powerful, influential men to get away with crimes. No, Ratson and his shitbirds didn't know who they were dealing with, and if Scar didn't turn up alive, they'd find out just how much that oversight would cost them.

He handed the shard of wood to Marley. "Put this in the storage compartment."

The Zodiac sliced through the rolling sea as it continued on an easterly course. Drake thought if there was one piece, there was more, and unfortunately, he was right, sort of. They didn't find another piece of Scar's boat, but what they did find disturbed Drake more.

A torn piece of cloth no bigger than an infant's hand floated on the surface surrounded by a thin oil slick. The fabric was red, with half a white beach poppy flower printed on it.

"Sure looks like that nasty Hawaiian shirt he wears," Drake said as he fished the cloth from the water with the net.

Marley nodded and took the fabric from the net when Drake offered it. He rubbed it between his forefinger and thumb. "He had that nasty thing on last time I saw him. What do you make of the chum slick?"

That was what it looked like, but Drake's mind went down a more horrible path, so he said nothing. The slick trailed west toward Kraken Island, and Deep Hollow Cove. A stream of white smoke puffed into the air off the tip of the island, the Mary Queen chugging north, outriggers swaying and bouncing.

"Bag that and tag it. Let's check in with Haley. You hungry?" The sun had climbed past noon, and it was time to dig into the sandwiches.

The kid stood watching Drake, the piece of Scar's shirt in his hand.

Drake raised an eyebrow as he popped a second beer and took a long pull.

"Bags and tags?"

Drake chuckled. "Sometimes I forget you're only sixteen. Put the fabric with the piece of the skiff. You want a sandwich?"

Marley nodded.

The pair sat on the bow cushions, eating, as Drake called Haley with the boy's cell. "How goes it?" he said over the light buzz of static caused by the wind.

"Just had a decent fight, but the dink lost it. Looked big," Haley said.

"Marlin?"

"Yup."

"You run a chum slick over this way?" he asked.

"Nope. Little bit on the leeward side, but anything by the strait usually gets washed out pretty fast, so I rarely chum there," she said. "Why? You find something?"

Drake looked at Marley, who shrugged. "Don't know yet. We're going to finish canvasing and then we'll come find you."

"That's a 10-4. Talk later." She closed the line.

For the next three hours, Drake trolled slowly over a two-square-mile grid off the northeast tip of Kraken Island, checking every dead fish, questioning boat captains, and investigating the gleam of every seashell and fish scale.

Vader was done. The black beast panted, a thick stream of drool creating a puddle on the fiberglass deck. Marley didn't look much better. He sat on the bow cushions, binoculars pinned to his eyes as he scanned the sea which was getting rough. A crosswind gusted from the east, pushing across the strait and creating swirling pools of seawater like eddies at the bottom of a waterfall.

Drake was about to call it a day when Marley shouted, "Eleven o'clock."

The moan of the outboards lessoned as Drake drew back the throttle, the Sand Dollar rocking and listing.

A mass of tangled seaweed floated off the port bow like a miniature island, appearing and disappearing with the roll of the ocean. Drake inched the Zodiac as close as he could get, then he snapped the throttle into neutral and shut down the engines.

Marley grabbed the net and went to work scooping up the mess.

"Hold up," Drake said. "Let's take a look before we dump all that stinking crap on my deck."

Marley nodded and pulled back.

The ocean tumbleweed was a mess of tangled seaweed, most of it black, but there were a few strands of yellow and green. Drake plucked another shard of wood from the ocean snot, and handed it to Marley.

"Sure looks the same as the other," the young Jamaican said.

Drake nodded, probing the seaweed with the net. The tangled mass started to break up as Drake prodded it, and a brown piece of what looked like skin floated away from the seaweed. He leaned over the gunnel and plucked it from the water. The shred was an inch long and half an inch wide, and all the edges were tattered and frayed. He turned it over in his hand, the way the color was blackened with mold or rot ensuring it wasn't plastic.

He turned the object over and gasped. A black hair protruded from the piece of skin. A bolt of angst coursed through him like electricity, and he shook himself and rolled his shoulders.

"What is it?" Marley said.

Drake showed the boy the hair.

"Oh shit, mon." Marley covered his nose as if the shred of skin smelled rancid, but it didn't.

"Grab one of our sandwich wrappers from the trash," Drake said.

Marley pushed away from the gunnel.

Vader got up and stretched, staring at Drake with vacant eyes as he squinted in the sunlight.

Drake wrapped the skin and Marley put it with the boards and fabric.

"That should do it then, eh, mate?" Marley said.

Drake hiked his shoulders and the kid frowned. He went back to searching the flotsam, breaking apart the tightly wound ball of seaweed that smelled like it had floated out of a sewer.

"You see that?" Marley said.

He pointed toward something white floating in the mess of seaweed and debris that trailed away with the current.

Drake plucked a piece of paper from the water. "This is the most important piece of evidence. It seals the deal."

The paper was a coated cardstock with black writing, though it was blurred and smudged. The slip of paper was pasted to a chunk of seaweed, fishing line, and man-of-war goo. He peeled the shred of paper free and held it up to the light.

It was the uppermost corner of an identification tag. The words name and address were visible, and written in black marker was half an S, the jagged torn edge leaving only the upper and lower curls.

"That's the tag from Scar's camera case," Marley said.

"You sure?"

Marley nodded. "It just said Scar."

Drake said nothing as he turned the paper over in his hand.

"I busted his shoes about it once. I asked him if someone found the bag, where would they bring it, since he didn't list an address." Marley chuckled. "He just laughed and said, 'Everyone knows Scar's place is Dugan's.'"

A thin stream of oil trailed away from the broken ball of seaweed, and the slick floated west toward Deep Hollow Cove.

"I've had just about enough of this shit," Drake said as he spun up the motors. The Zodiac sprang from the sea, and he set course for Kraken Island.

6

The entrance to Deep Hollow Cove was a narrow serpentine channel that twisted through mangroves and waist high beach grass. Drake stared through the binoculars, Kraken Island still half a mile off. He knew guards watched, though he couldn't see them. If he tried to enter the cove, he'd be met by a stern security guard who would warn him off with increasing hostility until he complied. Conning towers and flying bridges bobbed above the mangroves as boats moved around in the small bay, but he couldn't see what they were doing.

The mid-afternoon sun turned the Caribbean Sea into a desert, the wind having fallen off like the effort teenagers put into their chores. Bands of heat rolled off the churning water, the wind shifting yet again. Water slapped and popped against the hull, and Vader whimpered.

"You hungry, boy?" Marley asked.

Vader grunted. Marley knew the dog wouldn't eat on the boat—it was one of Vader's 'things', but they always brought food and offered it anyway because Drake believed that's what good owners did. "Would you not bring a bottle with you because you thought the baby wouldn't drink?" he'd said to Marley more than once.

Drake's anger flared when they came across what looked like a diluted blood slick.

A faint pink cloud tainted the water, and globules of what looked like specks of fat floated on the surface. Insects danced and jumped on the thin slick, creating tiny dimples.

"That what I think it is?" Marley said. "Where are the scavengers?"

Great White sharks could smell a drop of blood in the water a mile away, and Barracuda and many sea predators were drawn to the possibility of food.

Drake fought back a surge of worry and sorrow, and said, "Let's not jump to conclusions. Maybe someone gaffed a tuna?"

Marley looked up at Drake, but he didn't meet the boy's eye. "Maybe."

"I'm sure the sharks were here, but there's nothing left if there ever was anything," Drake said.

Marley harrumphed and sat on the bench before the command console.

Vader bleat-barked.

"I know. I know," Drake said.

The Zodiac drifted west toward the mouth of the cove.

"I've got a mind to slip on my dive gear and check out that cove," Drake said.

"I heard they've got fancy sensor things on the bottom that pick up vibrations or some such," Marley said.

Drake said nothing. He'd heard the same rumors, and believed them. The technology existed, and Ratson had the funds, but what was his motive? Privacy? Protecting trade secrets?

"I know it sounds crazy, mon, but that don't make it not true."

Drake said, "I know."

"Ratson's people definitely had something to do with this," Marley said.

"Hard to deny at this point, you know? The trail literally leads to their doorstep."

"But it's not enough, is it?"

Drake shook his head no.

"So what now, mate?"

"We poke the shark," Drake said. "Grab another sample. If the case progresses, and it is human blood, maybe the big heads will be able to get some identifying information from it."

Drake let the wind and current take him toward Kraken Island. He had the motor turned to starboard, and with the wind catching his Bimini top like a sail, the Sand Dollar was making a steady three knots.

The pink cloud dissipated and gave way to the crystal-clear water that made the Caribbean the envy of the world. The boat slid past a tiny red buoy that marked the private channel. There was a white sign on the marker that read 'No Trespassing. Private Property. All trespassers will be prosecuted to the fullest extent of the law'.

"Real friendly," Marley said. "And not true."

"Only sign like that I've ever seen down here, but they're all over the place up north."

"They should make him take the sign down. Ratson has no right putting it there. He doesn't—"

Vader barked three times, got up, and stretched.

"Sorry, we wake you?" Drake joked.

The big black dog walked to the port gunnel, all four sea legs steady, gray eyes squinting as he searched the western horizon and the channel that led to Deep Hollow Cove.

Marley said, "He senses something. This guy should've been a drug sniffer."

The sun was dropping to the horizon, the sky fading to an indigo hue that left a blazing orange glow just above the water. The humidity had eased, the temperature a manageable eighty degrees. The Zodiac floated west with the wind, aimed directly at the channel. The sea slid past, small waves snapping against the gunnels. The light sea spray felt good on his face.

Drake's nerves danced on a wire as the sea began to change.

The water thickened, the ripples rolling over the surface became larger, and moved slower. The light sea spray arcing over the gunnels was deep red, and it splashed on the bow cushions making the area look like a grisly murder scene. No dorsal fins knifed through the area, so it wasn't blood. Tiny specks sparkled in the sludge, and they moved and shifted in an unnatural way, against the pitch and roll of the boat.

The clear sea clouded like an oil spill, choking the ocean and everything in it.

"Looks like red tide," Marley said.

Drake sniffed the air. "Can't be." There was no stench, but the cloud moved and shifted against the current, like unseen fish were controlling the plume's direction. Metal-like specks glowed in the thick ooze that moved as though it was alive. The slick trailed away toward the entrance to Deep Hollow Cove like a boat wake.

"This is bullshit, man," Marley said. "They aint even trying to hide what they're doing."

"What are they doing?" Drake said.

"They're…" Marley's gaze shifted from the slick choking the sea, to Drake, and then to Kraken Island. "They're poisoning our water, mate. It's clear as day to anyone who has eyes."

"Third time's the charm," Drake said.

Marley's eyes narrowed and his forehead wrinkled.

Drake held up an empty water bottle.

Marley took a sample of the slick while Drake got two fishing poles set and baited.

"Here you go," Marley said. He held out the sample like it was burning his hands.

Drake accepted the water bottle filled with the mystery substance. He held it up to the light, and it reminded Drake of the fancy hand sanitizer that had different colored scent flecks mixed within. He shifted the bottle, testing the liquid's viscosity, and the deep red fluid sloshed like half-frozen vodka.

Drake lifted the handset from the UHF radio, then slammed it back down as he glared at Kraken Island. He pulled out his phone. No messages. No bars. "WTF?" he said.

"What now, mate?"

"I've got no service."

Marley rolled his eyes as he produced his own device. "Dude, we always get a fine signal out here. The tower up on…" He looked up from his phone. "Shit, you're right, mate. I got nothing."

Drake and Marley stared at Kraken Island.

As with the blood slick, the strange cloud of unknown sludge dissipated and faded, and the entrance to Deep Hollow Cove loomed before them like an open mouth as the channel twisted away into mangroves.

"I'm gonna risk it," Drake said.

Marley's forehead scrunched and he pursed his lips.

Vader barked.

Drake lifted the UHF radio's handset, adjusted the channel to the one Haley monitored, and called her.

"Copy, Sand Dollar," she said, light static crackling under the transmission. "Everything O.K.? Over."

"Everything's copasetic, but my phone is de…" He paused, remembering their code. "Go to Betty's address," he said. Drake shifted the UHF channel to eight-one. That was the number of her friend Betty's house.

A short pause as Haley changed channels, then, "Copy, SD."

"My phone's not dead, but suddenly I've got no service. You?"

There was a pause of thirty seconds, then, "Odd. We've got no signal either. Like zero. You think the tower is down?"

"Maybe. Switch to Glenn's social security," Drake said as he shifted the channel to twenty-six.

Static, then, "Copy, SD."

"Why don't you come around to the eastern side? We're getting all kinds of hits over this way." Hits referred to biting fish.

Another pause. "I've got you, Sand Dollar. Have you caught anything? Do you need my live well?"

Drake looked at Marley, who hiked his shoulders. Drake said, "We've got it covered. Might need backup. Going in close. Over."

"On my way. Out."

Drake nodded as he replaced the handset in its cradle.

Marley watched him, suspicion lines spidering around his eyes, a thin coating of sweat making his dark face shine in the fading sunlight.

Vader dropped to the deck before the command console and yawned.

Dusk was the best time to fish, and Drake and Marley tended their poles as the Zodiac drifted the last hundred yards into the mouth of Deep Hollow Cove.

Vader got up and went to the bow, sniffing the air, thin rivulets of pink seawater running down the deck through his legs.

Nothing moved along the island's shoreline. There were no cabanas. No beach chairs or umbrellas dotting the pristine white sand beach. No tiki bars packed with tourists. There was nothing except tranquil blue water, and a ribbon of paradise that faded into mangroves, then on into forest.

The rumble of an outboard sparking to life echoed over the channel, thickets of dense mangroves sliding past on both sides.

Vader barked.

"Here we go," Drake said. "Let me do the talking."

Marley nodded.

Drake opened the storage cabinet beneath the center console, and a light came on. There was fishing tackle, spare life-preservers, snorkel equipment, but he wasn't interested in any of that. Wires of various colors ran along the edge of the compartment, held together with zip ties and affixed to the fiberglass with snap-clamps. He traced the wires to the deck, where he found a black inline fuse housing. He twisted it, popped out the ignition fuse, tapped it on the deck until it cracked, then replaced the fuse back in its housing and snapped it closed.

Marley watched him with concern etched on his face.

"No worries," Drake said. "I've got spares."

An outboard screamed, and a moment later a boat knifed into the channel ahead of the Sand Dollar.

It was a twenty-one-foot Parker with an enclosed cabin that had a row of lights mounted on the forward edge of its roof. The craft arced across the channel, and the engine wheezed as the boat's pilot eased back on the throttle. The boat came to a bobbing stop in the center of the channel, blocking the Sand Dollar's path.

Four men exited the Parker's pilothouse, and they spread out, each taking position around the boat. A man with a dark black beard put his foot on the boat's gunnel and stared at Drake like he had lasers for eyes and was looking to barbecue him.

Vader went to Drake's side, the low gurgle of his growling barely audible above the wind.

Drake waved his arms. "Ahoy there. Ahoy!"

The two boats were fifty yards apart, the channel a jumble of rolling whitecaps caused by the Parker's abrupt stop.

The bearded man said nothing, but he put his hand on his sidearm and anger rose in Drake. Who the hell did this asshole think he was? Ratson didn't own the ocean, or the cove, and Drake could fish there whenever the hell he wanted.

Drake got to his feet, planting one foot on the gunnel, copying the bearded man's pose. The two men stood like that, the man's hand on his gun, Drake staring right at him, daring him to draw it.

Beard Boy didn't draw down, however, and when the Zodiac bumped into the Parker, Drake got a friendlier greeting than he'd expected.

"Are you in need of help?" The guy's accent sounded Russian.

Drake did his best fake laugh. Louise said it sounded like a seal in pain. "I don't know. Got any rum?" Drake laughed again.

Nothing. The bearded man looked over his shoulder and he was joined by his three friends. They lined the Parker's gunnel like the advancing frontline of an army readying for battle.

"Yeah, well, my guide here," Drake said as he jerked a thumb in Marley's direction, "He said the fishing over this way is great, but that we need to stay clear of the island. Private property and all that. I say, hey, that's fine. What kind of–"

"Sir, do you require assistance?" the man interrupted. His eyes slid over the series of registration stickers and permits plastered all over the side of the command console.

Drake drew back his head as if offended. "I was getting to that." He shook his head with mock annoyance. "Anywaaaay, the engines won't start, and I didn't want to run aground on your precious island."

No response.

"And I have no signal out here for some odd reason," Drake said. He stared at the bearded man for several seconds, then continued, "I can't call SeaMate. What's that all about?"

As Drake bantered with the man, he scanned the area.

To the north there was a long dock that extended into the cove, and boats of various sizes were docked there. A boathouse, a storage shed, and a large brick building with no windows or doors sat nestled back among the mangroves. To the west, a widow's watch stood above the trees, and to the south, mangroves encroached into the water, their spider-like trunks casting thin shadows across the fading day.

Off the port bow, four large metal circles rose above the waterline, the sea within a roiling mess of whitecaps and whitewater as something within churned the cove.

"Well, you cannot stay here," Beard Boy said. "Throw me a line and we'll tow you out. I will call SeaMate for you."

"That's OK. We want to fish a little. I hear there's big Hogfish in here. That true?" Drake said.

Beard Boy nodded, and one of the men standing beside him strode aft and attached a rope to the port cleat of the Parker. Then he moved along the Parker's starboard gunnel and tied the rope to the Sand Dollar's forward bow cleat.

"Hey, what the hell are you—"

Vader barked several times. Hard, teeth bared.

Beard Boy undid his holster snap.

"Easy, buddy, easy." Drake patted Vader's head without taking his eyes off the bearded man.

"You are very welcome for the assistance," Beard Boy said. He retreated into the pilothouse, his three goons watching Drake and Marley. The Parker's outboard rumbled to life and the boat spun, Beard Boy being careful not to tangle the towline in the prop.

"Hold on," Drake said, just as the towline went taught and the Zodiac jerked into motion.

"Szar!" Beard Boy yelled as he stared at the cove's entrance.

The Mary Queen chugged through the channel, blocking the exit.

7

"Marley, get that fuse replaced. Some dumbass cracked it," Drake said. The Zodiac lurched and twisted as it was pulled by the Parker. "They're in the tool kit. It's a number five."

Marley buried his head beneath the command console.

Vader chirped, putting his paws on the bow cushions, eyes locked on the Parker as it dragged the Sand Dollar from Deep Hollow Cove.

White smoke poured from the Mary Queen's exhaust stack, the fishing trawler chugging at full steam, its old diesel engine working overtime.

The UHF crackled to life. "Sand Dollar, this is the Mary Queen. Are you in need of assistance?"

Drake pulled the handset from its cradle, then paused.

Beard Boy watched him through the rear window of the Parker's wheelhouse, ignoring the chaos in his boat's path. Two men stood on the bow of the Parker, guns at the ready as they watched the Mary Queen power into the cove.

Marley's head emerged from beneath the command console. "Should be good to go," he said.

"Mary Queen, full stop."

"Please verify instruction, SD. You want me to stop?"

"10-4."

To the east, the white smoke streaming from the Mary Queen's stack eased, whitewater roiling around its bow. In the west, a drone buzzed over the mangroves and hung in the air, its four rotors holding the flying camera in place.

"Hold on, Marley," Drake said.

Drake lit the motors, slammed them into gear, and pinned the throttle, all in one smooth motion that took two seconds. The Yamahas screamed as they tore at the water, kicking up a massive mound of whitewater and sucking the rear of the Zodiac down, the deck tilting.

For several tense seconds the two boats fought, the line connecting the vessels twanging, stretching and pulling.

Fiberglass cracked and popped as the cleat tore from the Parker, flying at the Zodiac at the end of the rope. It missed Drake by a foot and smashed into the plexiglass windshield above the command console, just missing the NAV monitor, and fell onto the dashboard.

The line was a bigger problem. It snapped back like a rubber band, laying out across the water. Drake spun the wheel and backed down on the throttle, pulling around the starboard side of the Parker, hoping Beard Boy would follow.

"Just like on Whale Wars," Marley said, and laughed.

"Get that line off our bow cleat," Drake yelled.

"Shit," Marley said as he realized if Drake's plan worked the two vessels would be attached again.

The Parker spun and gave chase.

Marley undid the hitch knot and the line trailed over the gunnel into the water.

The Parker powered across the rope as it floated on the surface, and the boat's engine sputtered, wheezed and coughed, then died. The boat bucked and listed as the vessel stopped, a thin tendril of black smoke rising from beneath the engine cover.

That's when Drake heard the faint sound of the helicopter approaching from the north. He spun the wheel, putting the Sand Dollar on course for the Mary Queen.

The drone buzzed Drake, coming so close he lifted his arms to protect his face, then it disappeared over the mangroves.

Beard Boy was yelling and screaming in a language Drake didn't understand, but he didn't need to be a linguist to know the man was pissed. Drake pushed down on the throttle and the motors whined as the Sand Dollar moved away from the disabled Parker.

The *womp womp* of the chopper was like thunder as the small MD 500 buzzed the mangroves and hovered over the scene.

Drake saw Feddi staring down at him through the chopper's clear nosecone, the pilot working the yoke beside him.

Ratson's people had called the police and the lackeys had come running, and all because Drake had floated into the cove, where he had every right to be. Anger fought its way forward, his stomach churning. It was like the night he decided to rat on the captain. His stomach felt like that. A deep cold pain that spidered out to his extremities like poison.

This fight was over. What did he have to gain by throwing fuel on the fire? Feddi definitely wouldn't listen to him if he thought Drake and his crew were harassing one of the most powerful men on Tetu. At least he'd won his little tussle with Ratson's men. Drake looked over at the Parker, and Beard Boy stood on the forward deck, watching the Zodiac power away as his goons worked on his outboard.

The rumble of the Mary Queen's engine coming to life snapped Drake from his reverie. Smoke cycled from her stack as the boat backed out of the channel. No instructions from Drake needed. The police could pull Haley's license. They didn't even need to give her a reason until her hearing, and even that didn't matter. There were many subjective areas—like safety—where the police had tremendous discretion. Haley had to protect herself, her business.

The UHF emergency channel sparked to life. "To the Sand Dollar. Please clear the scene immediately. There is an active experiment underway. Leave the area immediately or you will be—"

Drake shut off the radio. To Marley, he said, "So they admit there's some kind of experiment happening. Feddi needed some excuse to run us off public waters, and they just unwittingly verified a part of Scar's story."

Julian and Jillian stood on the aft deck of the Mary Queen. Julian raised his hand and put it by his ear in the 'call me' gesture. The fishing boat churned into the mangroves and disappeared around a bend, leaving only a thin trail of white smoke behind.

"Time to make like a tree," Drake said.

Marley stared at him wide-eyed.

Vader barked.

"And leave," Drake said as he spun-up the motors and tore from the cove. Right before he passed into the channel and out of view of the Parker, Drake turned and gave Beard Boy a single finger salute.

Mangroves and beach grass slid past on both sides as the Zodiac tore through the channel, its fifteen-foot wake sending waves rolling and crashing into the foliage. A cloud of gulls sprayed from the mangroves, squawking and yelling. Schools of shiners jumped from the water, crabs dove from their perches, and water reeds swayed.

The Sand Dollar broke free into the Caribbean Sea, and Drake arced the boat toward the channel buoy and slowed. A bruised sky clouded the western horizon as the last rays of the setting sun sent dancing shadows across the clear water. Tattered clouds floated across the sky, beams of light cutting through them like divine spotlights.

The chopper thundered overhead as it followed the Sand Dollar, nose down, rotors tearing at the air, churning the sea.

The Mary Queen chugged northeast, ignoring the channel markers as it headed for home.

Drake pulled back the throttle and snapped it in neutral, the outboards sputtering and coughing. "Take the wheel a second, will you?" Drake said.

Marley's eyes went wide as he slid across the bench seat until he sat before the wheel.

The Zodiac's inflatable port gunnel bumped into the red buoy they'd passed on their way in.

Drake grabbed pliers from the toolbox and leaned over the side.

Marley said, "What are you doing, mate?"

The whirlybird hovered, rotors flattening the sea, its turbine whining.

Drake snipped the zip ties that held Ratson's Private Property sign to the buoy. He held it up so Feddi could see it, then tossed it on the bow cushions.

Marley hooted. "You the man, Drake. You the man."

Drake took the wheel and Marley slid back into position beside him.

Vader howled, then barked hard three times.

Drake didn't feel like the man. He felt like an ass. What had he accomplished?

He'd seen the cove, the buildings and boats, the strange metal cage-like contraptions in the water and the tumultuous sea within them. He dropped the hammer, arcing the boat toward Boot Tip.

The copter's external speaker blared over the Caribbean Sea. "This is Feddi. You will return to the harbor for questioning. Do you copy? Over."

Drake rolled his eyes at Marley. Just what he needed. He considered ignoring the order, then recalled the nagging feeling he'd had only moments before that being antagonistic wouldn't help Scar. He had little hope his friend was alive, but until he had proof, he wouldn't let it go. He'd find out what happened and let the chips fall where they may.

Drake gave Feddi a thumbs-up and arced the boat east toward port.

The helicopter dipped its nose, and tore away, the pounding of its rotors fading as its red running light disappeared into a cloud.

Drake wanted to hightail it home, but Feddi would only come out to the house, and he'd likely be significantly more pissed than he was at the moment. Putting down his fourth coffee to take a joy ride on a whirlybird and see a sunset was one thing. Making him miss his dinner and refusing the direct order of a police officer was another thing and would only cause more trouble, and his dance card was full. Plus, Louise was probably at his place working on dinner. That was another problem with their relationship. She was such a great cook, he couldn't complain when she turned up uninvited.

Most of the day fisherman and tourist related vessels were already in for the night, but Drake still slowed when he entered the channel that would take them to Fredricksville Harbor. The channel was littered with sunset cruises, party boats, and kayakers looking to catch the sight of a dolphin or the glow of shrimp.

He brought the Zodiac to a crawl and called to Vader.

The animal had been silent since they'd been run off, and Drake thought the pounding of the helicopter's rotors hurt the beast's ears. Vader planted himself at Drake's side and he reached down and stroked the animal's head.

"Marley, you set for tonight?" he asked.

The boy nodded. "I'm going to break out my best flowered shirt and spin tales of reefs packed with colorful fish."

"Don't forget the unlimited rum punch," Drake said.

Marley nodded.

"Listen, as soon as the Sand Dollar bumps the dock, I want you gone. Comprende?"

Marley started to protest.

Drake held up a hand. "I don't want you involved in this. I'm white and have a few bucks. You..." Drake threw up a hand. "Go take care of business at The Deck, then meet us at Dugan's. Got me?"

The kid nodded sullenly.

Drake knew Feddi would want to question the boy because he'd figure the young man might let something slip. Drake was more worried about himself, but they didn't have anything to hide anyway.

Darkness fell, and boats slid by, some portholes filled with light, others dark. People sat on deck chairs drinking expensive cocktails, and smoking cigars. The whine of small outboards echoed over the water as tenders moved within the maze of moored boats. The tinkle of steel drum music, and the faint hum and chatter of people floated on the breeze. Drake sniffed and caught the scent of charred meat, spices, and under it all he thought he caught the scent of roasting fish.

Feddi waited at the end of Ozzie's fuel dock, hands on hips as he stared into the gloom.

The Sand Dollar's NAV lights cast green and red clouds of light across the still surface, the outboards wheezing as they were shut down.

Marley went to the bow and grabbed a line, and Drake went aft. The Sand Dollar bumped the floating dock and Feddi reached out to steady the craft as it swayed and bobbed in its own wake wash.

Marley jumped from the boat, tied the bow line off on a cleat, and kept going. He didn't look back or say goodbye.

Feddi threw up his hands.

"What?"

Feddi motioned toward the kid.

"He culls shellfish and untangles fishing line for me. Where we were or weren't supposed to be today is on me," Drake said.

"And you figure that's your call, how?" Feddi said. He put his hands on his hips, his face a mask of frustration and anger.

"You might have told me you wanted to speak with him," Drake said, as if it would have mattered. "He's running an urgent errand for me. A problem created because I had to come to port. What do you want?"

"What the hell happened out there today? Ratson's chief of security called. Said you tore into the cove and interfered with their research."

Drake tied off the aft cleat and fished the evidence they'd collected from the storage compartment in the command console. Three water samples of various composition and hue, two pieces from Scar's boat, the slip of paper from his camera bag and the shred of what he believed to be skin. He showed Feddi the items and described the scene, told how they floated into the cove and didn't bother anyone.

"And I'm supposed to believe your engines... plural, were down and that you floated right into the cove? The mouth of which is fifty yards wide."

Drake hiked his shoulders. He didn't owe this man anything. Then Drake remembered Feddi was a cop and worked for him. "I understand you're worried about whatever illegal shit your buddy Ratson is doing. You don't want it to get out. I get it, but I just showed you compelling evidence that proves—"

"Nothing!" Feddi yelled. He looked over his shoulder as if expecting to see Captain James, but when he wasn't standing there, Feddi turned back to Drake and sighed. "You've got nothing of substance. We don't even know for sure that Scar is missing. He's a vagrant, for shit's sake. And you better be careful with the accusations you're throwing around, Drake. I know you think you're a bigshot because those losers are impressed by you. I'm not. You're sticking your nose in business that doesn't concern you. I suggest—"

"Piss off!" Drake had heard enough. "If you're not going to look for Scar, I'll contact St. Croix myself."

"You do that and I can't help you."

"Oh, like you're helping me now? Go call your boss Ratson and give your report. I'm sure you don't want to keep him waiting."

"Drake," Feddi took a step forward so he and Drake were inches apart. "If you accuse me again of—"

"What's going on here? Drake? Is that you?" called a man's voice from the shadows. Trevor Linday walked into a cone of light that spilled across the dock.

"Mr. Linday," Feddi said. "A pleasure to see you, sir. No problem. Drake and I were just having..."

"A disagreement," Drake said. Trevor was a good guy. Drake liked him. He was one of the few rich tourists welcome at Dugan's, and Drake and the man had enjoyed many a drink and good conversation. Trevor was a Wall Street pit trader, and his life partner, John, was in the fashion industry. Drake took them fishing at his secret spots, and in return Trevor let Drake use his jet skis and promised to take him on his new luxury submarine.

"Sounded like you were being a bit rude, Officer Feddi," Trevor said.

Drake and Trevor exchanged smirks.

"It's O.K., Trev. He was just leaving," Drake said.

Feddi's eyes went wide and he dipped his head. "Evening to you both." He turned to leave, then stopped and locked eyes with Drake. "Remember what I said. I might not be able to help you next time." Feddi tipped his hat to Trevor and disappeared into the darkness.

"What the hell was that all about?" Trevor asked.

"Bad news. Scar is missing. I was trying to get—"

Trevor put up a hand. "I think I'm going to need a martini for this."

8

Drake left the Sand Dollar in port and caught a ride to Dugan's with Trevor. His fancy Range Rover glided over the pothole pocked streets, Drake in the passenger seat. Water reeds slid by on both sides of the road, walls of green with brown cotton-like escarpments. There were no streetlights, and the truck's headlight beams lit the desolate road like a klieg light. Stars blinked above, a thin haze stretching to the horizon the only remnant of the day's earlier bad weather. Wind whistled through the open windows, bringing the scent of low tide, hibiscus, and the sea.

Trevor made a left onto an unnamed road. There were no signs. No markers at all directing people to one of the island's oldest gin mills, and that was exactly how its owner, Chance Dugan, liked it. The place had been in the Dugan family for three generations, Chance's great grandfather having squatted on the choice piece of bay front real estate before official records were kept on the American side of the island.

Dugan's was a landmark, a place tourists searched for, like a hidden treasure they felt they were missing. They weren't missing anything, unless they liked stale beer and mosquitoes. They came to take selfies so they could tell tall tales at their resort bar. Preach about how they'd been to Dugan's and it was nothing special. Islanders gave wrong directions, and it was considered a major breach of island etiquette to reveal the local's prized hangout. Tourists who did find the place were served, and weren't treated rudely, but the silence when they entered, and a continued cold shoulder from all the bar's patrons usually sent a clear message and produced the desired effect. Few tourists who found Dugan's returned.

Trevor and John were exceptions.

The dark maw of a white crushed-shell driveway opened in the water reeds and Trevor turned onto the narrow lane. Broken shells popped and snapped as the truck rolled slowly down the drive, a thin strip of hardpan separating the vehicle from thick mangroves that arced over the road and blotted out the stars.

Dugan's had originally been a fishing shack, and it sat perched above the tide line, a field of tumbled boulders and fallen trees littering the slope that ran down to Simpson Bay. The lights of Fredericksville glowed in the east, the bay filled with slow moving vessels as the evening sunset cruises and party boats steamed in for the night.

The Land Rover crunched to a stop, and the two men jumped out.

"Can you give me a minute? I've got to make a call," Drake said.

"Meet you inside," Trevor said.

Drake waved and pulled out his phone. Louise picked up on the first ring.

"Hello?" She sounded mildly annoyed, as if she'd been expecting the call. She knew it was him from her cellphone caller ID.

"Hey, babe. What's happening?" he said.

"Made a salad. I've got two chunks of Hogfish ready to throw on the grill. Just waiting on you," she said.

"Yeah, that's why I called. I'm not going to be home for a while. Don't count on me for dinner."

Silence.

"You there?" he said.

"Not for much longer, Drake. Where are you? Dugan's?" she said.

"Yes, but it's not like—"

"You don't need to explain anything to me," she said.

"Apparently I do. I had a crazy day and we… I need to talk some things through," he said. As excuses go, he knew he'd failed, so he added, "We're planning a tour for tomorrow, also."

"See you around, Drake," Louise said, and hung up.

Drake sighed and pocketed his phone.

Dugan's was a ramshackle building covered in dark shingles, an occasional new cedar shake standing out like eyes. The view was amazing, and Chance had been offered millions for the property. He always said no, his favorite line being, "What the hell would I do with that much money?" Drake could think of a few things, but the bar was so entrenched in Chance's family history it was the foundation of his life. Drake didn't think Chance would sell the place for any price.

The scent of charred meat wafted from within as Drake pulled open the old ship's door.

Thumping bass guitar galloped through the place like the four horsemen of the apocalypse, and Drake's heart pumped, the rolling march of the song Barracuda by the iconic band Heart pounding through him like blood.

Ann Wilson's voice boomed about lying in the weeds, her stunning sound running through Dugan's like an anthem.

A chorus of customary hellos rose above the throbbing beat. The place's version of "everybody knows your name" and it always made Drake feel like he belonged, like Tetu was his home, even though he was a transplant.

Drake waved to Chance.

"How are we today, mate?"

"Better now," Drake said.

"Whatcha be having this evening? Your mates have already got a pitcher of martinis going. You want a glass? Olives?"

"That'd be great. You get Trevor one already?"

"Yes, sir." Chance handed over a chilled martini glass with olives impaled on a toothpick. "Enjoy. Just holler when you need a refill."

Drake nodded and accepted the glass.

"Yo!" Julian said as Drake exited the rear of the restaurant onto the deck. Two person tables lined the railing, and half of them were occupied. Large round tables were set back under a blue awning, and only one was in use. Past the railing, a rock-strewn hill packed with mangroves and beach grass stretched down to a field of boulders, a dark sand, seaweed-covered beach separated the bay from the thick vegetation. Simpson Bay glistened in the moonlight.

Drake took a seat between Haley and Trevor. Then came Helen, Jillian, Julian, and two open seats.

Haley said, "Everything OK? What took you so long?"

Drake sighed as he plunked his martini glass on the table.

A clear pitcher of vodka martini sat at the center of the table, a long glass stirrer sticking from its mouth at an odd angle. Trevor lifted the pitcher, condensation dripping on the old, stained, cable-spool table. He filled his glass and Drake's, then lifted his own.

"To Feddi," Trevor said. "Screw him!"

"Here, here," Julian said.

Everyone took pulls on their martinis.

They sat in silence for a time, sipping their drinks. The group exchanged glances, waiting for Drake, who savored his martini. The vodka seeped through him like elixir, and his muscle aches faded, the burn in his stomach driving the weariness from his bones.

Drake refilled everyone's glass and flagged down Chance.

"Another, mate?" the bartender asked as he bustled over to the table.

Drake put a hand on the man's arm. That was Drake's go to move when he really wanted someone to listen to what he was going to say, or when he was going to make a request. "You got a sec? I think you should hear this."

Trevor and Haley nodded.

Chance picked up the empty pitcher, looked around, and said, "Yeah, sure. For you I got two secs, Drake."

Crickets chirped, frogs bleated, an owl hooted, the bar music thumping in the background.

"What the hell happened out there today, Drake?" Haley said.

"You saw most of it," Drake said. He told the story from beginning to end. What he and Marley had found, what they'd seen, the confrontation with Ratson's men, and his subsequent conversation with Feddi.

"This is ten kinds of wrong," Chance said. "No way Scar would take off without telling us. Just not possible."

"That's exactly what we thought," Helen said.

"What do you think Scar stumbled on? Must have been important if they'd…" Jillian let the thought go unfinished.

Drake said nothing. He wasn't ready to admit his friend was gone. On that point, he agreed with Feddi. Was there enough evidence to warrant an investigation? Yes. Was the evidence solid enough to say with 100% surety that Scar had been kidnapped or killed? No.

"Do you think he's… he's dead?" Julian asked, his tone devoid of its constant mirth.

"I don't know," Drake said.

"Let's review what we do know," Haley said.

Drake and the others nodded.

"Well, I think we know his skiff went down when he was watching Kraken Island. We know there was blood in the water, but not where it came from. It doesn't look good, but I'm not ready to say he's gone. Not yet."

Helen said, "He's a tough SOB."

"Did you search the shoreline?" Jillian said. "To see if he washed up on shore? Maybe he was able to swim to safety."

That was possible, but unlikely. The current in the strait was intense, and Scar had been a mile offshore. It was more likely he'd wash up on St. Croix, that's if the sharks, Barracuda, and other scavengers didn't get him first. What he said was, "We should check. Can't hurt."

"If he's not dead, where the hell is he? Do they have him?" Jillian's chin nodded west toward Kraken Island.

"I don't see another explanation. Do you, Drake?" Haley said.

Drake shook his head no. "Not if he's alive. If he's in the water, who knows. A chopper could hunt for days and not find him because of the sun glare."

The group sipped their drinks. A foghorn sounded.

Chance stirred the martini pitcher and leveled everyone off.

"So what's next?" Helen said. The woman's face was burnt, her eyes red as cinders. Her dyed blonde hair was in a knot atop her head and held in place with a black banana clip. One of her tank-top straps hung off her shoulder, and reading glasses hung around her neck on a gold chain.

Drake leaned back and looked at his friends. Five sets of eyes watched him, waiting for him to lead, but this time he had no answers, and one crazy idea. "There's only one thing I can think of, and it's stupid."

Julian hooted. "Yes. Yes. Yes. Assault on Kraken Island."

Drake patted the air and looked over his shoulder at the bar and surrounding tables. "Lower your voice. Even in here I'm sure Ratson has ears."

Julian jerked back like he'd been punched, and his smile slid away from his face as he looked around at the other patrons.

"Unfortunately, I think you're right. I think I need to pay a visit to the island. Take a look around for myself," Drake said.

"You're right, that is stupid," Haley said.

"No, it's not," Chance said. "It's trying to be a flame thrower at your family picnic by spitting moonshine on a Bic stupid. There are guards all over the place. You know that."

"Forced to agree, mate," Jillian said. "What makes you think you'll be able to sneak by the guards? And even if you can, don't you think the buildings will be secured? The boats?"

"All excellent points. Other ideas?" Drake said.

Helen said, "Why not fly a drone in there? We can get a decent one cheap and I—"

Julian laughed. "They'll blow it out of the sky like they're skeet shooting, mate. All you'll do is waste dinero."

"Forced to agree," Haley said. "I've seen it. Maybe wait until it's dark to fly one in?"

"For that you'd need a much more expensive drone, right?" Drake said. He didn't know anything about the mini-robotic flies that seemed to be taking over the world.

"I'll look into it," Trevor said.

Crickets chirped, the faint sound of boat wake rolling onto the shore below.

"What do you think was in those water cage things?" Trevor asked.

Drake hiked his shoulders.

"Not to be an ass, but maybe if I go down to the station, the fuzz might do something? I go to the governor's fundraiser every year, and I've supported his political campaigns," Trevor said.

"Can't hurt. Thank you."

Trevor nodded.

"What's up, boss?" Marley said as he strode out onto the deck.

"Can I get you anything, Marley my boy? Water? Pop?" Chance said.

Marley looked at Drake, who ignored him, then he turned to Chance and said, "No thank you."

Chance let the kid hangout at the bar. Even though Marley was only sixteen, he was more mature than most forty-year-olds Drake knew. Still the crew discouraged the boy's drinking, everyone treating the kid as family, trying to teach him right from wrong. He was underage and couldn't afford to get in trouble. That wasn't to say Drake and the others didn't let the kid have a sniff now and then, but generally they kept things on the level because they didn't want to cause any problems for Chance or the boy.

Marley took the empty seat.

"What's the good word? You're here early," Drake said.

"I used Julian's theory, mate. Worked like a charm," Marley said.

The group turned to Julian and he hiked his shoulders.

"The theory of GUE, dude," Marley said.

Drake and Julian laughed, but the rest of the party stared at the boy with blank faces.

"Go ugly early," Marley said.

"What the hell is he talking about?" Helen said.

"What are you teaching him?" Haley said.

Julian looked like he'd just gotten caught sticking his finger in the wedding cake.

"I saw these three ug... physically challenged tourists. They were all alone in a corner, so I made some jokes, told them about the reef, how the guides would love little hotties like them," Marley said.

"And?" Drake said. "You closed?"

Marley nodded. "The three of them are meeting us on the dock at 0900. Half day tour at $200 each."

"$200." Drake whistled. "Sweet. Well done."

"What the hell did you tell them?" Jillian said. "That Julian would sleep with them?"

Julian's face twisted, then he nodded and smiled.

"Promised them run punch, colorful fish, guys in swim trunks, oh, and lunch."

"Good job, my padawan. Good job," Drake said. He sipped on his martini until there was a shot left and passed Marley the glass under the table. The kid's eyes lit up and he quickly downed the dregs and handed Drake back the empty glass.

Helen sighed and harrumphed, but it was only for effect. Her smile was wide, her cheeks red with vodka.

Chance held up the pitcher and said, "Another round?"

Drake said, "No thanks."

Everyone else said, "Yes please."

Three pitchers of martinis deep, nobody was in a position to drive, though Marley offered to drive Trevor's Land Rover. The kid was still riding his sip of vodka, all smiles and confidence.

"Chance, any chance..." Trevor said.

He looked around and everyone laughed except Chance.

"Very original," Chance said, but he was grinning ear-to-ear.

"Can you spare someone to drive us home?" Trevor said.

Chance raised an eyebrow and rolled his eyes.

"Five bucks from each of us. That's…" Trevor turned to count the group and Helen burp-laughed.

Drake sighed. He was feeling no pain, but he knew what five times seven was, and it was too much. "Tell Ronda $20 and she can drive Trevor's truck."

Trevor turned, smiled, and said, "Tell her she can—"

Chance held up a hand. "She's already gone. I can drop Marley and Helen. Trevor, call John."

Trevor rocked back, smiled, and gave a thumbs up.

The group dispersed, Helen heading to the bathroom, and Marley and Chance closing the hurricane shutters and locking up. Julian and Jillian retreated to the beach to smoke a joint, and Haley and Drake moved across the deck, collecting silverware.

When John arrived, everyone retreated to the parking lot where Drake recapped the next day's plan. Surprisingly, not everyone remembered the entire conversation. "Helen, you're going to walk the likely wash-up spots on the west coast. Haley, you'll fish south at the drop off, where the straits end, and J&J, Marley and I will take these tourists out to the wreck, then swing by the reef, and finish over by Kraken Island again and see what's to be seen."

9

Drake sat on the bench seat before the command console, watching the three tourists frolic in the shallows with Marley and Julian. Tiny waves washed over the sandspit, and Drake cracked his neck when he saw his snorkel gear tossed on the sand. The Sand Dollar was anchored off Boot Tip Point in six feet of water, Kraken Island a dark green stain to the southwest. A sweet breeze redolent of hibiscus and barbeque smoke floated on the wind, the small hibachi Jillian was tending sending plumes of black smoke rolling over the pristine Caribbean Sea.

"Marley, can I get another punch, please?" asked Crissy, one of the tourists. Her voice had the tone of politeness tinged with the haughty privilege of knowing she wasn't really asking a question. The big-boned lady from New York wore a gold bathing suit that hurt Drake's eyes when he looked at the woman.

"Coming right up," Jillian said as she worked her way toward the boat, handing out burgers as she went.

Crissy frowned at Marley, then realizing that meant the shirtless young Jamaican wouldn't have to leave her side, she smiled and handed her cup to Jillian. "Thank you," she said. Drake didn't think the woman could've been more condescending if she'd tried.

Tourists. Can't live with them, can't live without them.

Julian was teaching Lexi, the youngest of the tourist-trio, how to fish. He had his arms around her, working the reel as she held the pole's handle, a smile splitting her head. Stacey, a blonde who wore a one-piece Micky Mouse bathing suit, sipped on her punch as she lounged in a chair half buried in the sandspit, gentle waves breaking over her toes.

They'd snorkeled the reef, and the plane wreck off Heel Rock, but the three girls were more interested in eating burgers, drinking rum, and pretending Julian and Marley were interested in them.

Julian hooted and laughed as Lexi pulled a six-inch shiner from the sea, its scales glistening in the bright sunlight. There wasn't a cloud in the sky, and endless blue stretched to the horizon in every direction.

"How you doing, boss?" Jillian said as she squeezed the white plastic tap on the rum punch container.

"There's worse things I could be doing," he said. "Can you grab one of those for me?"

She lifted an eyebrow. "Little early, Captain, isn't it?" But she was smiling. She'd made the punch herself and to say it was watered down would be an understatement.

Drake inched sunglasses down to the end of his nose and stared at her above their rims.

"Just kidding. Give me a minute." Jillian climbed back into the sea to deliver her cocktail.

Drake shifted position, gazing southwest toward Kraken Island. He lifted binoculars to his eyes. Nothing stirred along the island's shoreline, no conning towers moved above the mangroves, and no smoke rose from Deep Hollow Cove.

Lexi shrieked as Julian handed her the wriggling fish. She screamed and dropped it back into the sea. As she stepped back, she slipped on a rock and fell with a splash, her friends laughing so hard rum punch poured from Stacey's nose and Crissy dropped to her knees.

Jillian sat next to Drake and handed him a rum punch.

"Thanks." He downed the entire contents of the small plastic cup with one pull.

"Something bothering you, boss?"

Drake nodded at Kraken Island. "Rich asshole thinks he can get away with whatever he wants. If I find out Ratson or his people harmed Scar, I'll…" Drake didn't make threats. They served no purpose other than to notify your enemy of your intentions and document your animosity.

"I'm worried about Scar too," Jillian said. She put a hand on his knee.

Jillian was twenty-eight, blonde, trim and muscular, but she had a boyish quality about her, like a piece of her fraternal twin Julian never totally separated from her. He felt no tingle, no attraction at her touch. Drake saw his reflection in Jillian's sunglasses. His hair was a bird's nest, white t-shirt stained with mud.

The laughing and splashing stopped.

Julian stood at the end of the sandspit, staring at the western horizon, Crissy behind him holding the fishing pole.

Stacey leaned forward in her chair, staring west.

Marley and Crissy waded through the shoals, and both of them had stopped picking up shells and were also staring west.

The surface of the Caribbean beyond a few feet away was white with sun glare. Drake peered through the binoculars, searching the western horizon. He saw only the white glare of the sun and heat rolling over the water in invisible waves.

A field of dimpled whitewater emerged from the glare, a chaotic jumble of fast-moving whitecaps that rippled over the sea like an invisible hailstorm pelted the ocean.

"What is it?" Jillian said.

Drake leaned in and handed her the binoculars, the lanyard still around his neck.

She said, "A school of fish?" She handed him back the field glasses.

"If so, it's a large school, and they're big and moving fast," Drake said.

The wind shifted, strands of blonde hair blowing across Jillian's face.

Drake scanned the horizon, but the Caribbean was once again tranquil and undisturbed. Seagulls cried, and small fish leapt from the water.

"You want them on the boat?" Jillian asked, gesturing toward the tourists, Marley and Julian.

"Naw, not yet. Give them a little extra time. They've been an easy group, and they paid top dollar. Maybe they'll come back or tell their friends," he said. Drake didn't really care if they did, he didn't need the money. But his crew did, and he didn't mind hauling tourists around. At least during daylight.

She nodded toward his empty plastic cup and he handed it to her. "So what's the deal with you and Louise?" Jillian filled his cup and handed it back.

"Deal?"

"Don't be a dork."

He sighed. "I don't know." He took a long pull of punch. "I like her. She's beautiful, we like hanging out together, no problems between the sheets, it's just..."

"She can be a bitch?" Jillian said.

"I was going to say possessive, but yeah, she can certainly be a bitch, but who can't?" he said.

"True," she said. "Question is, are you happy?"

Drake said nothing.

"Because, you've got options, you know."

Drake's eyes went wide, and he drained his punch and held out the empty glass.

She laughed. "You don't know who I'm talking about?"

He did, but he couldn't bring himself to say it. If he admitted he knew Haley had feelings for him, and that he might have feelings for her, everything would change, their group dynamic forever altered. Is that what he wanted? Is that what Haley wanted? She hadn't made a move, but neither had he, and then there was Louise.

Drake said nothing.

A shriek came from the water.

Marley had Crissy on his shoulders, and they were fighting Julian who had Lexi on his. The women shrieked and clawed at each other in their drunken merriment, Stacey doing what she always seemed to do, sitting on the side watching.

"O.K.," Jillian said, and got up. "You don't need to…" Her voice trailed away as she focused on the horizon to the west.

Drake followed her gaze.

The patch of turbulent water had returned, and it was closer.

A football field-sized area of roiling whitecaps surged over the ocean, building whitewater rising several inches above the sea's surface. The disturbance glistened in the sunlight, fish scales visible in the knot of water.

"Drake, I think we should pull them in," Jillian said.

Drake turned his attention back to the tourists.

The chicken fight had broken up, and Stacey, Crissy, and Julian were crossing the sandspit and wading through knee-high water toward the Sand Dollar.

Marley and Lexi were floating on their backs in the gentle surf, staring up at the crystal-clear blue sky.

"Not good." Drake yelled, "Julian, double-time it up here."

The young man looked confused, but he knew better than to question an order, especially in front of tourists. Julian picked up his pace, putting out his arms and gently guiding the two semi-drunk women to the dive platforms on the rear of the Sand Dollar.

A rank stench wafted over the Caribbean, the sound of rushing water rising above the push of the sea breeze. The field of rippling whitewater was a hundred yards off the port bow. Barracuda jumped from the churning water, dark eyes focused, long curved needle-like teeth bared.

"Marley! Marley!" Jillian yelled, trying to get the kid's attention, but he and Lexi still floated on their backs, ears beneath the water's surface.

Drake ran to a bag of beach games he kept for tourists— giant chess, bocce, and an assortment of balls and kites. He grabbed a football and ran across the deck, slipped in a wet spot, and slid like he was on a skateboard, arms stretched out for balance, goofy left foot out before him. He hit the gunnel and came to a stop, reared back, and fired a bullet at Marley, flexing his hips and putting everything he had into the throw.

It missed and missiled into the sea five feet from Marley, but it was enough.

Thinking someone was messing with him, Marley rolled and surged from the ocean, ready to rush whoever had thrown the ball. Instead, he saw the swarm of teeth and whitewater surging toward him and froze, staring west like his feet were stuck in the sand.

"Marley! Marley!" Drake and Jillian screamed.

Julian and the tourists scrambled onto the Sand Dollar, their eyes locked on the patch of white roiling sea foam advancing on their position.

"What is that?" Crissy asked.

Marley helped Lexi to her feet. She struggled and fought at first, but when Marley pointed at the knot of water coming at them, she screamed and ran.

"They're not gonna make it," Julian said. He dove into the sea and stroked hard, not heeding Drake's calls.

Julian swam, and Marley and Lexi splashed across the shoals toward the boat.

The swarm changed direction, knifing south toward the entrance to Simpson Bay.

Drake breathed deep, and it felt like that was the first breath he'd taken in hours.

"What the hell was that?" Jillian said.

"A Barracuda swarm."

"A what now?" she said.

Julian reached Marley and patted the kid on the head. Drake's mates had realized the immediate danger had passed, but they didn't waste any time gathering the gear, dousing the coals, and heading back toward the boat.

"Did you see the…" Jillian's eyes were still wide as she stared south toward the fading field of dimpled sea. "The teeth? Did you see the teeth? I've never seen a Barracuda act like that. They hide in rocks and bite your hand off, they don't work together to attack humans."

Drake said nothing. He hadn't taken his eyes off Marley and the others.

"Why do you think they took off? Water too shallow?" Jillian pressed on.

Drake didn't have answers, just more questions.

Lexi climbed aboard with Marley's help, then the young Jamaican followed.

When Julian stepped onto the Sand Dollar's deck, Jillian punched him hard on the shoulder.

"Easy. That hurt," Julian said as he rubbed where she'd hit him.

"What the hell were you thinking? You want to be a hero? What about me? What the hell would I do if you got killed?" She hit him again.

"Maybe find a man," Crissy said.

Everyone stared at the woman.

She burped, and said, "Excuse me."

"Take a seat, please," Jillian said as she corralled the tourists to the bow.

Drake fired up the outboards and brought the Sand Dollar up on plane, the Zodiac slicing through the light surf.

The entrance to the Fredericksville Harbor loomed in the distance, and the tourists sipped rum punch and chatted, content in the glow that only a day on the Caribbean Sea can deliver.

The UHF crackled to life. "Mayday. This is Dive Rental Fred in need of assistance. Diver under attack. Mayday. Mayday. We're off Simpson Bay."

Drake grabbed the handset. "We've got you DR Fred. What's your exact location?"

"Dive marker eight, just north of Teapot Cove. Over."

Drake addressed his crew. "They're close. I'm going to respond. Your jobs are to look after them," he said as he pointed to the bow where the tourists sat. He spun the wheel, the outboards coughing and sputtering, the Zodiac throwing spray as the craft arced southeast.

"On our way DR Fred. Out." Drake put the handset back in its cradle. He was familiar with Des Krispin's fleet of rental dive boats. He had seven eighteen-foot Boston Whalers, and they were all named after children or grandchildren.

He dropped the hammer, and the twin Yamahas screamed as the Sand Dollar leapt from the water, driving through the sea and shooting two fifteen-foot rooster tails.

The DR Fred was surrounded by tumultuous sea, long slender fish mounding on one another, launching from the ocean, teeth shining in the harsh sunlight. The Barracuda were in a feeding frenzy, and they squeezed, chomped and slithered as one, a mass of roiling scales and teeth.

"Dear God," Jillian said.

A diver struggled in the water, the man's black hooded head bobbing in the waves, arms thrashing. He screamed and wailed, legs churning as Barracuda bit him, sharp teeth tearing through the thin wetsuit.

Drake spun the wheel and the Sand Dollar knifed into the swarm, the engine coughing and choking as Barracuda were diced and sliced, leaving a wake of blood, bones, and gristle. He snapped the throttle into neutral, and the Zodiac bumped into the DR Fred's port gunnel and came to a rocking stop amidst the churning horde of fish.

A woman with short blonde hair ran across the DR Fred's deck. "Help him. Please! Help him."

The diver in the water was getting pulled under as he fought to keep himself above the surging sea, the fish making strafing runs, some locking on, jaws clamped closed, tails writhing, others taking glancing bites out of the man as he screamed and struggled.

Barracuda covered the guy like ants on a fallen lollipop, caudal fins thrashing, jaws snapping and tearing. The diver yelled as a fish clamped down on his neck, a stream of dark blood spraying over the sea's surface. The man yelled one last time, a strangling cry that fell silent as he went under, the thrashing knot of Barracuda biting and ripping. The diver surged from the sea one last time, arms reaching for the sky, his wetsuit shredded, right arm missing, blood covering his face.

A loud sucking sound echoed off the water as the diver went under as he was devoured by the swarm.

Drake ran for the gaff, but stopped. What could he do? There were so many.

Barracuda writhed and swam, the swarm surging from the area as fast as it had appeared. Blood bubbles popped and snapped as the sea flattened, the whitewater settling.

The woman cried and wailed, and Jillian jumped from the Sand Dollar to the DR Fred to comfort the woman, but she wouldn't stop yelling and screaming.

The clear Caribbean Sea turned crimson.

10

Helen walked alone on the desolate, windswept white sand beach the locals called Lonely Run. On maps it was called Two Mile Beach, though it was longer than two miles. Islanders called it lonely because it ran from the southern side of the channel that ran into Teapot Cove, down to the English fishing village of New London. There were no access roads, no parking lots, and authorities warned tourists away from the deserted stretch of beach. That's why it was a favorite of locals.

Waves crashed, whitewater rolling toward her, only to be sucked back into the ocean. Beyond the breakers the Caribbean Sea flowed swiftly south, the current in the strait between Tetu and Kraken Islands strong and consistent. To the north, Boot Tip Point jutted into the sea like an arm, the town of Fredericksville nestled within Simpson Bay. Small crafts flowed in and out of Teapot Bay, a foghorn sounded, and Helen looked at her watch.

It was 5:19PM, and the sun had started its fall to Earth. She'd walked all day and her legs ached. She was used to being on her feet. She'd been a crossing guard up north for forty-two years, and her old liver spot-stained legs were taut and muscular, but she'd walked the entire border of Simpson Bay, threaded through tourists down to Teapot Cove, around its entire circumference, and found nothing of interest.

When she reached New London, she'd have a couple of drinks and catch a cab to Dugan's.

Helen waved as she passed a family lounging on the beach, two little children riding boogieboards in the gentle surf. The dunes fell away, and New London sparkled in the late afternoon sun, daggers of bright light cutting through the incoming cloud cover and sending errant rays across the beach.

The closer she got to New London, the more people she saw. Houses, resorts, and hotels sprung up beyond the dunes, surrounding the quaint fishing town. Helen saw folks sitting on their decks, heard the faint tinkle of chatter, smelled the sharp scent of charred meat and smoke.

She threaded through groups of beach goers as they packed up their stuff, everyone looking to get a jump on the next stage of fun. Helen didn't understand tourists. She'd been one many times, of course, but she didn't understand people that followed a stricter schedule on vacation than they did at home. Hurry and pack up, we've got a dinner reservation. We have to pick up this, and that, and we've got tours, and meetings, and... It hurt Helen's head just thinking about it, and to her it was no surprise most people who visited Tetu left happy and fulfilled, but in need of a rest.

A child screamed and Helen gazed west toward the sea.

Several kids frolicked and swam in the ocean, and one of the children floated just beyond the breakers, the current tugging him out to sea.

Helen's hackles rose. A stench washed over the beach, like low tide baking in Summer heat, and everything Drake said the prior night came rushing back. She glanced around, looking for parents, and there were many possibilities. Bars, hotels, and restaurants lined the eastern edge of the beach now, and people drank and talked under umbrellas and in blue cabanas. She'd never find them.

The stink got stronger, and people started covering their noses, looking around in disbelief.

Just inside the breakers, moving fast along the shoreline, a field of whitewater surged over the sea like a watery avalanche.

Her first year on the job, Helen was almost fired. It had been one of the most stressful and painful situations she'd ever gone through in her sixty-six years. She'd been standing roadside, arms out, whistle in her mouth, when little Kimmy Drapper stepped from the crowd of children behind her and started to cross the road, cars still streaming in both directions. Horns blared, and Helen had reached out and grabbed the child, jerking her back with such force she left bruises on the kid's arm. In a day and age when children below the age of five can do no wrong, the parents complained, and it had only been a traffic camera mounted on a nearby light pole that had saved her. She'd been so upset and demoralized. To be treated like a criminal for saving someone's life.

The old anger grew in her as she watched the field of dimpled water roll over the ocean toward the children.

She ran toward the sea, screaming. "Get out of the water. Now! Get out!"

Heads turned, mothers vaulted to their feet, spilling frozen drinks. The lifeguard on duty woke from her daze and leapt down onto the pile of sand at the foot of her lifeguard stand and charged into the sea.

Helen didn't stop. She ran into the water and grabbed children by the arms, dragging them to shore.

Parents protested and screamed, but when they saw the roiling mass of whitewater surging toward their kids, they joined the effort.

The lone child out in the breakers hadn't heard the commotion, and he swam lazily in the churning sea, head appearing and disappearing in the crashing waves.

The swarm was a hundred yards away from the boy.

Helen dove into the face of a breaking wave and swam hard, arms stroking smoothly, legs kicking. She lifted her head and yelled when she got close to the boy.

He heard her, and his head jerked above the waterline, his gaze shifting to Helen as she powered toward him, arms and legs aching, lungs burning from the exertion.

She stopped swimming and tread water, waving at the boy, beckoning him to come to her.

The kid did. He swam hard, the current pulling at him.

He wasn't going to make it. The field of roiling whitewater was almost on the boy and a large set of waves rolled in, the sea lifting.

The kid disappeared.

Helen closed her eyes, tears leaking down her face, the ocean popping and snapping around her.

Someone screamed, and Helen's eyes snapped open, but what she saw put a smile on her face.

It hadn't been the boy who'd screamed. It was someone on the beach—most likely the boy's mother. The kid belly-surfed the face of a breaking wave, and when he zipped past Helen, she figured it was time to get the hell out of the water.

She turned and swam, and when the water got shallow, she let her feet hit the sandy sea floor. She waded through the surf and collapsed on the beach.

"What the hell did you do that for?" an adult asked. "The kids were having fun."

Helen rolled over and looked out to sea, but there was nothing there except the glare of the falling sun.

***

The Mary Queen chugged south, the current in the strait helping pull the boat along. The tourists had lines out, but nothing was hitting. They'd been floating all day under the hot glare of the sun, but other than dolphins and seagulls, they'd seen nothing.

This group of butterflies didn't seem to care. They drank beer, laughed, chatting and enjoying the sun and not really paying attention to the fishing. Haley got it. It was more about being out on the Caribbean than fishing or catching anything. Half the people she brought out wouldn't know how to clean a fish, and the other half didn't want to learn.

The water got murky, and a foul stench wafted over the boat.

"Who farted?" said one of the men, and everyone laughed.

Helen went to the bow, scanning the sea. A greenish-gray cloud the size of a football field filled the ocean, dark black and white strands running through the cloud like snotty entrails.

The tourists covered their noses and bitched as Haley changed course, turning the Mary Queen around and heading back north. Smoke poured from the boat's stack as the old diesel engine rumbled, the deck vibrating. The fishing boat cut through the growing surf, throwing spray, building up to a speed of twelve knots.

"Ms. Haley, what's that?" asked a teenage girl. Haley was amazed to see the child had put away her phone. She pointed north toward a rolling fist of whitewater that cut across the strait toward Kraken Island.

Haley searched for her eye scope and found it in the pouch on the fish fighting chair. She pulled it free and peered through it, but with the sun glare she didn't see much. The dorsal fins of two dolphins fifty yards off, a few birds flying in a tight formation just above the water, a patch of leaping minnows, but no field of churning whitewater.

She took the scope away from her eye and scanned the sea unaided, but saw nothing unusual.

***

Drake stood in stunned silence, the screams of the dead diver's friend like an icepick in his brain. Lexi cried and whimpered, and even the warm sunlight on Drake's face didn't ease his fighting nerves. A pink cloud spread through the sea, pieces of black rubber, fat, and gristle floating on a slick of dark blood, strands of veins and muscle running through what was left of the diver.

"Ma'am, please stop screaming," Jillian said. She guided the woman to a deck chair and sat her in it, but the woman's wailing only got louder.

Stacey and Crissy sat on the bow cushions, eyes wide as quarters.

Drake grabbed the UHF handset. He went to the emergency channel, gave his hull number, location, and briefly recounted what he'd seen. The dispatcher said he'd already sent a vessel when he heard the Mayday, and he ordered Drake to stay in place until the police boat arrived.

Drake brought up the binoculars.

The sun settled on the western horizon. Sun glare covered the Caribbean Sea like a blanket, and if the swarm was out there, Drake couldn't see it. He let the binoculars fall to his chest in frustration, and said, "Julian, get a line on the Fred."

Julian nodded and went about tying the dive boat and the Sand Dollar together.

The woman on the Fred with Jillian was sobbing, and Drake stepped over the gunnel and went to the woman.

"The police are on the way," Drake said. "Can I get you anything? Water? Some bread? Snacks?"

Julian added, "Rum punch."

Drake shot him a dirty look, but his face softened when the woman said, "That might settle my nerves. Thank you."

Drake nodded to Julian.

"The police are going to want to know what happened," Drake said to the woman. He looked at each of his crew in turn, his unwritten, unspoken command to keep their traps shut overwhelmingly clear. Drake knew the woman was upset, but he needed to hear what happened, because Feddi sure wouldn't tell him.

Julian returned with the rum punch and handed it over the gunnel to Drake, who relayed it to the woman.

She nodded her thanks and downed the punch with one pull and handed the cup back to Drake. Shit flows down, so Drake handed the cup over to Julian, who needed no instructions.

The woman hooted and snorted. "Feel a little better now," she said.

"What happened?"

She accepted another cup of rum punch, and said, "Well, you saw most of it."

Drake waited and said nothing. He'd learned that trick from an officer on his first tour. Stay silent, and people talk.

"Jimmy wanted to dive for lobsters. He's never been deeper than twenty feet, but Krispin said the water depth here is perfect for spear fishing. He was hunting for fish and lobsters. We were going to have what he caught for dinner." She started to wail and cry.

Drake patted her back. "Easy now. Easy." He waited, the pop and crack of the sea pelting the boats filling the silence.

"I was just reading, when I caught this nasty smell. Like the biggest pile of shi… waste ever was floating toward me." She sniffled, drank her rum punch, and passed over the empty cup.

Marley leaned across the gap between boats, tapped Drake's shoulder, and nodded to the east.

The Fredericksville police boat was skipping over the sea, heading right toward them. He had two minutes.

Drake didn't want to push her, but he had no choice. "Then what?"

"You saw it," she said. "The swarm surrounded the boat. Jumping. Biting. I was so scared, but when I remembered Jimmy was in the water I freaked. That's when I sent out the Mayday."

Drake nodded and got to his feet, the DR Fred listing in the gentle surf. "I'm very sorry, Mrs.?"

"Please call me Kendra. Kendra Longly," she said, and held out her slender hand.

Drake took it gently, and said, "I'm very sorry for your loss."

She nodded, and the tears came again, and that led to wailing as she dropped back into the deck chair and let her head fall in her hands.

The incoming SAFE boat screamed to a stop and two officers boarded the DR Fred before the police boat's engine went still.

Drake retreated to the Sand Dollar with Jillian, and he, his crew, and the tourists watched as the two officers questioned Kendra, the woman giving the same exact story she'd told Drake. They questioned Drake and his crew, the ladies, and asked if one of his crew could bring the DR Fred back to the harbor.

Julian volunteered. "Never hurts to score some points with the boys in blue," he said as he spun the Fred around and sped off, leaving the police boat and the Sand Dollar rocking in its wake.

The cops thanked Drake, and he gave Kendra one of his business cards. "If you need anything, day or night, please call me," Drake told her, and strangely, it was Haley's aggravated face he saw in his mind's eye, not Louise's.

She nodded.

The police SAFE boat pulled away and disappeared into the dusk.

The sun went down in the west, leaving only a bruised sky of purple-orange over black. The Sand Dollar skipped and hopped over the two-foot waves, sea spray coating the boat in a fine layer of mist.

The tourists sat on the bow cushions, huddled together like they'd been through a war. He figured he'd never see them again. Drake pushed down the throttle, the outboards whining as he headed for port, his mind spinning. He kept coming back to Ratson. In his gut he knew the rabid Barracuda were somehow connected to the rich asshole, and when he had proof, Ratson would pay, even if it cost Drake everything he had. He'd given it all up before to do what he thought was right, and he'd do it again if he had to.

11

Saturday and Sunday were usually off days for Drake because tourists traveled on weekends, and with many locals off from work or dealing with the flow of off-islanders, booking tours was impossible. After dropping the butterflies and crew off in Simpson Harbor, Drake and Marley brought the Sand Dollar around so he could moor it offshore behind Drake's place.

The Zodiac screamed past Heel Rock, and Drake pulled back on the throttle, searching for the mooring buoy in the darkness. Stars blinked, and tattered clouds drifted lazily across the horizon, beams of moonlight slicing into the clear Caribbean Sea like spotlights. The ocean was inky black glass, and hardly a ripple disturbed its tranquility. A warm breeze redolent of roasting garlic pushed across the water.

Drake's small house was a shadow behind the spidery mangroves and swaying beach grass. The place was dark, save for the kitchen light above the sink. Drake sighed. He wasn't in the mood for company. He was exhausted, every joint ached, and his throat felt like sandpaper rubbed with peanut butter. He stiffened, anger and frustration building.

Marley said, "Smells good."

Drake looked hard at the boy and Marley's eyes fell to the deck.

"You worry about the mooring line," Drake said.

Marley nodded in the darkness.

Instantly Drake felt like a shit. Not only because his friend was trying to lighten the mood and make him feel better, but because the kid was poor, and that was his way of asking for food. "I'm sorry, mate." He patted the kid on the back.

Marley smiled, his white teeth standing out in the darkness against his black face. "It's all good, Mr. Drake. Everybody has bad days, and seeing a guy get eaten qualifies."

Drake nodded. "I'm sorry you had to see that."

The kid shrugged.

Marley didn't realize what he'd seen yet. He hadn't woken-up in the middle of the night screaming, the memory of the blood, the wails of pain. That was something Drake couldn't help the boy with, and like all wounds, as time passed the memory would fade, but never fully heal. What Marley had seen would haunt him his entire life. The boy was just too young and inexperienced to know it yet.

Marley grabbed the boat pole and hooked the mooring buoy.

Drake cut the engines, the sound of servos echoing over the sea as he raised the motors. The NAV lights blinked out as Marley tied the mooring rope to the forward bow cleat. Then he started pulling the Sand Dollar toward shore, six-inch waves tinkling on the hull.

"Why don't you hang for dinner?" Drake said.

"Don't you want to head to Dugan's? See if the others saw anything? Don't you want to tell them—"

"Easy, Tonto, easy," Drake said.

"What the hell is a Tonto?" the kid said.

Drake sighed. Marley acted so mature he often forgot the kid was sixteen and didn't grow up in America. "A sidekick."

Marley's eyes rose and he smiled. "Sidekick. I like the sound of that." The pully sang as Marley pulled on the mooring line until the Zodiac crunched onto the rock beach. Small waves smacked the transom, and it was then Drake saw Louise sitting on the deck, a candle on the table before her.

"Let me head up. Stay here and tidy-up while I get the lay of the land. Maybe we'll eat fast, then go to Dugan's."

Marley nodded vigorously.

Drake hopped over the gunnel, the slight undertow sucking at his feet when he hit the pebble beach. Sharp shells and stones rolled against his ankles, seaweed tangling between his toes as the sea retreated, only to surge forward again. Beach grass whispered and sighed as he made his way up to the house.

"Howdy," Louise said as Drake emerged from the mangroves.

"Howdy to you," he said as he climbed the steps to the deck and sat before her.

Vader sat next to her.

A loud clang reverberated up from the shoreline, Marley putting away the anchor.

Vader puff-barked.

Louise frowned. "You're not alone?"

He shook his head no, and took a pull off her wine.

"Made roast chicken with garlic," she said. Her eyes narrowed and her tone was glacial.

"Smells good," Drake said. He was having trouble containing his frustration, but he knew she meant well, and he kept telling himself not to be an ass.

"Do you have to drop Marley—I assume that's who's down there, because I'm sure the rest of the crew is already at Dugan's—do you have to bring him home? Drop him someplace?" She left no doubts with the harshness of her voice that when she said 'someplace' she meant Dugan's.

"Actually, I'm not done for the night. Had a really long day. We—"

"Yeah, a long day. Sitting on the Caribbean with bikini clad tourists," Louise said. She stood and paced back and forth along the picnic table as she ranted, Vader's eyes following her. "You make this too hard, Drake. I try to be—"

"We saw a diver devoured by a swarm of rabid Barracuda," Drake said.

She stared at him, eyes wide, mouth open a crack. Her face softened, and she said, "Rabid Barracuda?"

He nodded. "We think. I've got to talk to Helen and Haley and see if they found anything today so we can go back to Feddi in the morning."

"Haley," Louise said in the same way people said IRS.

"Look, this is getting—"

Vader barked twice and lifted his head from his paws.

"William? Are you there?" A woman's voice floated from the mangroves like the call of a dove.

Louise's hands went to her hips.

Drake shrugged.

"Mr. Drake? Are you here? I need to see you," the female voice said.

"Back here," Louise yelled. She turned her eyes on Drake, shrugged and threw up her hands in a 'let's see what the hell this is now' motion.

The click of the gate being opened, the latch clanging as it fell back into place, then the snap of the motion detector as it turned on the floodlight on the corner of the house. A slender, attractive woman with short blonde hair wearing a floral sundress walked into the cone of light, raising her arm to cover her eyes. "Drake?"

Louise drew her head back as if preparing to yell, but instead she folded her arms across her chest.

"Mrs. Longly," Drake said. He vaulted from his chair and went to the woman, concern growing in him like fungus.

"Thank God I found you. I didn't know what to do," she said.

Out on the sea, in the panic of the moment and with the stress of the swarm, Drake hadn't noticed how beautiful the woman was. Her eyes gleamed in the moonlight, the white flowers on her dress glowing.

Louise cleared her throat.

"Yes," Drake said. "This is Mrs. Kendra Longly. She..." Drake paused. He didn't want to blurt out Kendra was the wife of the diver that had been killed.

That second of thoughtful hesitation sealed the fate of Drake and Louise's relationship.

Before Drake answered, Louise went on the attack. "Did he tell you he's in a relationship? With me!" She stabbed her own chest with a finger.

"Oh, I don't think you understand. Drake..."

"I think I do understand," Louise looked Kendra up and down like she was a bug she wanted to squash.

"That's enough," Drake boomed.

Both women took a step back and stared at him.

"Mrs. Longly, I apologize for Louise's behavior," Drake said.

Louise harrumphed and started to speak but Drake put up a hand.

"Not that it matters at this point, but you didn't even give me a chance to explain."

Louise refolded her arms.

"Her husband was the diver killed today," Drake said.

Louise deflated like a balloon, her eyes falling to the ground. When she looked at Drake again, he saw in her face she knew what was coming next.

"I think we need to take a break. I didn't invite you here tonight. I explained I had a rough day, but I understand you're looking for a real companion. Right now, that isn't me," he said.

Kendra Longly stood by, face blurring red.

The motion light clicked off and Drake waved his arm, and it came back on. "I think maybe you should leave," he said.

Louise nodded and retreated to the house.

Drake sighed.

"I'm sorry, I didn't mean to start an argument, but the cops are blowing me off and I don't know what to do," Kendra said.

He waved a hand. "No worries. What you just saw was going to happen whether you came over tonight or not. It really had nothing to do with you."

She nodded.

Louise's car started, and gravel crunched and popped as her Jeep rolled down the driveway. Drake felt good, like business had been settled and now he could move on to new things, new... He thought of Haley. Now he had no excuses.

"What'd I miss?" Marley said as he came up from the beach.

Drake fed Vader as Marley and Kendra packed up the chicken and macaroni salad Louise had made. Then the trio headed down to Dugan's where the rest of the crew waited patiently for Drake's arrival like a line of ducklings awaiting their mother.

"Drake!" came the chorus of voices as he entered Dugan's with Marley and Kendra in tow.

"And who be this flower you've brought with you?" Chance said.

"This is Mrs. Longly..." Drake said, then quickly added, "...she lost her husband today."

Chance's eyes went wide. "I heard something happened," he said.

Drake put the food on the bar. "You eat yet?"

"I could eat," Chance said.

The bartender grabbed plates, napkins, and plastic utensils, and when he arrived at the crew's table, Drake was already on his second rum punch. The whole group was there, and they let Drake choke down some food before they pestered him with questions.

"Kendra, I'm going to tell my friends what happened today. Do you think you can hear it? You can wait by the bar if—"

She was shaking her head no. "I need to do something. I want to know what's happening," she said.

Drake nodded. He told his tale from first to last, Marley nodding the entire time.

When Drake was done, Julian whistled.

"Damn," Jillian said. "I'm very sorry for your loss, Mrs. Longly."

A chorus of sorrys and my condolences.

"I saw it," Helen said. "The swarm I mean. It almost got a little boy." Helen told the party what she'd seen, then Haley spoke. With the day's efforts laid bare, the ragtag group ate in silence.

The front door to Dugan's slammed, but there was no chorus of 'hellos', no chant of someone's name.

Chance lifted an eyebrow.

"Shit," Drake said.

Beard Boy strode up to the bar like he owned the place, and a waitress pointed to Drake's table.

"Looks like trouble," Jillian said.

"That's the guy from Deep Hollow Cove?" Marley said.

Drake nodded.

"Stay cool. I don't want the cops here," Chance said.

"Appreciate your concern for my safety," Drake said.

Beard Boy looked younger than Drake remembered. His black hair was short and wild, his dark beard tight, but unkept. Hazel eyes locked on Drake as the man approached. He stopped before the group's table and held his hands out, palms up. "Mr. Drake?"

Drake said nothing.

"Surely you recognize me, no?" The man's voice sounded Russian, but like a weak copy.

"You've got balls coming in here," Drake said. "After that bullshit you pulled today."

A flash of anger crinkled the man's face, but he mastered himself and said, "That is why I am here."

"Do tell," Drake said.

"My employer, Mr. Ratson, has agreed not to file trespassing charges if you'll agree to stay away from Deep Hollow Cove. We're conducting sensitive research there that is costing my employer much money and you're causing needless problems. Have I been clear?"

"As mud," Drake said.

Marley snickered.

Drake and Beard Boy shot Marley harsh looks and he wilted.

"You will not come back. Do you understand?" He paused and looked around the table. "Otherwise there will be consequences."

Drake wasn't a violent person by nature, and he rarely picked a fight or argued unless it was important and necessary. But today was different. He'd seen a guy eaten alive, fought and broken up with his girl because she couldn't trust him, and now he was being threatened by an overpaid lackey that had no business even being in Dugan's, let alone telling him what he could and couldn't do. Drake pushed his chair back and got to his feet.

Screeching and scraping echoed through the bar as all the chairs around the table slid back, the entire group surveying the alpha males with wide eyes.

Drake strode forward until he was a foot from Beard Boy, and the guy did exactly what Drake had hoped.

Beard Boy reached behind him, and Drake didn't wait to see what he was going for.

Drake swept his right leg low; a fast, powerful strike that took Beard Boy's legs out from under him and sent him to the floor. Drake was on the man like a spider, sitting on his legs and pinning his arms to the floor. Beard Boy thrashed and fought, but Drake held him fast.

The guy spit a curse Drake didn't understand as Haley stepped forward and pulled a snub-nosed revolver from the thug's waistband.

"Gun," she said as she held it up and snapped open the cylinder. "Not loaded."

"Lucky for you, dipshit," Drake said.

Guns were serious in the Caribbean, especially pistols, and possession of an unlicensed handgun carried stiff punishments, especially if you were a butterfly or off-islander.

Chance said, "Should I call the police?"

"Not yet," Drake said. He pressed Beard Boy's face to the ground, and got low, whispering in his ear. "Tell your boss I'm coming for him."

Drake released the man and Beard Boy vaulted to his feet, ready to fight, but when he saw the crowd arrayed against him, he grimaced. "This isn't over," he said.

"Not by a long road," Drake said.

The thug turned on his heel and left.

"Damn. You made quite an impression," Haley said.

"You aint seen nothing yet," Drake said. "Tomorrow we're calling St. Croix and I'm gonna get proof of the swarm's existence. Pictures or video. We'll lay a slick."

Nodding heads and murmurs of agreement.

"Then tomorrow night after dark, I'm searching Kraken Island," Drake said.

12

The chirp and buzz of Drake's phone brought him awake, sunlight streaming through the bedroom window, tracing dancing shadows on the walls. His stomach gurgled and growled, and his muscles screamed as if he hadn't slept at all. Pain knifed through his head, like a nail in his forehead. He rubbed his temples, and regretted that last shot of Kraken rum.

Vader lay beside the bed, dark eyes closed, chest rising and falling. With twice the traffic of a normal day as tourists were shuttled out and a new crop brought in, the thunder of planes coming and going at Ventras International Airport was a constant rumble above the crashing surf and the crackle and pop of pebbles and shells as they were sucked back into the sea.

Drake fumbled for his phone and tapped 'Accept Call'. "Yeah."

"Drake? It's Kendra."

"Yeah."

"I'm sorry to wake you, but I don't know what to do and I have nobody else to turn to. My brother and his wife won't be here until late tomorrow," Kendra said. People from up north talked so damn fast. Drake remembered when he'd talked that fast. The locals had made fun of him for two years until he naturally adjusted, and now everyone made fun of him when he visited home.

He looked at his phone. 8:19AM. He was already late. "No. No," he said. He needed to show this woman some compassion, which wasn't one of his areas of strength. "As you know, it was a late night. What's wrong?"

"As you predicted, Governor Trainer's PR team is in full damage control mode. They're not even acknowledging my husband's death. They're saying the facts need to be verified."

"The cops spoke with everyone at the scene. Are you saying they don't believe us?" Drake's hackles rose, hunger pains churning into overdrive.

"Not exactly. Feddi won't take my calls, but the desk sergeant said everything is still under investigation, and that a formal statement will be made in the next few days."

Drake harrumphed. "Right, when it's old news. Trainer doesn't want this getting picked up by the major news outlets. Tourists getting eaten is bad for business." He put his free hand to his forehead and tapped that nail. He was such an ass. "Mrs. Longly, you have my apologies. I haven't had my coffee yet and I'm working on one brain cell at the moment."

"Call me Kendra, please," she said. "And don't worry about it. I'm from Long Island, and most folks feel the same things about the tourists who come to the island during the Summer."

"Still," he said. "It was insensitive, and that's not what you need right now. I'm very sorry."

She said nothing, a snap of static filling the line.

"What is it you do need, Kendra?" he asked.

She started to cry, faint halting sobs that built like a raging storm until the woman was shrieking and wailing. "I... don't know... what I'm going to do without him."

Drake tried to put himself in the woman's shoes. Less than twenty-four hours ago she'd been enjoying a day on the Caribbean Sea as her partner dove for dinner, what to do on her vacation in paradise her only worry. Now she was alone on the island, her life forever altered, her vacation over. He said, "I need all the help I can get today. Where are you?"

"Back at my hotel," she said.

"Have breakfast and sit tight for a bit. Let me get things going over here. I'm sure there'll be plenty of things you can do to help," he said.

"That's another reason I called," she said. "I want in on everything you're planning."

"I don't think that's—"

"Drake, if you didn't want me in this, you shouldn't have told me everything you did last night. I'm not going to let Ratson get away with this. Like Scar for you, this is personal."

"O.K.," he said. "I understand."

Silence.

"Is there anything else I can do for you right now, Kendra?"

"If you try and give me the slip, I'll tell Feddi what you're up to," she said.

"No need to threaten anyone. I'm trying to help you here," he said. He was a little aggravated at her lack of trust, but he understood. Hell, giving her the slip had already crossed his mind, but he had an idea how she could help. A task that was made for her, but he needed to give Feddi one last chance to do the right thing first.

"Please don't be offended," she said. "But I know honorable men like you, Drake, and they justify all kinds of bullshit in the name of keeping women safe. I want in on this."

"Understood. No offense taken," he said. "Call you soon."

Drake clicked off and rolled over as he searched his contact list for Marley's number. When he found it, he texted, "GOHNWF," and got up.

The phone trilled a heartbeat later. "On way, what u want from The Hub?"

"Eggwhich w/ bacon," he texted back. Then, "And don't forget the bucket of special sauce." Before they'd left Dugan's the prior night, they'd made a bucket of the foulest smelling chum Drake had ever concocted. Chance contributed the food grade bucket and a bunch of rotten food from the bar's garbage.

With breakfast on the way, he shuffled into the bathroom. Once on the porcelain throne, he dialed Feddi's direct line. When the officer didn't pick up, he called the main number.

"Tetu Island Police. Officer Tesha Harries here. How may I be of service?" said a sweet female voice.

"Thank you, Officer Harries," Drake said. He explained he was trying to get Feddi on the line and why.

"Yes, he is well aware of Mrs. Longly, Mr. Drake. She's called several times. We're doing everything—"

"Yes, I know," Drake said. He took a deep breath, anger and frustration building like a clogged waterpipe, overflow and flooding imminent. "I know you're doing all you can, but I need to speak with Officer Feddi."

"I'm afraid he's not here at the moment," the officer said, all honey gone from her voice. "I can send you to his voicemail?"

"Sure," Drake said. No sense threatening the desk sergeant. He'd save that for Feddi.

The cop transferred Drake and when Feddi's prerecorded message ended, Drake said, "Where are you hiding, Feddi? What is all this shit coming out of the governor's office? There's no mystery and you know it. We need to get the word out about the swarm before someone else is hurt. If I don't hear back from you within the hour, I'm calling St. Croix myself, and then I'm going to call a press conference, so you better get back to me."

Drake left his number and clicked off. He knew his threats were in vain. The stations wouldn't come if he called. His opinion meant nothing. He was a transplanted northerner, and even the locals who loved him would turn against him if he messed with the tourist trade.

The scent of coffee wafted through the house. He wasn't a big fan of technology, but being able to start his coffeemaker with his phone was pretty cool. He cleaned up, pulled on shorts and a Tetu Island Adventures t-shirt, and dusted off his father's Remington 870 twelve-gauge shotgun. There were eight shells left in the box of twelve, and they were over a year old. He inspected the bullets, and they looked fine. He thought of packing the cooler with supplies, but the empty fridge settled that.

It was a stunning day. Not humid, a gentle breeze making the eighty-five-degree heat feel like seventy-five. He sipped on his coffee as he and Vader threaded through the beach grass, across Heel Rock, and down to the rock beach. He leaned the Remington against a stone, put down his mug, and pulled in the Sand Dollar and loaded Vader aboard.

When he was floating on the Zodiac, sipping the dregs of his coffee, gun hidden safely in the command console, he called Kendra back. She picked up on the first ring. "Hi, Mrs. Lo— Kendra, it's Drake."

"That was fast," she said.

Show concern, said his mother's voice from the back of his brain. "Did you eat?"

"Not very hungry. I feel kind of—sick, you know? I can't get the image of my husband getting sucked under out of my mind; the screams."

He said nothing and let her talk.

"I've never heard someone in such pain, and I've seen people give birth," she said.

Drake waited, but when she didn't go on, he said, "Kendra, I need you to harass central police command, the governor's office, everyone. Go to the U.S. Virgin Islands government website and start calling and emailing everyone. Then when you think you've hit them all, do it again. And again. Keep harassing them until I tell you to stop."

Silence at the other end.

"Tell anyone who will listen that we have proof. Pictures of a rabid Barracuda swarm that's killing people."

The faint buzz of a small outboard motor echoed over the ocean, and still Kendra said nothing.

"You there?" he said.

"We don't have proof, do we?" she said. "I mean, other than our eyewitness accounts. Isn't that why you're heading out today? To get proof?"

"Yes," he said. "I'll have the proof we need by sundown, and I want St. Croix involved ASAP. Things on St. Croix move slow. Not Jamaican slow, but slow."

"What if you don't get proof?" she said. Before he could answer, she said, "What am I saying. We're doing more than the cops."

"Right," he said. "Any questions?"

"Not now," she said. "But this isn't enough."

"Excuse me?" he said.

"This is busy work. I want in on the real thing tonight, we clear?"

"As the Caribbean before a storm," he said. "And you're wrong. The calls you're making might be the most important thing we're doing today. And who better to do it than the widow of the diver killed by the swarm? They'll have to listen to you."

"Hope so," she said.

"Me too. Talk later. Call me if you learn anything new," he said.

"Please do the same," she said.

"I will."

"God speed," she said, and the line went dead.

The rumble and cough of the small outboard was now a roar, and Marley came around Heel Rock in the small Mercury dinghy Drake had loaned him.

Vader got up, put his front paws on the Sand Dollar's gunnel, and barked three times. That was hello.

Marley killed the motor and the small inflatable bumped into the Sand Dollar. The kid handed Drake a paper bag and said, "You pack the cooler?"

"Nope. Nothing in the fridge. We've got some warm waters left over from yesterday," he said.

Marley's face wrinkled. "Great. Here," he said as he handed the white sealed food bucket to Drake, who instinctively crinkled his nose.

Drake secured the chum bucket to the transom with a bungie cord and opened his sandwich. He took a bite, egg yolk dripping down his chin, then placed it on the dash atop waxed paper as he dropped the motors.

Marley undid the bow line, attached the dinghy to the buoy, and jumped aboard the Sand Dollar.

"You mind taking us out as I eat?" Drake said as he slid over on the bench seat.

"Where to?" Marley said as he took Drake's place and spun up the motors.

Drake tapped the NAV screen and brought up the prior day's marked locations. "We'll start where Mr. Longly was killed," Drake said as a red line charted a course around Boot Tip Point, and south along the strait.

The outboards screamed as Marley brought the Zodiac up on plane, sea spray coating everything, the gentle bounce and lift of the hull comforting. Vader lay before the command console, head on paws, eyes closed.

Drake pulled his phone with the intention of texting Haley and telling her she didn't need to worry about calling St. Croix, but decided against it and let the phone slide back into his pocket. Haley had nothing but time while Jillian observed Kraken Island and Julian dealt with the tourists. Couldn't hurt having two people shaking every palm tree on St. Croix.

Marley slowly turned the wheel, arcing the Sand Dollar west, around the shoals that extended off Boot Tip Point like an extra toe. Less than twenty-four hours earlier they'd been anchored off the sandspit, sitting in the Caribbean's gentle undertow. It seemed like a long time ago.

Twenty minutes later, Marley slowed the Sand Dollar as they reached the end of the red line on the NAV screen. The engine sputtered to a stop and the wind spun the boat around, pushing the Zodiac west toward Kraken Island. The binoculars hung from the throttle control arm, and Drake grabbed them. He couldn't see the Mary Queen, but a thin tendril of white smoke rose from the western side of Kraken Island.

"Time to catch a… some fish," Drake said.

The Sand Dollar floated with the current as Drake undid the bungie-cord holding the chum bucket.

Marley pulled up his t-shirt and covered his mouth and nose.

Drake felt the eggs he'd eaten moving around in his stomach like worms.

The chum was a concoction of three-day old fish, the blood and entrails of several Hogfish that were used in the daily special of fish tacos, rotten muscles that had washed up on the beach and baked in the sun, bad chicken set aside for crabbing, garbage, rotten fruit, and a brine of alcohol and salted water. They'd mixed it up good in the food-grade container and snapped on the top.

The strange brew they'd dubbed 'special sauce' had percolated overnight, and the smell that escaped the bucket as Drake peeled off the cover made him choke and sputter as he fought back nausea. He lifted the container and poured a thin stream of the foul liquid into the sea, the stench spreading like a disease. The steady stream of nasty brown sludge gurgled as it hit the surface, turning the clear Caribbean Sea the color of mud. The slick spread out behind the boat like a giant had puked, rotten bits of fish and chicken floating on the calm water like marshmallows on hot chocolate.

When the bucket was half empty, Drake sealed it. The wind picked up and a line of dark clouds marched across the western horizon.

"There's a storm coming," Marley said.

"You got that right," Drake said as he settled in to wait.

13

The sun arced past noon and the Caribbean Sea became the Sahara.

Clouds marched in from the east, a dark bulging smudge covering the horizon. The sea breeze died away, the air cycling upward before the storm, and waves of heat rolled across the clear water. The scent of the chum slick was nauseating, and other than attracting a few sand sharks, the special sauce hadn't brought the swarm or anything else. The Sand Dollar floated south with the current, the Mary Queen a dot to the north of Kraken Island. Knots of fishing boats and pleasure crafts filled the mouth of Teapot Cove, and a line of small sailboats with yellow sails tacked back and forth along Two Mile Beach.

Marley lay sprawled on the bow cushions beneath the forward Bimini top. Every few moments he'd rip a snore, and Vader would lift his head, then let it drop back to his paws in frustration. After he'd lifted his head seven times… not six or eight…. seven times, he'd puff-bark, and the process would start again.

Drake and Marley were grabbing naps when they could because it was going to be a long night, and that's if everything went perfect, which he knew it wouldn't. Plans never survive implementation, and there were so many moving parts, so many unknowns, that angst constantly gnawed at Drake. What did they really hope to achieve, anyway? Prove that Ratson created the swarm? That he killed Scar and Kendra's husband? In the light of day, the idea seemed crazy, but he had to do something. Sitting around waiting for St. Croix wasn't an option. He owed Scar at least that much.

The waterproof digital camera Drake and the others used to take pictures of tourists making memories sat on the dashboard. If there's no picture, it didn't happen, was the motto of the twenty-first century, and Marley posted their tour pictures on the company website. Drake began charging when folks started asking for copies of the pictures, and if he had packages. The camera was a Canon with an excellent zoom and video capability, and along with their cellphones, Drake was confident he'd get the proof they needed.

Marley snored and Vader barked. Not a low energy puff-bark, a full-throated get off my lawn bark.

Marley sat up and rubbed his eyes. "We get something?"

"Sunburn," Drake said.

"You want to grab some zzzs?" Marley said.

Drake gazed north, scanning the surface of the sea. The slick was getting thin. "Yeah," he said. "Put out the rest of the chum, then I'll see if I can get some rest."

"What happens if the swarm doesn't show?" Marley asked as he unstrapped the chum bucket from the aft gunnel.

Drake said nothing. He'd been turning that question over in his mind all day, second guessing his decision to tell St. Croix they had proof. He was starting to think he'd miscalculated. If the swarm didn't show and he didn't get pictures, all the work Haley and Kendra did would be dismissed and they'd be in a worse position with the authorities than they had been when the day started. He'd been so sure he'd be able to find the swarm, but in retrospect that had been the rum and frustration talking. The sea was vast, and if Ratson did have something to do with the deaths and the swarm, he might be laying low.

Drake covered his nose at the sound of the lid popping off the chum bucket.

Marley had his t-shirt pulled over his face, and the kid's eyes watered as he poured a steady stream of the foul liquid into the bath-like sea. The brown cloud of blood, fat, and rotten fish and chicken spread-out like an oil spill, the scent as thick as smoke. The bilge pump snapped on and a steady stream of water jetted from the side of the boat, and it sounded like a horse urinating into a puddle.

When the chum bucket was empty, Marley leaned over the gunnel and dipped the pail into the sea and rinsed it out. "Surprised no great whites or bulls have shown. We're in thirty feet of water here."

"I was thinking the same thing," Drake said. The apex predators rarely missed an opportunity to feed, and the scent of blood normally brought the beasts from miles away.

The bilge pump went off and silence spread across the Sand Dollar, the only sound the tinkle and pop of the sea lapping against the hull.

Drake said, "Wake me if—" His cellphone buzzed and vibrated, and he answered it.

"Drake?" said Haley.

He chuckled. "Your timing is better than my mom's. What's up?"

"Just wanted to check in," she said. "We were right. You can set your watch by the guard patrols. We've got it all down."

"Is there a window?"

"For the first part, I think so. It takes some time for them to walk around the point and back. Takes the average guy fifteen minutes. I think that's enough time," she said.

Drake lowered his voice, his eyes shifting to Marley. The kid gazed out to sea, trying to look like he wasn't listening. "What about my part?"

Haley sighed. "That's going to be harder, but I think we can work something out. You might have to change the drop off point, which would mean coming in from another angle. You think Trevor will have a problem with that?"

Drake hadn't asked his rich friend if he'd take him out on his new luxury sub. He wanted to keep things as tight as possible, for as long as possible. Plus, he knew Trevor would come through, but he needed to make that call. The sub required prep, Trevor and John might have plans that they needed to change, and if for some reason he couldn't help, they'd have to change the plan. He said, "I don't see why it would matter."

"Nothing on your end?" Haley asked.

"Nada," he said. "I'm gonna take a nap. Touch base in a couple of hours."

"K," she said, and clicked off.

Drake drank a warm water and stretched out on the bow cushions in the shade. He called Trevor, who having been present the prior night at Dugan's asked only one question. "What time?"

"Midnight. Where do you want us to meet you?" Drake said.

"Come up to my place. The Georgia Ann is in the boathouse. John and I will be ready."

"Georgia Ann?"

"Named the sub after my mum," Trevor said.

"Ah, my mother would have said, 'Why would you name such a thing after your mother? Why not a flower, or a scholarship,'" Drake said.

Trevor chuckled. "Not too far from what my mother said. See you at midnight."

"Thank you," Drake said. "I really appreciate this, and... shoot, if you weren't already an honorary local, I'd make it my mission to make sure you were."

"Say nothing of it. Do you need anything else? Dive equipment?" Trevor asked.

"Not that I can think of."

"Later," Trevor said.

Drake lay back, staring up at the blue canvas. The Sand Dollar rocked gently in the growing wind, the pop and snap of the sea hitting the hull lulling Drake to sleep. He closed his eyes, and the gentle rocking of the Caribbean ushered him off into the white clouds.

"Boss. Boss. Wake up," Marley said.

Drake rubbed his eyes and sat up.

The sun was falling in the west and a raspberry-orange sky glowed above the dark line of the horizon. Stray clouds fleeted past, the front edge of the storm inching across Tetu. The grey haze of dusk pushed over the sea, stray beams from the setting sun cutting through the clouds like searchlights from Heaven.

The kid had the binoculars pressed to his eyes as he stared west into the growing gloom.

A two-foot dorsal fin streaked through the sea, leaving a thin wake. The shark was moving fast as it knifed through the thickest section of the chum slick, caudal fin swaying back and forth, dark eyes scanning the sea, massive jaws open, rows of teeth on display.

"What do we do?" the kid said.

The shark was coming straight at the Zodiac.

"Don't worry, it won't—"

The shark bumped the boat, tail splashing as it pushed the Sand Dollar. Then it peeled off and circled, jaws flexing, caudal fin sweeping like a pendulum.

"And now?" Marley said.

Drake's nerves danced on a wire. He didn't like the idea of a fifteen-foot Great White this close to the Zodiac, which had inflatable gunnels. The shark didn't know the Zodiac's vulnerabilities, and as the beast swam in its ceaseless circle, Drake felt a kinship with the creature built on the shark's futility. He felt like that often, like he was swimming in circles, not going anywhere.

"Ruh oh," Marley said. The boy pointed west, the binoculars pressed to his eyes again.

Without the white glare of the sun blanketing the sea, it was easier to see. A mass of undulating whitewater rolled across the ocean, two-foot waves snapping and breaking in every direction.

"It's moving fast," Marley said.

The swarm was still several hundred yards off, the froth and bubbles of its churning power rising from the sea like a leviathan climbing from the depths.

The Great White didn't appear to notice the swarm as it swam circles around the boat, the Zodiac spinning slowly as the beast created a whirlpool with its massive girth.

Drake had seen enough. He fired up the Yamahas and adjusted to the UHF radio to the emergency channel. "Mayday. Mayday. This is the Sand Dollar. We are under attack. I repeat, we are under attack."

No response. Haley wouldn't respond because she knew Drake was trying to pull the police in, force them to see what was right in front of them.

The swarm writhed and slithered through the water, the rabid fish climbing and mounding on each other, a gigantic rolling knot of teeth and scales. The cloud of predators was two hundred yards off the port bow.

"Sand Dollar, this is Island PD, over. What is your situation?" a male voice boomed from the radio.

"We are under attack by a school of rabid Barracuda," Drake said. He read the coordinates from the NAV screen and the cops said a boat was being scrambled. On Tetu, that meant at least a fifteen-minute wait.

Drake pulled the Remington from the storage compartment in the command console and fed the weapon four shells, which left four in the box. He pumped the gun and jacked a shell into the firing chamber. He said, "Let me see."

Marley handed him the binoculars.

An army of black red-rimmed eyes stared out from a tangle of curved teeth and scales as the fish pushed and jumped through the sea.

The Barracuda horde was upon them.

Drake yelled, "Get the—"

Marley already had the camera in his hands, focusing on the roiling mass of teeth and eyes. "Video or stills?"

"Video." Drake pulled his phone and tapped the camera app.

The Great White broke off from its patrol and raced toward the swarm, the primeval apex predator unaware that it was outnumbered and outmatched. The shark swam hard, twisting and slithering through the sea, caudal fin jerking back and forth as it distended its jaws, flexing to strike.

The swarm and the Great White met in a thunderous clash of teeth, scales, flesh and bone. The shark didn't have a chance, and the beast realized its doom and attempted to escape, caudal fin sweeping, the beast driving through the sea of fish and teeth. With one last pulse of survival born from thousands of years of instinct and evolution, the shark breached, trying to shake off the Barracuda that had attached themselves all along the shark's length.

The Great White disappeared under a mound of Barracuda, the clear Caribbean Sea turning blood red. Like a buzz saw that had cut through a nail, the swarm came on, the roiling chum remains of the shark in its wake.

Drake dropped the hammer and the engines wailed as the Sand Dollar leapt from the sea, both props digging in, kicking up whitewater and spray.

Vader planted his feet as the Zodiac hopped across the ocean. The beast barked and snarled at the oncoming storm, and for a minute Drake played chicken with the field of whitewater. Except in a game of chicken usually one of the competitors pulls up chicken, but not this time.

The Sand Dollar and the swarm met in a crushing, thunderous collision, and Drake was forced to grip the handrail on the command console to stop himself from falling. Barracuda launched from the ocean, sailing across the Sand Dollar, jaws chomping, teeth glinting as they smacked into the windshield. Several fish flopped around on the deck, and Marley tracked the carnage with the camera. Barracuda bounced off the hull, the Bimini top, the stench of rotten flesh thick in the air.

Drake eyed the shotgun where it sat on the dash, but there were too many fish, and he'd end up shooting the boat, so he resisted the urge to start blasting the Barracuda to hell.

The Zodiac broke free of the swarm, but the rolling mass of fish was already shifting, turning and giving chase.

Drake jerked the wheel back and forth like he was going through a thick patch of seaweed, trying to keep the props from getting tangled in the sea's quicksand. The maneuver didn't fool the swarm, it undulated and shifted like oil in water, locking in on the Sand Dollar.

"Are they slowing?" Marley asked.

As the sun disappeared below the horizon, a thick cloud passed overhead, thin dusk shifting momentarily to gray darkness.

The sea flattened and blood bubbles popped on the surface as the swarm retreated.

"You get all that?" Drake said.

Marley smiled, held up the camera, and nodded.

14

"So, what do you make of that, mate?" Marley said. He sat next to Drake behind the command console, Vader sitting dutifully by his side.

"I've never heard of anything taking down a fifteen-foot Great White," Drake said. "Orcas, maybe, if there was more than one. Maybe."

"Why didn't they finish us?"

"Not sure," Drake said. The kid had a point. The swarm could have easily brought down the Sand Dollar. "Might have something to do with the sun going down. Many animals' circadian clocks get scrambled a bit at dusk and dawn."

"Good to know, yeah?" Marley said.

"Another good point. Like the one on the top of your head," Drake said. "Do you ever stop thinking?"

"When I'm looking at Tina at the bakery, or Karen at—"

"Tina!" Drake laughed as he gently arced the wheel, falling in behind the Mary Queen, which was chugging toward the channel to Fredericksville Harbor. "Tina is so out of your league, dude. She might as well be the First Lady."

"What?" The kid looked genuinely offended.

"She's rich, and you're not. She has powerful parents, you've got none. She's going to an Ivy League school in the states next year, you're staying here with me. Her father—"

"Got it. Got it. Can't you just let me enjoy fantasizing about it?" Marley said.

"No, because you're a good kid and there's a girl out there for you. One that will love you for you."

"Says the guy who can't keep a woman for more than a week, and who can't see what's right in front of him."

"You too with the Haley shit?"

Marley frowned at him. "I just want you to be happy, and it's sickeningly obvious that you guys like each other."

"We're friends."

"Sure. And you left the Merchant Marine by choice. Yeah. Got it," Marley said.

Drake felt anger rise in him, but he pushed it down. The kid was asking because he cared, and there weren't many people that gave a shit about Drake these days. He said nothing.

"Look, I'm sorry, but are we friends? I think... thought we were. But I don't know anything about where you came from, why you're hiding on this rock. You know my entire history from the moment my mum dumped me until this instant."

"I'm not hiding. Know that." Drake waved a hand. "Don't be an ass. I love it here on this crazy rock." He paused and turned to look at the boy. "As to the rest... you're right. When we've got a little time, you can ask me whatever you want. Deal?"

Marley nodded. "So, before we get back with the others, I don't want an argument. I'm coming with you tonight."

Drake laughed. "You most certainly aren't."

"Scar's my friend—"

Drake held up a hand. "I know, but you're not coming. That's final."

The kid deflated.

"Look, I get it. I do. But do you think you're the only one that's going to hit me with that in the next hour? The best chance of success is me going in alone. You know that."

"Fine. But I'm on the sailboat then."

"Fine," Drake barked. Then he turned to look at the kid, who couldn't contain a slight smirk. "You knew I'd say no to coming with me, then you hit me with your next option. You're going to do just fine in life kid, just fine."

He backed off on the throttle, slowly cruising through the white line of churned ocean behind the Mary Queen, the channel's red entrance buoy on his right.

"Right, red, return," Marley said. "That was one of the first things you taught me. Don't think I don't appreciate everything you do for me, Drake. I'll repay you someday. I promise."

"No need, but I know you'll try." Drake rubbed the top of the kid's head and he leaned away, just like Drake had done as a teenager when his dad touched him.

The Mary Queen tied off on its mooring in the harbor, and when the Sand Dollar bumped the fishing boat's side, Julian and Jillian were there to help Drake and Marley aboard and secure the Sand Dollar.

"How'd you make out?" Jillian asked.

Marley held up the camera. "I think we're good to go. The things took down a shark."

"What are you saying?" Julian said.

"A big mother," Drake said. "Ate it like it was canned tuna. What about you guys?"

Jillian rolled her eyes. "The captain is pissed 'cause she spent the whole day getting the runaround, but I think we got everything you asked for."

"Solid."

They worked their way across the flat aft deck of the Mary Queen, traversing piles of netting, buoys, and a fifteen-foot tender that sat on angled blocks of wood. The group found Haley chowing down on chili in the galley.

"Grab a bowl. There's waters in the fridge," she said.

Drake and the others retrieved bowls, filled them with Julian's famous three bean chili, and when they were seated around the table, Haley wasted no time opening her steam valve. "It's amazing the Virgin Islands don't slip beneath the sea with the collection of clowns running this place. Guess how many people I spoke to? Guess?"

"Twenty-three," Marley said.

Drake winced. The boy wasn't experienced enough to know Haley wasn't really asking a question.

Haley turned her fiery eyes on the kid, and Marley flinched. She said, "Three. Now guess how many calls I made?"

Silence as Haley bored holes into Marley, but the kid learned from his mistake and kept his mouth pasted shut.

"I lost count. That's how many." She went back to eating, her cheeks red.

"Who were the three?" Drake ventured.

"Some lackey in the governor's office, the desk sergeant at headquarters, and a plebe named Filipe Grandiouser. On the job six months."

"And?"

"All three said they'd kick it up the chain. Make some inquiries and call Feddi," Haley said.

"Who will take his sweet time returning the calls," Jillian said.

"Did you talk with Kendra? She have any luck?" Drake asked.

Haley dropped her spoon and it hit the rim of her bowl with a clang. "Yeah, I did. Nice woman, and she had a bit more luck, seeing she's the widow and all. She's waiting for a call back from the governor's office, but she said the aides are waiting on our proof. I also mentioned we had samples of that strange shit you found in the ocean." She reached into a breast pocket and brought out a slip of paper. "She gave me this email address. Said to send the pictures ASAP. That was four hours ago."

Drake nodded. "What about your friend Professor Wexford?"

"I sent him some samples like you asked. He said he'd take a look and get back to me," Haley said.

"Marley, where are we with that?" Drake asked.

The kid wasn't eating. He was watching the video he'd shot on the camera's small display screen, a sour look spreading over his face.

"What is it?" Drake said.

Marley handed over the camera without a word and started eating.

"That thing have Bluetooth?" Julian asked.

Drake looked at Marley, who nodded.

A thirty-inch flat panel TV was mounted on the bulkhead at the head of the table, its screen dark.

Jillian grabbed the remote and tossed it to Drake, who turned on the monitor and adjusted the inputs as he handed the digital camera back to Marley.

The boy fumbled with the camera, his glance shifting back and forth from the TV to the camera.

A blurry image appeared on the screen, smudges of blue and white coming together like a puzzle. The group watched in silence, the picture jumping and shaking. Every few seconds the churning water would clear for an instant, and dark, red-rimmed eyes and teeth appeared as Barracuda slithered through the sea. The Sand Dollar was moving fast, bouncing as it knifed into the swarm. The image shook, rabid Barracuda missiling from the ocean and flopping onto the deck.

Drake's heart sank. He knew the danger because he'd been there, but the video wasn't the smoking gun they needed. It was clear there was something wrong with the fish, but the Barracuda looked small as they thrashed and fought. Based only on the video, Drake didn't think they had enough, but at least they had something to send, and maybe that, along with the complaints of Haley and Kendra, might be enough, but the rock of ice in the pit of his stomach told Drake otherwise.

"Anyone heard from Helen?" Drake asked.

Jillian nodded. "Just a few minutes ago. She was able to borrow a small sailboat. A sunfish. It's perfect for us. Even has the rental logo on the sail."

"Good." All that was left to be decided was who would do what, and Drake knew that's where he'd get his biggest fight. "Marley, when you're done eating, send that video to Feddi, the address Haley has, and any other addresses Haley and Kendra can give you. Then go get the sailboat."

The boy nodded, but didn't look up from his bowl.

"I've got one more call to make," Drake said as he pulled his phone. "If he takes my call." He went to Latimor on his contact list and stabbed it with his middle finger. The phone rang three times.

"Drake?"

"Yup. How are you, sir?"

The cackle of laughter didn't sound happy. "Sir? Now that's some funny shit. What do you want?"

"I know—"

"Wait. How the hell did you get my number?"

"Siggy. I saw him—"

"That prick."

"You saw my name on the caller ID and picked up. What the hell—"

Haley paused in her eating and put a hand on his shoulder.

"Yeah, sorry. I know you're pissed, but when I heard you were down here, I've been meaning to reach out, but... you know."

Silence on the line.

"You know anyone in headquarters over there? I'm sure you drink in Dinghy's."

Nothing.

"I've got a real situation down here. People are dying."

The line went dead. Drake dropped the phone onto the table.

"You're a popular guy, huh?" Jillian said.

Drake shrugged. He was surprised his old shipmate had even taken the call. Latimor had gotten caught up in the sting that brought down the captain, and he'd gone down with him. Drake had been sorry for that, but it wasn't his fault his old friend had been helping the captain smuggle guns.

"You chew like a cow," Haley said.

Marley didn't even look up.

Julian and Jillian watched Drake, their eyes shifting from him to the table.

Drake's crew was awaiting final orders.

"So, tonight," Drake said.

"Here it comes," Haley said.

"What?"

"The part where you say you're doing this alone," Jillian said.

Marley chuckled, pushed away his empty bowl, and got to his feet.

"I'm not doing anything alone," Drake said. "I need help from all of you, Helen, Kendra, and obviously Trevor and John."

"Trevor taking you out on the sub?" Haley said.

Drake nodded. "Meeting them at midnight. Alone."

Everyone started talking at once. Haley saying he didn't have the right to make that decision, Jillian and Julian complaining, making their arguments. Only Marley stood quietly by, and when Haley noticed, she said, "Marley, why the hell are you so calm?"

Marley's eyebrows rose.

"Leave him alone," Drake said. "Haley, you'll take the Sand Dollar and sit off Kraken Island. You're our emergency backup and escape plan. Helen's with you and tell her to bring her gun."

Haley started to protest but Drake put up a hand. "Marley and Jillian will take the sailboat, and Trevor will dump me at the drop off point. That leaves Julian and Kendra to take out the Mary Queen. She's going to be our safe place."

When Drake didn't continue, Haley said, "I understand you not wanting to put any of us in danger, but going in alone is nuts. You need someone to watch your back. I agree more than two makes no sense, but I think I should come with you."

"Not a chance," Julian said. "I'm faster, younger, a better swimmer, a better shot. I don't wear reading glasses and I—"

"That's enough, dipshit," Haley said. "You're young and stupid, prone to rash decisions."

Drake listened to his team argue, worry building in him like a tumor. It did make sense to have someone with him, but who? Regardless of who he picked, the others would be pissed.

Marley had paused in the doorway, sensing the shift in the tide. "Drake, I want to go with you. I asked first."

"This isn't a democracy, now get going," Drake said.

Marley's chin hit his chest, but he stepped through the bulkhead door into the corridor beyond. His head popped through the open door, "Jillian, I'll call you with the meeting spot when I'm ready."

Jillian nodded.

"You guys make some good points," Drake said. "Someone should come with me. Do we need to draw straws, or do you all trust my judgement?"

"Depends on who you pick," Haley said.

Julian was the clear choice; he was young, strong, all the things he'd stated, though Drake would never let the kid know he was right, or they'd all never hear the end of it. Haley was older, more experienced, but physically she was no match for Julian, and then there was the nagging feeling that he didn't want her to get hurt, didn't really want her involved in any of this.

Nobody spoke and Drake took that as tacit acceptance of his implied authority. "Julian, you're with—"

"Oh, hell no," Jillian said.

"What? A kid?" Haley said.

"If Julian is with me, you'll need to take out the Mary Queen," Drake said.

Haley sighed. "I guess I can take it out and anchor it off Kraken. Helen can bring the Sand Dollar around, and Kendra can stay on the Mary Queen, handle communications."

Drake nodded. They were a team again, working together, one goal. "What about the comms?"

"I was able to get three two-way radios with earpiece cables, but they're no more than walkie-talkies and they're not waterproof," Haley said.

"That's good, though. We can pick a channel and since our signal won't be going through a repeater our transmissions will be harder to find and listen in on."

"I recommend radio silence unless absolutely necessary," Haley said.

"Starting," Drake looked at his watch for effect, "now."

15

The winding crushed shell driveway that led to Trevor and John's place looked like it was weeded and raked daily, and there were patches of tended wildflowers, yucca, and aloe among the beach grass that lined the drive. The house was modest, but new, and Drake whistled when he saw the immense glass entryway. He'd never been to Trevor's place before, though he'd been invited several times. The place was like Trevor; neat, well put together. Not flashy like most of the transplant houses, which were monuments to personal success. Trevor knew he was rich, and didn't care if anyone knew.

Julian drove Drake's dented 2007 Chevy pickup, shells popping and cracking beneath the tires. "Do you know how Trevor made his money? I know it wasn't an inheritance. Computers is my guess," Julian said.

Trevor's luxury sub cost $2.3 million. Quite a purchase for a toy. As Trevor told the story he was just lucky, but Drake knew there was more to it than that. The guy was smart—real smart—and people make their own luck. He said, "Computers might be part of it. He started a bakery with a friend when he was twenty, and in five years they had six places."

The pickup crunched to a stop and Julian slapped his leg. "That's why he's such a pain in the ass about the bread being warm when we eat someplace."

Drake said, "Maybe, but he hasn't done that in a long time. He sold his share to his partner and used the money to invest in several other businesses. Now he runs a venture capital firm."

Julian wasn't stupid, but island education didn't have a core curriculum covering the stock market.

"He invests in startups. New businesses he thinks will take off. He was in on several tech companies, as well as a bunch of environmental resource companies."

"That why he doesn't like Ratson?"

"You could say they're natural enemies, yeah. If Ratson is doing what we think he is," Drake said.

He and Julian got out of the truck, and Trevor appeared behind the house's huge glass front door. He waved them on.

Julian grabbed a backpack from the pick-up's bed and slipped it on.

"Does he know the whole plan?" Julian whispered.

"Most of it. Only big thing I left out is exactly where we need to be dropped. Oh, and that we're being dropped," Drake said.

Julian grabbed his arm. "He doesn't know he's leaving us?"

"Not yet," Drake said.

"Hey, guys," Trevor said as he pulled open the heavy door.

Drake shot Julian a look that said, "Keep your trap shut. I'll pick the right time to tell him."

The duo entered an expansive foyer opulently decorated. John waited behind his partner, drink in hand, white shirt and pink shorts making it clear the trip was also a social event. "You both know John," Trevor said.

John waved.

"Of course," Drake said. "How are you, John?"

The man took a long pull on his drink, and said, "Looking forward to going twenty thousand leagues under the sea."

Trevor chuckled. "Not twenty thousand leagues... whatever that even means. No, the Georgia Ann has a depth limit of a thousand feet. Not a problem in the Caribbean since the waters around Kraken Island top-out at eighty feet."

"Can I get you boys anything before we go? Cocktail? Food?" John asked.

Trevor looked at Drake with lidded eyes. He hadn't told his partner the situation, or at least not all of it. "No, thank you."

Trevor said, "I've never had her out at night, but the bulk of the storm hasn't reached us yet and the sea is still relatively calm."

"Should we go then?" Drake said. "We're losing moonlight."

"The sub has very good photographic capability above and below the water. Even has an infrared periscope. So, I'm going to get really close and we should be able to see what they're having for dinner."

"If they eat outside," Julian said.

The group made their way through a vast kitchen with a stainless steel zero-g, a commercial stove, and a round wood table with brass edges that looked like it had come from an old ship. They exited onto the deck, an infinity pool stretching into the beach grass, Simpson Bay beyond, moonlight shining on the bay's inky black surface. A thin path led through a garden down to the boathouse.

"Your place is amazing," Julian said. He walked next to John.

"It's all Trevor. I'm just a passenger on his tilt-a-whirl," John said. "And happy for it."

The boathouse's huge bay doors stood closed. Trevor held open a side door as the team passed inside and flicked on the lights.

"Wow," Drake said.

The Georgia Ann was white with three sets of red stripes cutting diagonally across the hull. It looked like a small jet, but instead of wings, two powerful electric motors were housed outside the pressure hull in missile-like housings ending in four-foot props. A dorsal fin conning tower rose ten feet above the command level, which sat above the waterline, and four short vertical rudders, two forward and two aft, floated just below the surface. A four-foot tail fin with red stripes cast a long shadow across the dock.

"I made him get the nosecone cutout," John said.

Trevor laughed. "True that. $367,000 upgrade. The basic design called for a normal forward pressure hull, but the cut-out option provides a clear Lexan nose with two command chairs for optimal viewing. I can control the sub from there as well."

"$367,000 for an upgrade?" Julian said.

Trevor said, "Disgraceful, I know. The whole shooting match cost over two million. I donated twice that to The Society for the Conservation of the World's Oceans to assuage my guilt. And I agreed to a month of research cruises every year."

"I didn't mean to—"

Trevor held up a hand. "I know you didn't. For some reason I feel compelled to tell people I'm not a rich asshole."

Drake said, "How long is she?"

"Sixty-one feet," Trevor said.

"Did you have to go to training or something to pilot this thing?" Julian said.

"Yeah," Trevor said. "It was like fast-food college. I was there two days and all I really wanted to know was how to set a course and work the autopilot. But you know businesses; safety, maintenance, all such a bore."

"It's easy to pilot then?" Drake asked.

"A monkey could do it. Really," Trevor said. He stepped down onto the floating dock that ran along the sub's port side. A control panel was mounted to a yellow stanchion and Trevor flipped open a clear plastic lid and stabbed a red button.

The boathouse's large bay doors began to slide open.

Trevor said, "I really wanted—"

A loud screeching and braying and shrieking tore through the boathouse, the pounding of wings creating dancing shadows on the boathouse walls. A flock of bats darted through the darkness, and knifed through the widening gap between the bay doors.

"Sorry about that. Damnable flying rats," Trevor said.

"I thought you said you were taking care of that?" John said.

Trevor rolled his eyes at Drake.

A dock ran all around the boathouse's edge, except on the southern exit end. A big pleasure craft and two smaller boats, a V hull center console and a small Zodiac, were docked across from the sub.

"Really wanted one of those penis boats. You know, one of those yachts that says look at me. Thing was, John and I started looking and I didn't see anything new. Nothing exciting and fun. I'd been on plenty of big boats, and plenty of people have them. Not a unique toy at all." Trevor mounted the short metal ladder that led to the sub's exterior topside deck, the narrow conning tower to his right. "Now this baby," Trevor said as he patted the metal hull. "She's different. Nobody else on the island has anything close. And it's fun, and the boat will do meaningful research that could help save the reefs and oceans." He bent and pulled back the hatch in the deck, the scraping of metal on metal echoing through the boathouse.

The group climbed down onto a bridge that resembled a spaceship. Windows ran around the entire cabin, the retracted periscope tucked away next to the ladder. Safety equipment, fire extinguishers, and storage compartments were mounted on the aft bulkhead. The port and starboard bulkheads had an array of monitors and control panels filled with levers and buttons. Forward, there were two command chairs with swivel touchscreens, and the chair on the right had access to a control yoke.

"Very impressive," Drake said.

"Thank you, Mr.?" a deep male voice intoned.

"Um," Drake said.

Trevor stared up at him, frozen on the metal ladder, doing a bad job of containing his laughter.

"Andy?" Trevor said.

"Captain Trevor," Andy said.

"I told you not to call me that," Trevor said.

"Sir?" the computer voice intoned.

"Just prepare for departure, will you?" Trevor said. He turned to Drake. "Hard to get good computer simulated help these days."

"Sir, how far will our cruise be? What depth should I prepare the ballast for? Will your guests require—"

"Local cruise, less than fifty feet," Trevor said as he continued down the access ladder.

John was the last one down and he handed Trevor his drink as he climbed down the final two rungs. Trevor said, "You really should use both hands."

John waved him away and took back his drink.

"All lights," Trevor said.

"Yes, sir," Andy intoned.

"Don't blink or you might miss the tour," Trevor said. "Main deck has five compartments, each with a bulkhead door that can be sealed in an emergency. The mechanical room and living quarters, which can accommodate six people and include a camper-style bathroom, is that way." He pointed aft. "This is the main guest observation area." He waved forward. The main compartment had a series of seats and couches, all arranged before large portholes, with a bar in the forward port corner and a conversation pit with a large monitoring screen mounted on the bulkhead before it on the starboard side.

Trevor threaded through the cabin toward the front of the ship and stopped at the bulkhead door. "We've got a fully functioning galley with storage that allows for cruises of up to two months."

John shook the ice in his empty glass.

Trevor took the glass and stepped behind the bar and made John a whisky and soda. "Can I get anyone anything?"

Drake didn't answer. He peered forward through the bulkhead door at the open nosecone.

"Yes, as I said, the highlight of the ship," Trevor said. He handed John his drink and disappeared through the bulkhead door. "Come see."

The nose of the sub was dark, and Trevor dropped into one of the command chairs and swung the monitor on its arm until it was before him. He tapped the panel and the exterior LED lights came on, illuminating the murky water.

Julian jumped and Drake laughed.

The huge sullen eyes of a Manatee stared through the observation window, tiny schools of shiners darting around it as though the sea cow was their sun. The sea marshmallow floated just below the surface, flippers gently pumping up and down. Moonlight streamed through the open bay doors, shards of pale light cutting through the water. The bottom was mud, and crabs scuttled about, black puffs of silt rising from the bottom like toxic clouds.

The voice of the autopilot bleated through the onboard speakers. "We are ready for departure, sir."

"Shall we get underway?" Trevor said.

Drake nodded.

"Let's head back up to the command deck. Take a look at the charts," Trevor said.

John plopped into one of the nosecone chairs, sipping on his drink.

Julian looked at Drake, who in turn looked to Trevor. "I don't need him if you don't," he said.

Drake nodded, and Julian sat in the second chair.

"Best seats in the house," John said.

Trevor stopped at the bar and grabbed a beer and held one out to Drake, who accepted it. His nerves were jumping and biting like fleas, pain arcing out from his chest to his extremities. Suddenly he felt like the entire plan was a bad idea.

"You look like you've seen a ghost," Trevor said. He took a pull on his beer and headed for the access ladder.

"Actually, there's something I need to tell you," Drake said.

Trevor's face brightened. "Ah. A wrinkle. I love it," he said.

"We're doing more than just poking around tonight. You're dropping me off," Drake said.

Trevor clapped. "Excellent."

16

Drake sat in the co-pilot seat, a control screen angled before him. A larger screen was mounted between the two command chairs, and Drake traced his finger across the digitally enhanced SONAR image.

"See how the channel gets wider here," Drake said. He was pointing toward a dark slash of blue that marked a narrow depression in the seafloor. "You go in that way, slow and silent. You should be able to get us within a couple hundred yards without being seen."

Trevor wagged his head. "Don't see any problems on my end except light."

"Excuse me?"

"We'll have to go in dark. The Caribbean is clear, and in twenty feet of water the Georgia Ann will make the surface glow like that alien spacecraft from The Abyss is coming up from the depths."

"Is going in without lights a problem?" Drake recalled the man saying he'd never taken the sub out in the dark.

Trevor shook his head no. "We're going to run on autopilot. Might be a bit weird for us, but the computer doesn't need light to see."

"You trust the NAV computer that much, huh?" Drake said.

"The software was developed by the Navy for drones and pilotless planes and warships, so yeah, I trust it. There are hundreds of sensors that constantly monitor conditions in and around the boat. Look here." Trevor tapped Drake's screen. "As you can see, we don't need to do much. The screen displays the rear and side cameras, and you can remove the system's status bar at the bottom with a swipe of your finger if you want the camera images bigger. The dummy lights on the status bar monitor interior and exterior pressure, battery strength, sub speed, angle of descent, depth, and life support, which has four separate icons for oxygen flow control, CO_2 monitoring, oxygen percentage, and sensor status."

Trevor tapped on his control panel, adjusting systems as he prepared to dive.

The onboard computer said, "All hatches and intakes are closed."

Trevor tapped his monitor. "Pressure up." The autopilot released air into the Georgia Ann and Drake's ears popped. "Opening vents. We're not going deep, and most of the safety precautions are for when the sub goes below a hundred and fifty feet."

"How deep have you had her?"

Trevor chuckled. "On our second tour we headed northeast toward the shelf. Went down real slow. Shit got eerie when the sea went dark, but we went down eight hundred feet. It was like being in space."

"Thinking about the pressure of all that water makes my head hurt," Drake said.

"We didn't do it again. We use the sub for fun, rarely go deeper than a hundred feet as we look at the wildlife."

The sub listed slightly as the ballast tanks partially filled with water and the sub settled.

"Are we good to go, Andy?" Trevor said.

"Yes, sir."

Trevor tapped his panel and said, "John, Julian, prepare for departure." He started the electric engines, and a slight tremor ran through the hull. "All systems are go. Release mooring lines."

Two pops echoed through the ship.

"Turning control over to Andy," Trevor said. He tapped his screen and fell back into his chair, finishing his beer with one long final pull.

"Yes, sir," the NAV computer said. "Engaging maneuvering thrusters."

A whirring echoed through the sub as it eased into motion, the gentle whine of the thrusters buzzing. Seawater bubbled over the observation windows as the Georgia Ann settled.

Trevor said, "We'll stay on the surface until we get into open water."

The sub eased through the bay doors, knifing silently into the bay, tiny waves breaking on the nosecone. Moonlight lit Simpson Bay, a white glow that coated the inky surface and bled into the mangroves and water reeds, thin spidery shadows creeping across the sub's exterior deck.

Drake's stomach ached, his nerves on puppet strings of adrenaline. He'd built this plan in his head, a flawless succession of events that would lead to finding Scar and taking down Ratson, but now that the time had arrived his legs felt like Jell-O.

"Nothing left for us to do here. Do you want to get the dive equipment ready?" Trevor said.

Drake shook his head. "We'll take snorkels and masks, but that's it. We only have to swim a hundred yards or so and I want to keep this simple. No tanks or gear to hide and be found, no air bubbles. We go in silent as gators."

Trevor said, "Any way I can convince you to let me come?"

Drake said, "Here's the thing. I think you're more qualified than Julian, but..."

"Spit it out."

"You've got way more to lose and looking at the big picture you bring resources and other expertise that makes you valuable to our cause here."

Trevor said nothing.

The sub exited the thin estuary that led to the boathouse and the onboard computer said, "Engaging engines." The props created slight cavitation as the electric engines cycled up, the props digging into the bay as they drove the Georgia Ann through the water. The submersible's nose dove beneath the waves as the rudder and trim tabs angled the craft downward. Bay water washed over the cockpit and the sub leveled out, the weak waves slapping the conning tower.

LED floodlights cut through the clear Caribbean Sea. Crabs scuttled along the sand bottom, fish of various sizes and colors darting past the observation windows.

"Andy, what's our depth?" Trevor said.

"Fifteen feet. Entering the channel now, sir."

Drake eyed the NAV screen. The red line that marked their charted route led two miles north of Boot Tip Point and circled back southwest to a position on the leeward side of Kraken Island.

The sub leveled out and glided through the ocean, the purr of the motors, the slosh and pop of the sea, and the push of oxygen being pressed into the cabin filling the silence.

"It's quiet down here," Drake said. "I'm so used to the cacophony of the surface."

Trevor nodded vigorously. "Like I said, first time we went deep was very strange. Alien."

"Doesn't sound fun, but why do I want to go?"

Trevor smiled. "It would be a great story for Dugan's."

Drake had spent most of his seafaring days on the surface, but he knew what it meant to be five hundred miles offshore at the edge of the Blake Plateau, where the sea floor plummets several thousand feet to the abyssal plane. He'd wanted to be an astronaut when he was a boy—what kid didn't? There was something alluring about going to a hostile environment where you can't breathe, can't move without assistance, and where you're so far away from your fellow humans there was no way anyone could assist you. It's the ultimate thrill ride. One Drake had never had an interest in riding after age twelve. But taking a luxury sub to the edge of the abyss for cocktails? That was something altogether different. He said, "You pick the day and time and I'm there."

"You can bring Louise. We'll make a day of it."

"I'm afraid we've decided to take some time apart."

Good thing Trevor wasn't a poker player, because he couldn't keep a joyous smirk from peeling across his face.

Twenty minutes later the sub was running silent and dark along the western edge of Kraken Island. The water around the island was shallow, but dropped off a few hundred yards from shore.

John and Julian had come to the bridge, and Trevor prepared to send up the periscope. Drake examined a sea chart on the large LED screen between the command chairs.

Drake said, "See here?" He pointed to a spot at the head of the dark blue cut in the seafloor. "Can we stop and take a look there?"

Trevor ran a finger over the screen and relayed the coordinates to the NAV computer.

The engines whined and cycled down, and the thrusters came on as the sub slowly came to a stop.

Trevor undogged the latch and swung the periscope out of its holding bracket and flipped down the maneuvering arms. "Andy, light the scope."

"Yes, sir," the mechanical voice said.

Trevor pressed his eye to the scope, and slowly panned it back and forth. Then he threw up his hands and stepped away. "The forest and the damn mangroves are in the way."

"May I?" Drake asked.

Trevor held out a hand and Drake took control of the scope.

The fluorescent green landscape looked alien, and it struck Drake how close the island was. A red light atop a conning tower swayed in the cove, a light on the widow's watch of the main house glowed, but other than that the island was still and quiet. He arced the scope right, scanning the beach, but saw nothing of interest.

Three minutes passed, John coughed, and Drake sniffled.

The guard came around the bend and Drake said, "Julian, time."

The kid started his dive watch timer.

Drake stepped away from the periscope. "We'll wait until the guard completes this section of his rounds, then we'll get in position."

Trevor nodded.

The team waited in silence, Drake watching the guard meander down the beach and disappear around the bend. He said, "Good to go."

Trevor said, "Andy, take us to the final coordinates. Use only maneuvering thrusters. Do not engage the engines. All interior and exterior lights are to remain off."

"Yes, sir."

The sub dove deeper as it entered the depression in the sea floor, and when it reached the cut's end, the sub leveled out and came to a stop.

"Bring us up to a depth of ten feet," Trevor said.

"Yes, sir," said Andy. A rush of air and bubbles streamed past the observation windows as the onboard computer released ballast.

"OK, you still up for this, kid?" Drake said.

Julian's eyes were wide, his forehead knitted. He nodded yes.

"Let's get ready then," Drake said. "Trevor, can you keep an eye on the guard?"

Trevor nodded and pressed his eye to the scope.

Julian stripped off his backpack and opened it. There were two dry bags inside and he handed one to Drake, and took one for himself. Drake's waterproof pouch contained a Glock 19 he'd borrowed from Helen, water shoes, a ration of food, extra ammo, a black t-shirt and black sweatpants, a penlight, and a small radio with a wireless headset. Julian's had the same, minus the gun and radio. Both men had twelve-inch dive blades strapped to their legs.

Trevor's cell phone chirped and Drake stared at him.

"I have my iPhone routed through ship's comm," he said as he pulled out the device. "Yes?" he answered. Trevor's eyes shifted to Drake. "Yeah, he's here. One moment." Trevor handed over his phone. "Haley."

"Drake here."

"Hey, everything O.K.?" Haley asked.

"Just about to get wet. You tell me?"

"I'm just waiting for Kendra, and we'll be pushing off shortly. Figured I'd touch base because I heard back from Professor Wexford."

"That was fast."

"You know scientists. They get something stuck in their craw and everything else goes to the back burner." Wexford was a professor of marine biology at The Tetu Institute of Technology. The school focused on hospitality management, culinary, and security, but the College of Marine Science was strong, and several prominent Caribbean Sea researchers called the university their home base.

"And? What did he find?"

"And he was stumped and didn't have much to say. If you knew Wexford, you'd understand how big a deal that is. That guy can talk for hours about the derivations between snail species," Haley said.

"He didn't find anything?"

"Prof. said he's never seen anything like it. The sample contains an odd mixture of metals; tin, iron, silver, gold, and strange specks, a compound he can't identify. Dr. Wexford said there are formed particles in the liquid, but the stuff is so small he can't see any detail with his microscope. He took photos and sent the samples on to Miami University. They have an electron microscope, and he hopes to have results soon."

"Did he have any guesses?"

Haley sighed, and said, "The things, whatever the hell they are, appear to be moving under their own power."

"Their own power?" he said. Drake recalled the odd movement and shimmering colors when he collected the sample, but there was no time for that now.

Trevor cleared his throat and pointed to his watch.

"O.K. Thanks, Haley. See you when I see you." Drake clicked off and handed Trevor his phone.

Drake and Julian stripped down to their underwear and tied the bags to their waists via thin canvas dive belts.

John watched Julian with eager eyes.

"Hey," Trevor said, a smile splitting his head. "Eyes this way." Then he turned to Drake. "Our guy just reappeared."

"What time is it?" Drake said.

Julian said, "We're just shy of 1AM."

"OK," Drake said. "Perfect. Let's put this baby on the surface."

Trevor said, "Andy, prepare to surface on my command."

Several tense minutes passed, and finally, Trevor said, "Bring us up. Slowly."

Bubbles and whitewater streaked by the portholes and the faint sound of breaking waves and sloshing water echoed through the ship as the sub broke the surface. The boat listed and rocked, then went still.

Drake climbed the access ladder and undogged the hatch. It was freshly oiled and didn't make a sound as it swung on its large metal hinges. Moonlight arced into the cabin as Drake stepped out onto the deck, followed by Julian.

He closed the hatch and dogged it down.

Julian sat on the deck, slipped on his dive mask, and pushed off like he was sitting on a playground slide. He slipped across the deck and fell into the water with a faint splash.

The sea was oily black, and Drake couldn't see Julian floating on the surface. He pulled on his dive mask and dropped into the water.

The sea felt cold, despite the exterior temperature gauge showing a water temp of seventy-two degrees. White moonlight cast everything in flickering black and white, birds arcing silently in and out of the cones of light. Drake blew out his snorkel and searched for Julian. The kid was swimming hard toward the front of the sub and Drake followed.

The tinkle and pop of the sea was the only sound. Moonlight reached a few feet below the surface, the seafloor a dark abyss.

Drake saw Julian ahead. He had his facemask pressed to the bridge's forward observation window. Drake took a deep breath and went under, stroking hard.

Trevor and John waved from within the sub, and John lifted his glass.

Drake gave a thumbs up, and using the sub as leverage, he pushed off for the surface.

He inched his head from the water and slipped back his dive mask.

Julian's head popped up beside him.

The static of waves crashing on the shore and the chirp and buzz of the night symphony floated on the breeze.

The guard walked north, and Drake had five minutes before the guard turned around and restarted his march. If things were going as planned, Marley and Jillian were beaching the sunfish on the point. He strained to see them in the darkness, but it was way too far.

A football field doesn't sound very far. Shoot, guys could run it in fifteen seconds. But even in the relative calm and temperate Caribbean Sea, the swim was harder than Drake had envisioned when he'd been sipping in Dugan's.

He swam on his stomach, using only his arms, gently stroking the dark water as the shoreline got closer. The diversion hadn't appeared, so he was going slow, Julian pacing himself at his side. His muscles ached, and the beer he'd had sat in his stomach like a stone.

A loud pucker, then bubbles popping as the sub backed away and submerged. It would circle the island and act as backup support with the Sand Dollar and Mary Queen.

Drake floated on his back just beyond the wave break, Julian beside him in the darkness.

The guard walked on the beach. The man was diligent. Drake could see that in the darkness. The guy's head shifted back and forth as he scanned the sea and the inland forest, never breaking stride or pausing. He was a thick shadow against the line of palm trees that ran at the edge of the mangroves. If

Drake didn't know exactly where to look, he never would have seen the guard.

The faint glow of a fire sparked on the point to the south, a small flickering flame growing in intensity until it was like a candle in the darkest of places.

The guard saw it at once and ran toward the fire, the squawk of his radio echoing across the sea.

Drake and Julian swam hard for shore.

17

The Mary Queen's old diesel engine rumbled in the darkness, smoke puffing from the vessel's single stack. Patchy clouds raced across the sky, stars blinking through the gaps, the eastern horizon a roiling mass of dirty cotton candy. Every few moments a thin blue streak of lightning lit the night in the distance, and the faint roll of thunder sounded off like artillery fire from a war that was heading their way. The front edge of the storm was still eight hours off, but its specter loomed like an unwanted task.

The buzz of a tender echoed through the maze of moored boats, and a green aluminum dinghy pushed into view piloted by a young boy.

"Hello!" Kendra said, waving.

Haley peered over the gunnel. The blonde sat on the tender's front bench seat, staring up at the Mary Queen. "You must be Kendra?"

The woman nodded.

"Bring her around to the ladder, Ray Ray."

The kid waved and circled around to the port side of the Mary Queen where a boat ladder hung over the side.

Haley strode across the deck to greet her.

Jealousy stirred in Haley as she fought back her feelings. The woman's husband had been eaten by the swarm, and the last thing she was probably thinking about was finding another man, but strange things happened in the throes of sorrow, and Kendra was beautiful, vulnerable and in need of support, and Drake was only a man, and... She cursed herself. If she felt so strongly about Drake, why hadn't she told him? She knew the answer, even if it ate her up inside. What if he didn't feel the same way? What would that mean for the group? They were all she had.

Kendra reached main deck and held out her hand. "Kendra Longly. I really appreciate you allowing me to tag along."

Haley took her hand. "You'll be doing more than that. Change of plans."

Kendra's brow knitted.

"Helen is bringing out the Sand Dollar, and I'm going to patrol with that while you and Helen handle communication via the Mary Queen's bridge."

Kendra nodded. "At least I'll know what's going on."

"Don't sound so disappointed, I'm sure the plan will go to hell, and you'll be more involved than you want."

Haley went to the bridge and Kendra went to release the mooring lines.

The Mary Queen's bridge was a mix of new, old, and ancient. The boat was thirty-six years old, and it had been commissioned when Jimmy Carter was president. The deck was dimpled steel, the command console black, wires running in gray conduit down its side. The ship had an up-to-date SONAR fish finder, and solid GPS, but there was no autopilot. Haley piloted the trawler via a ship's wheel made of wood and scavenged from an old sailing vessel. The wheel was worth more than the boat's engine.

"Good to go," Kendra called from below.

Haley tapped the throttle arm an inch, and the motor grumbled as the vessel lurched into motion.

Simpson Bay was getting pushed around by trade winds out of the east. The calm before the storm was over, and lines of white foam streaked the undulating bay like tiger stripes. Haley notched the throttle down, and the motor groaned, and the deck trembled as the boat drove through growing surf.

Once out of the channel, she headed due west, Boot Tip Point a gray outline in the blackness.

"Do you think Drake will get caught?" Kendra asked when she joined Haley on the bridge.

Haley shrugged.

"How well do you know him?" Kendra said. "I have to admit, I felt guilty as hell when I first met him. I was..."

Good question. Haley said nothing. She was used to dealing with tourists. Some liked to talk, some didn't, either way the smart move for the charter captain was always silence.

"My husband was eaten by a school of zombie Barracuda, and I was attracted to him. A fleeting thought, but there, nonetheless. I felt horrible. Still do."

"And now?" Haley said. She hoped she'd kept the edge out of her voice.

She hadn't, because Kendra said, "I'm so sorry. Are the two of you…?"

Anger rose in her like the tide, but it drained just as fast. Haley sighed. "I don't know what we are, honestly. We've got a really cool group—you've met them—and we just dance around and around."

"Every relationship is a negotiation," she said. That thought appeared to bring back a bad memory, because a tear slipped down her cheek.

"I guess I'm scared," Haley said.

Kendra nodded, then began to sob hard.

Haley handed her a tissue.

"We're here," Haley said. She pulled back the throttle arm, the growl shifted to a tapping purr, and the deck ceased vibrating. Haley stabbed a button on the command console and the rattle of chain dragging over metal echoed over the ship as the anchor dropped into the sea. She killed the lights, and the Mary Queen listed in the growing surf, darkness blanketing the Caribbean.

A whirring buzz echoed over the water.

"That what I think it is?" Kendra said.

"Let's get some lines out. Fast," Haley said, and she darted from the bridge, Kendra in tow.

The buzzing got louder as a pinprick of red light approached from the south.

Haley handed Kendra a rod and pointed toward the gunnel.

The drone wheeled around the Mary Queen, not even attempting to be discreet. The flying robot pulled up above the bridge, then slowly cruised in a slow circle.

Haley reeled in her line and cast it again, ignoring the drone.

The drone's engines cycled up and it tore off, dropping low and disappearing in the darkness.

Haley's phone trilled. She tapped it and said, "Yo."

***

The mangroves creaked and chittered as Helen threaded through the beach grass down to the shoreline behind Drake's house. The wind worried her, but not much. She didn't like the ocean, wasn't a swimmer or diver, but when one lives on an island there were certain mandatory skills that must be obtained, and piloting pleasure boats was one of them.

The Sand Dollar wasn't a pleasure craft, but it served that purpose regularly, and Helen knew the boat well. She dropped her rucksack and looked for the mooring rope. The outgoing tide was minimal, and she found the line easily and pulled the boat in. She was sixty-one years old, but she was still a tightly wound strand of corded muscle from years of being on her feet.

Folks asked her regularly why she'd moved to an island if she didn't like the water, and it was a fair question, but one she didn't really have an answer for. She loved island life, just not the surrounding sea. Fred, her deceased husband, had been a water rat, swimming whenever he could. She thought that was where she'd gotten her love for the beach and the tropics. She'd spend many hours sitting on the beach or poolside watching her husband swim.

But Fred was gone, dead eleven years from a cancer that ate his brain. A day didn't pass without her thinking of him, and the pain in her stomach returned anytime she thought about him.

Fuck cancer.

She grabbed her sack of supplies and jumped aboard. Foot high waves rolled onto the rocky shore, crashing in the blackness, the thin line of whitewater visible in the faint moonlight. She tied off the mooring rope and let the Sand Dollar float with the current as she lowered the motors.

It was strange being on the boat without Drake. She'd taken the boat out without him only one other time when her daughter and family had come to visit. It had been a great day, the grandchildren thoroughly impressed with how she beached the boat on Boot Tip Point, and brought them to the reef.

She was about to turn the key and spin-up the motors when something caught her eye off the starboard bow.

A cone of moonlight knifed through the clouds, illuminating a section of the inky black sea like the center ring of a circus. Dimpled whitewater writhed and snapped, and the foul stench of rot floated on the wind. The field of whitewater left the cone of light and disappeared in darkness.

Helen stared into the blackness, but whatever had drawn her eye was gone. The wind died away, the sea around the boat going flat. Someone yelled from the back of her mind, "Run you fool! Run!"

She spun the engines and they fired up with a roar. She pushed the throttle arm all the way down, the Yamahas screamed, and the Sand Dollar jumped from the water and came up on plane. Helen spun the wheel and headed out to sea, looking over her shoulder only once, but there was no whitewater, no teeth, yet her nerves still did cartwheels.

She eased back on the throttle, pulled her phone, and called Haley.

"Yo."

"It's me," Helen said.

"Everything O.K.?"

"Yup," Helen said. "ETA is seven minutes."

"10-4. See you then. Mary Queen out."

***

The southern tip of Kraken Island was a faint dark line in the distance, and the growing surf broke across the bow of the sunfish, seawater running down the fiberglass deck and filling the footwell. The sail was down, and the boat floated south with the current. Jillian had her arms wrapped around the boom arm, keeping the sail from snapping.

Marley's watch glowed pale green in the darkness. "It's almost time. You ready?"

Jillian nodded as she pulled on the line that raised the sail.

The boat jerked into motion, slicing through the waves as the bow lifted and fell.

Marley worked the tiller, keeping one eye on the sea, the other on his watch.

Jillian tied off the main sheet, holding the sail in place. She peered through the night scope Drake had given them, scanning Kraken Island's dark shoreline.

"Got him?" Marley said.

"Yup," Jillian said. "Just turned around and he's moving north along the beach right on schedule."

"Any sign of the boys?"

They knew the location of the drop off, and Jillian searched the sea for Drake and Julian. She said, "Don't see them, but I wouldn't expect to."

Marley glanced at his watch again. It was time. He said, "Jillian, tighten that sheet."

Jillian pulled on the rope, reigning in the sail, creating more wind pressure. The sunfish zipped along at a steady four knots, slicing through the waves with ease, throwing little spray and making no noise.

Worry and doubt crept through Marley, and he felt like he'd done something wrong. That deep worry of waiting for the other shoe to drop. He trusted Drake—trusted him with his life—and he couldn't let him down. He scanned the shoreline and jerked the tiller left, and the boat arced to starboard on a direct course for Kraken Island.

"Let's do this," Jillian said. She tied off the sail and lifted a sealed package that contained matches dipped in wax, several small fire starter logs, and one walkie talkie and their cell phones. There was driftwood all along the shoreline, and Marley was confident he could get a fire going in seconds. He'd gotten fires started with much less.

The sunfish crunched onto the beach and Marley dragged the boat onto shore as Jillian lifted the centerboard. Then they were scrambling about, Marley on his knees digging a hole, Jillian collecting firewood. When Marley had the fire starters surrounded by a teepee of dried wood, he struck a match on a stone and the fire sparked to life. Flames licked the darkness, white smoke disappearing in the blackness.

"O.K.," Marley said.

Jillian turned on the radio, went to the emergency channel, and issued a Mayday. She repeated the call three times, but didn't say where she was. The call was for Ratson's men and to alert the rest of the team that they were in position. The signal strength wasn't strong enough to reach the Teto Command Center, and though Drake wouldn't have his radio on, he'd see the fire in the distance if he was where he was supposed to be.

The patrol guard arrived first, out of breath from the jog, an old AK47 pointed at them. "This is a private island. You're not allowed to be here. Now go, or things will not go well for you."

The guy sounded Russian to Marley, but not exactly. Like a pig Latin version. He said, "Thank God you're here. We went for a night sail, got caught in the current and ended up here. We were scared and didn't know what else to do," Jillian said.

"Not my problem," the guard said, but the tip of the rifle barrel fell slightly. "Who the hell goes sailing at night in a tiny boat, anyway?"

"Moonlight and all that. We went out at eight o'clock. We've been lost for hours," Jillian said.

Marley stayed silent. He knew if he opened his mouth things wouldn't go well.

The guy said something in his foreign language when his radio squawked. "Ya." The man's eyes shifted to Jillian and Marley and the tip of the AK47 came back up. "Yes, sir." He clipped the radio back on his belt and said, "Put that fire out. Now!"

Marley and Jillian kicked rocks and sand on the fire, and it sputtered out, dark smoke clouding the area. Rushing the man and taking his gun ran through Marley's young mind, and it was rejected immediately. They were a diversion, and their mission was to distract if they could, and then leave. If they were detained, Drake would intervene.

He searched the northern shoreline for his friends, but didn't see them. That meant nothing. The plan was for them to make sure Marley and Jillian were safe before they continued, but they'd be hiding in the trees, trying to be shadows.

Marley heard the quick crack of static, but he didn't look at Jillian. She'd opened a radio channel, but with the pounding surf and the rocks and shells tumbling in the undertow, the guard didn't appear to have heard it.

"What do we have here?" said a man with a dark beard as he emerged from the mangroves. He had four armed guards in tow.

Marley started. It was Beard Boy. He cursed himself. He'd pushed Drake to let him come, and neither of them had considered this possibility.

"You!" Beard Boy said.

"Sir?" said the original guard.

"This is no accident. This boy—" The bearded man grabbed Marley by the arm. "He was on that boat that accidently floated into the cove yesterday."

Marley struggled to pull free, but the man's hand was a vice-grip.

Jillian said, "Leave him alone." She surged forward and was met by two guards, who each took an arm.

"Now you two accidentally beach on Kraken Island? Bullshit." Beard Boy unclipped a radio from his belt and opened a channel. "Julius, you there?"

"Yes, sir."

"We're coming in with guests. Go to level red."

"10-4."

Beard Boy turned to his crew. "Search them."

"This one's got a radio, sir," one of the guards said.

Beard Boy turned his dark eyes on Marley and Jillian. "You two are coming with me. I think you need to meet the boss."

18

Drake crawled from the Caribbean, Marley and Jillian's small fire flickering like a candle in the distance. He pushed himself to his feet and darted across the thin stretch of beach to the cover of the mangroves. He crouched in the shadows and dug out night binoculars. A lone figure sprinted up the beach toward the fire. Everything was going according to plan.

First order of business was to make sure Marley and Jillian were safe. After that, Drake and Julian would creep around and see what they could see, maybe try and get into the buildings, though Drake thought that was doubtful. Everything he'd seen of Ratson so far displayed a 'spare no expense' attitude, and Drake was certain the man's facilities would have top level security.

Drake also knew there was a fault in every system, and that flaw was usually human.

"Hey," whispered Julian.

Drake nodded in the darkness, the sound of his own breathing like a bass drum in his head. He stowed the binoculars, took out the Glock, penlight, radio, black sweats, and t-shirt. He handed the radio to Julian, and the two men changed out of their wet clothes and hid their dry bags.

The kid studied the radio, then stuffed the earpiece in his ear and turned the on knob. He stared blankly into the darkness, listening.

"Anything?"

Julian shook his head no.

"Keep it off, but at the ready," Drake said. He lifted a hand and pointed down the beach, and the duo broke into a jog, moving down the shoreline just inside the shadows of the mangroves. Their rubber water shoes squeaked faintly as they ran, but the push and pull of the ocean covered the sound of their passage.

As the storm slid west, the cloud cover was getting thicker, cutting off most of the moonlight and starlight. Shadows danced across the beach, the mangroves and beach grass reaching out their long shadowy fingers. Crickets hummed, and a night owl hooted, the sweet scent of the sea and the rolling surf like a finely tuned symphony.

Yelling and screaming ahead, and Drake doubled his pace, digging in and running as fast as he could. Drake turned to Julian and put a fingertip to his ear.

The red light of the radio's power indicator cut through the darkness as Julian turned the unit on. He covered the light with his hand.

Three tense minutes flew by as the duo worked their way down the beach, sweat dripping down Drake's back, knees aching, stomach screaming, his mother's voice in his head yelling about what a bad idea it had been to come to the island. They were trespassing, and if he disappeared who would come looking for him?

Haley.

"Not good, boss," Julian said as they ran. "The guards are taking them in."

Drake had figured the 'we're lost and scared' ruse wouldn't garner help or sympathy, but the plan was for Marley to head back out on the sailboat as soon as the guard arrived. The thinking being the guard would be happy to have the problem removed from his plate, but that hadn't happened. He was a hundred yards from the fire when it abruptly went out, plunging the tip of the island into oily blackness.

The mangroves fell away to Drake's left, a thin carpet of beach grass thinning as he ran. They dove to the ground for cover, army crawling on their stomachs as they peered through the swaying vegetation.

Seven shadowy figures emerged from a patch of mangroves, four flashlight beams bobbing in the darkness as the group walked toward Drake and Julian.

Julian tapped Drake and pointed.

A path ran west to east fifty feet or so from their position, and the party's flashlight beams bounced and strayed. If Drake stayed where he was, he and Julian risked being seen, but if they moved there was an even greater chance they'd be discovered.

"Lay flat," Drake whispered.

The kid's eyes went wide in the blackness, but he stayed still.

Light bloomed in the night, the chatter of voices, and... Drake recognized one of the voices, but he couldn't place it. A radio chirped.

"Sir," said a deep male voice.

The beach grass all around filled with light and Drake felt like a spider crawling across the room when the lights come on.

But as fast as the light came, it was gone, the owner of the flashlight swinging its beam in a wide arc, illuminating the mangroves and forest beyond.

"The boy was on that boat yesterday, sir. The one we had to run off that caused all the trouble," the voice said.

Drake's heart sank. It was Beard Boy, and he had Marley and Julian.

He was no mastermind, but Drake had spent hours planning how to search Kraken Island. There were many inherent dangers, not the least of which being that Ratson's guards would shoot first and ask questions later, but he hadn't considered that Beard Boy himself might handle a simple beach intrusion, and that he would recognize Marley.

He considered pulling the plug, calling in the cops and telling them everything, but what good would it do? He'd end up in trouble and Ratson would still have his friends. He might even think it wise to eliminate the prisoners rather than deal with them being found. The memories of the metal rings in the cove came rushing back like the tide. The Barracuda swarm.

"I'll be there in a few moments," Beard Boy said. "I know he asked not to be disturbed, sir, but this is of the upmost importance." A large set of waves broke on the beach in the distance. "On my authority, sir." The man clicked off and ran off a long string of words that sounded like curses.

The party of seven shuffled by in the darkness, and Drake turned his head slightly so he might see. Marley and Jillian stood out because of their height, and their positions in the center of the guards, but he couldn't see their faces. They appeared unharmed, and that brought some hope, but not much.

Drake and Julian followed, staying back, using each bend and shift in the path to hide. The estate house rose from the tangle of vegetation to the north, one lone light atop a rise. The path plunged into a hollow, and mosquitoes attacked in force. He brushed them away, but it was like trying to take the salt out of the sea. Pools of water shined at the base of the mangroves, the rotten scent of low tide spreading over the island.

The flashlights ahead went out and Drake and Julian froze. A dense patch of water reeds blocked the way, and Drake figured they'd reached the southern edge of Deep Hollow Cove. He knew from the prior day's incursion that all the buildings, other than the house, were on the northern edge of the cove, tucked within a thick patch of mangroves and scrub pine.

A brief instant of panic surged through Drake because he thought he'd lost the trail, but a light flashed ahead, and Drake followed it. When the path reached the water reeds it forked right and left; the cove's eastern shore to the right, the left path meandering around the bay to the island's northern edge. He went left, Beard Boy and crew twenty yards ahead in the blackness.

The cove reflected moonlight and starlight that fought through the clouds. Shiners leapt from the water and frogs and lizards bleated from within the reeds.

The shortest figure, Marley, looked over his shoulder when Beard Boy and his group entered a small sand clearing. Perhaps he felt Drake's presence, but whatever it was, the guard to Marley's left didn't like it, and he cuffed the young Jamaican on the back of the head.

Drake brought up the Glock, anger burning through his carefully built layers of patience and cool. If Marley and Jillian were hurt in any way, he didn't know what he'd do.

Static, voices, but Drake couldn't make out what was being said, and he couldn't see in the inky blackness.

The mangroves gave way to Deep Hollow Cove, and four low buildings sat in a semicircle at the edge of a clearing, the largest and closest building only forty feet from the water. A steel sluiceway ran from an opening on the side of the largest building into the cove. The buildings had no lights. No visible windows or signage, and in the darkness the structures looked like giant bricks. There was a beeping sound, then the snap and click of an electronic lock, and the seven shadows passed into the building furthest from the cove.

Drake and Julian eased into the mangroves.

"What the hell do we do now? Check in with Helen?" Julian said.

"I know we said we weren't going to split up, but things have gotten real. I'm pulling the plug," Drake said.

"But they looked fine. Can't we—"

Drake held up a hand. "No, WE can't do shit. I want you to head back into the mangroves. Go to the center of the island where you'll be sure not to be heard. Call Helen. She probably heard what you did, but bring her up to speed and tell her to call the cops."

"Call the cops and tell them what?"

"That the Mary Queen got a Mayday from a sailboat beached on Kraken Island. She sent a tender to help them, and saw they were taken away at gun point."

Julian threw back his head in surprise. "You're kidding, right? Who the hell is going to believe that?"

"Don't worry, I'll make them believe," Drake said. He was better at breaking stuff than fixing it, and it was time for him to put his considerable destructive power to work.

"You're going to wait here?" Julian said.

"No," Drake said. "I'm going in there." He pointed at the metal channel that led from the nearest building into the cove, where it met one of the steel containment rings. "I bet that's how they move the Barracuda. That must be the lab."

"And you're going to walk right up its gullet?"

"Well, when you say it like that," Drake said. The kid had a point, but Drake was playing a hunch. He believed they moved the swarm during dusk and dawn, when the rabid Barracuda became docile. He'd seen it with his own eyes twice. He had four hours to sunup, and he saw no other way into the building. Red pinpricks of light pierced the darkness from the electronic locks on each door. Card access, and possibly keypads that required a code, but the sluiceway used to move the man-eating fish? Who in their right mind would try and enter the lab that way?

Julian patted Drake on the back and slipped into the mangroves.

He felt his nerves retreat with the kid away from the action, and Drake didn't look back as he worked his way around the cinderblock building closest to the water, keeping his back to the wall, avoiding the eyes of cameras mounted on the corners of the building. Boats bobbed and swayed in the cove, the beach grass whispered, and the mangroves snapped and popped, but nothing moved between the buildings.

Drake slipped from cover and walked toward the building's entrance. He didn't go slow, or fast, he walked briskly, like he belonged. He'd be nothing but a shadow to anyone who might be watching the cameras, and though he might get caught, he was confident Ratson's men wouldn't fire without knowing who or what they were shooting at.

The metal channel ran on a slight incline from the southern side of the building into the cove. The steel was scratched and dented, but dry. Drake stepped over the lip of the sluiceway and casually walked up the center of it.

"Hey," came a voice from the shadows.

Drake considered making a run for it, but he couldn't make it. Did it matter if he could? The guard would sound the alarm and that would be game over.

He turned and said, "They were having problems with the gate last night. Boss said to take a look."

Drake saw the outline of the guard in the blackness, so he assumed the man couldn't see his face. Drake hopped off the sluiceway, and headed straight for the guy.

A flashlight snapped on, its beam arcing across the compound and finding Drake.

The man was slow, and as he reached for his radio, Drake dove at the guy, fists forward like he was Superman flying.

The impact knocked the guard from his feet, and his old AK47 hit the ground, but didn't discharge. Drake scrambled across the hardpan on his hands and knees, weeds and wisps of young beach grass biting at his face. The guard's eyes went wide as Drake pounced like a spider, pinning the man's legs with his weight and momentum and slapping a hand over the guy's mouth.

Drake put the tip of the Glock to the guard's temple.

Whether it was the cold steel against his skin, or the realization that Ratson wasn't worth dying for, the guard's body went slack, and he dropped his radio.

"Shit. Thought I heard commotion," Julian said as he slipped from a thicket of mangroves.

"So you ran toward it!" Drake's voice leaked through clenched teeth. "Since you're here, give me a hand." Drake rolled the guard over, hand clamped over the guy's mouth as he dragged him into the cover of the mangroves. "Jul, give me your t-shirt."

"Drake, what the hell are you talking about?"

"Now! Give it to me."

Julian sighed in frustration and peeled off his shirt.

"Roll it for me," Drake said.

"Oh," the kid said when he realized what Drake was doing.

Drake tied the shirt around the guy's head, gagging him. Then he handed the Glock to Julian, and searched the guard, running his hands over his jeans. Nothing. "Where's your access card?"

The man said nothing.

Drake nodded to Julian and he pressed the Glock against the man's cheek.

The guard shook his head no.

"Bullshit." Drake punched the man hard, a vicious right cross that split the guy's lip. Blood dripped down his chin, and Drake asked again.

The guy frantically shook his head no.

Drake pulled back his fist, then he froze. "How do you get in there?" Drake pointed at the lab building.

"Kkkk… ooo…deaa," the guy squeaked through his gag.

"What the hell ar—" Drake started.

"Code," Julian said.

The guard wagged his head yes.

"Write it in the sand," Drake said.

The guard glanced back at Drake, then Julian, but the Glock and the punch hadn't been enough, and the man hesitated.

"Look." Drake put his arm around the guy. "You don't get paid enough to take the fall for all this, right? We won't hurt you—hell, we'll let you go. But first we've got something to do. Whatever is happening on this island is about to end, so unless you're a major stockholder, I suggest you give me the code."

The guard looked at the ground, and traced the code in the sand: 19, 23, 91, 19.

"Good boy," Drake said. "Jul, did you talk to Helen?"

Julian nodded. "Spoke with Kendra, actually. She was going to pass the message on. They're all going to harass Feddi and whoever else they can."

Drake nodded.

"She said just ring and Haley can blow into the cove with the Sand Dollar," Julian said as he handed Drake the radio.

In a pinch Drake could escape on the Sand Dollar, but those steel containment rings kept climbing back into his thoughts like a crazy girlfriend, and the idea of swimming with rabid Barracuda wasn't something that filled him with anticipation. He said, "March our friend here into the mangroves and wait. If he yells or tries to escape…" Drake got low and put his lips to the prisoner's ear. "Shoot him." He knew there was no way Julian could do that, and the kid's wry smirk let Drake know the kid knew he didn't expect him to. The goon looked scared shitless, but often courage is born from fear and Drake knew the guy was pondering what his boss was going to do to him.

Julian said, "I'm not cool with sta—"

"I don't give a shit," Drake said. "This whole thing was a bad idea and Marley and Jillian are in real danger. When the cops show in the cove, you get to them. Tell them where I am. Where Jillian and Marley are. Got it?"

Julian nodded. "But its O.K. for you to go in? Do as I say not as I do bullshit?"

"We've come this far, I've got to see what's in that building," Drake said.

"Then what?"

"I'm gonna burn it all down," Drake said. "Now go."

When Julian and the guard were gone, Drake pulled the magazine from the guard's AK47 and found it empty. He sighed and tossed the weapon into the mangroves as he strode purposefully toward the lab building's entrance. The light of the electronic lock marked the door and Drake tapped in the code, head down. The red light turned green, and the buzz of the lock releasing echoed over the distant crash of the surf as Drake slipped inside.

***

Across the compound in the main control room a red alarm light blinked on, and a guard dropped his sandwich onto wax paper and picked up his radio.

19

The cleaning closet smelled of bleach and floor wax, even though all the buckets, mops, rags, spray bottles and sealed containers were gone. All that remained was a slop-sink nestled into a corner which served as Scar's toilet and only source of water. He shivered in the darkness as he counted the drips leaking from the sink's faucet, the plop and crack echoing in the stillness. His stomach ached, and his shoulder thumped with pain. The thugs had bandaged him up, but the injury throbbed and pulsed, and Scar felt the wound growing tight with infection. Breakfast had been bread and water, and his comment about originality had been met with a backhanded slap to the face. It had been worth it.

The maglock snapped and the door opened. Scar covered his eyes with his arm as light spilled into the closet, and he ass-walked backwards, his long hair falling across his face.

"Don't be afraid," the man's voice said. "I'm not going to hurt you. I want to be friends. I'm Javier Ratson." The man stepped into the room and held out a hand.

Scar stared at it like it was a cobra head.

Two armed guards filled the open door behind Ratson, and the pompous a-hole looked over his shoulder and smiled, the message clear. "Try anything, and they'll gun you down like a dog."

Ratson wasn't big, nor was he small. Average described him in every way. His hair was wispy, as if he went to a lot of trouble to make it look messy, his face scrunched up like there hadn't been enough skin to cover it when he'd been born. He wore beach sandals, cotton sailing slacks, and a blue golf shirt with that annoying alligator on it. He dropped onto his haunches, resting his elbows on his knees like a catcher waiting on a pitcher.

Scar looked into the man's eyes. This wasn't a compassionate man. A caring man. A person that would show sympathy. This was a trash man, and he tossed anything he didn't have a use for in the garbage.

"What is your name?" Ratson said. "I've told you mine."

"I know you," Scar said, his voice breaking up.

"Yes, I'm sure you do. Why are you spying on my island? Trying to steal my trade secrets?"

"I was fishing," Scar said.

"Yes, sure. That's what the camera equipment was for? Taking photos—in the dark—for a Fishing Magazine."

"Never know when the big one's gonna bite." Scar was doing his best to sound stupid. Wasn't hard most days.

Ratson smiled. "Indeed. So, are you going to tell me your name? Why you're taking pictures?"

"That against the law?"

"Alright, I thought maybe we could talk like men. Settle things. Come to an understanding," Ratson said. He pushed to his feet so quickly Scar jumped.

Ratson lashed out and smacked Scar across the face.

Scar looked up at him, blood leaking through his teeth, and smiled.

Ratson's face grew red and he pulled a dive knife from a sheath on his belt. It was a short blade, eight inches, made of gray carbon fiber steel, its back notched. The handle looked to be made of driftwood.

"Sir," came a voice from outside the closet.

Ratson whirled.

A man with a dark black beard squeezed between the two guards blocking the entrance.

"Dimitri, I thought I told you I didn't..." Ratson's eyes tracked beyond Beard Boy to something outside the room. "Where the hell did they come from?"

"They claim they were out for a night sail. Got turned around and lost so they beached on the southern end of the island and lit a fire. My men found them there."

"Have they called for assistance?" Ratson asked.

"They sent out a Mayday, but nobody responded." Dimitri, A.K.A. Beard Boy, handed Ratson a radio, the thin black wire trailing from it ending in an earpiece. "Not a very strong signal."

Ratson's gaze turned back to Scar, rage spreading across his face.

"There's more," Dimitri said. "One of the people is the boy that was on that boat we had to run off yesterday."

Ratson tossed his head side-to-side as he tried to crack his neck. "Why didn't you run them off? The last thing I want right now is more prisoners," Ratson said with a sideways glance at Scar. "Did they see anything?"

"I don't see how they could have," Dimitri said.

"O.K. Apologize, feed them, and bring them around and retrieve their boat. Then dump them in Simpson Bay with continued apologies."

"Got it," Beard Boy said.

Ratson turned his attention back to Scar. "I don't know what you and your little band of miscreants are up to, but I assure you, it's over. You've got one choice. Tell me why you are here, and I won't use you for fish food."

"Piss off, mate," Scar said.

This time Ratson didn't slap him, but instead turned away.

Scar sagged.

Ratson spun, pirouetting like a ballerina, and kicked Scar in the head.

Scar went down, head ringing, vision blurry, shoulder wound pounding in rhythm with his galloping heart.

"Is that how it is, huh?" Ratson said. "My men save you, pull you from the drink and this is how you repay me? I should have left you for the horde and you'd be nothing but a slick on the surface of the sea, like your boat."

Scar knew his time was coming to an end, so he threw a Hail Mary. "We know what you're up to. The authorities have been notified and are on the way. We sent samples of the pollution you're dumping in the Caribbean, and soon you'll be the one held against your will."

The anger drained from Ratson's face. "Sir, my new friend, I own the police, and nobody cares about you." Ratson brought up the knife, the gray blade glinting in the fluorescent light.

Dimitri was back, and he cleared his throat.

Ratson whirled, his anger returning as fast as it had fled. "Again? What the hell is it now? I don't want to be disturbed," he screamed.

Beard Boy wrung his hands and looked at the floor. "I know, sir, but we've got an unusual alarm in the lab."

20

Drake closed the door behind him and squinted as his eyes adjusted. Daggers of red and green light cut through the blackness, and the faint hum of equipment and the ripple and slosh of water replaced the crackle of mangroves and breaking surf. The white glow of a light switch called out to him and Drake reached out to tap it, then thought better of it. Several yellow hazmat-type suits hung from stainless steel pegs next to the door, and Drake ran his hand over one.

If Ratson and his men felt the suits were necessary, who was he to argue? Drake pulled one down and slipped it on, the zipper closing and the squeak of rubber like cannon booms in the stillness. He put on boots and a hood, and was disappointed to discover the entire face-shield was clear, and would provide little camouflage.

He pulled free the penlight and radio, clicked on the light, and slipped the radio in a pocket.

Pipes and conduits lined the walls, and a raised gangway ran around an open space. He stepped onto the metal walkway and arced the light around.

Below, a large pool filled the center of the facility, the dark water still, silver flashes of scales glinting in the dim light. The tank was large and covered most of the building's footprint. Below the gangway the sluiceway ran from the pool to the closed metal doors. The channel was empty and dry like the section outside.

Drake worked his way to a metal staircase that ran down into darkness. He descended slowly, expecting the lights to be turned on by men with machine guns.

A dock ran around the large pool, and at its edges smaller tanks gurgled and snapped, the water within moving back and forth, stimulated by wood paddles that brushed the water and simulated incoming and outgoing tides. Drake had seen such machines in labs before. They were used to test ocean currents, the formation of sandspits and landmasses, as well as to study water power.

He arced the light across the nearest tank. A red cloud moved and shifted with the simulated current as if under power.

Tiny metal specks, like sediment in clear water, sparkled in the thick paint-like ooze that polluted the tank. The scent of rot and decay hung over the tank.

On the far side of the space a command console glowed with a myriad of control lights, and Drake headed for it. He gave the large pool a wide berth, never taking his eyes off the moving water. Yellow fifty-gallon drums with the words DANGER marked on them in red letters lined one wall, and sealed crates, stacks of plastic containers, and vats of what looked like water lined another.

Drake shined the light on the pool. It was separated into two holding areas, a steel curtain connected to the concrete walls of the pool via stainless steel rings running side to side in the tank's center. The tank was filled with Barracuda, but even in the dim light Drake saw the two groups weren't the same.

The fish on the right were docile and calm. They swam around each other lazily, winding and dipping into each other as though performing an intricate dance. Scales shimmered in Drake's flashlight beam, hundreds of black eyes with white rings staring into the cone of light.

The left side of the tank was chaos, fish writhing and fighting as they climbed on each other. Barracuda surged, black eyes rimmed in red. The beasts' jaws snapped, long needle-like teeth curving over pouting lips as they pressed against the metal netting that covered the pool. Every few seconds the Barracuda horde would surge upward and the steel rings holding the netting would clink and clang as the metal stretched and pulled.

He went to the control board, but he had no idea what he was looking at. Wires trailed away from the console into conduits that met larger pipes that ran along the walls. Several screens were mounted on angle brackets, and the control board had a series of switches, knobs, and levers. Many of the lights blinked green, a couple red and yellow. All the monitoring screens were dark save for two. One showed a split screen of both sides of the holding tank, dark eyes, teeth and scales filling the screen. The other display showed a status board: water temperature, chemical composition of the water, and a slew of other numbers and readings he didn't understand.

Drake had worked on a ship most of his adult life, and he'd been in many marine biology labs, but he'd never seen anything like this. He panned the light around and it fell on a computer printout tacked between two of the dark display screens.

The thing depicted in the diagram was bug-like, but immediately Drake saw it wasn't an animal, at least not fully. The subject had a mechanical look, all its edges sharp and defined. It resembled a spider with ten long arms extending off a main torso, each with a tiny claw at its end. The two rear appendages were larger than the others, and shaped like a fish tail. There were markings; what looked like a serial number, and thin red veins, like wires, wrapped around the entire creature, dipping in and out of the metal-like skin.

Drake thought the thing looked like a computer chip, and somewhere in the back of his mind a memory struggled forward, only to be pushed back.

Harsh fluorescent light filled every dark space. Drake froze in place like a kid who'd been caught searching for his birthday presents, then he reached for the Glock, only to remember he'd given it to Julian. Instead, he eased his thumb down on his radio's talk button and opened a channel.

"Do not move, or I will shoot you." The voice was Beard Boy's.

Drake raised his hands, keeping his thumb pressed to the radio. "I'm unarmed. Don't shoot."

The walkie-talkie chose that moment to let loose with a squawk of static, and one of the guards fired a warning shot, and the shell plunked into the control console.

Drake dropped to his knees, let the radio fall to the floor with a crash, and put his hands behind his head.

"Hold your fire!" came a new voice. "Are you crazy? If you hit one of those containers and release the nano, I'll order it to eat you. Pay attention!" Beard Boy rushed forward and pushed Drake to the ground, digging his knee into his back. "Not so big without your boat, huh? Mr. Toughness."

"If you're going to insult someone, at least get it right. Dipshit."

Beard Boy cracked Drake on the back of the head and his vision blurred, then cleared. The knot on his head throbbed, and Drake felt nauseous. He opened his mouth to tell the guy how tough he was, then thought better of it. He needed to start thinking smart, or he'd end up like Scar.

Boss man peered around the lab, checking the command console, trying to identify if anything had been tampered with or was missing. Finally, he sighed loud and strolled over to Drake, hands on hips like a mother about to scold a child.

"Where is the guard you got the code from?" the boss said.

"Well, I don't know, Ratson. Maybe you should pay more attention to where you put them," Drake said.

Ratson rolled his eyes and Beard Boy hit Drake again, but the blow had a governor on it. Clearly the thug didn't want to knock him out.

"So you know me," Ratson said. "Good, then I can skip the bullshit pleasantries."

"Awesome," Drake said. He tightened, waiting for a blow that didn't come.

"Why are you here? Taking pictures of my island?"

Pictures? He was worried about pictures? Drake said nothing.

Ratson's face scrunched when he saw Drake's consternation. "I have trade secrets on this island worth billions, so I need to know why you're so interested in my dealings."

"Because you killed my friend," Drake blurted.

Ratson smiled. "You'll have to be a little more specific."

"Scar," he said. "You know damn well who I'm talking about."

Ratson laughed, and he and Beard Boy exchanged a glance. Beard Boy looked at the floor. "Indeed," said the boss. "So you and your little sailor friends, you're all just trying to save, who?"

"Don't play games. I know your men took him out. I found the remains of his boat."

"And you know I was involved, how?"

Drake jutted out his chin in the direction of the large tank. Metal clinked and clanged as the fish pushed and heaved against the metal mesh covering the pool.

Ratson nodded. "Well," he said as he went to the control console. He tapped a few buttons and all the screens came to life. "You want to know what we're doing here? I think I'll give you a full, interactive demonstration."

Beard Boy stepped forward and whispered in Ratson's ear.

Ratson jerked back in frustration and looked at his watch. "Yes, I know what time it is in the Ukraine." He approached Drake, putting his face in close. "I think I want to question you a bit more after my meeting. I'm not buying your shit. Dimitri, put him on ice."

Drake's nerves danced on hot coals, and he was shitting enough bricks to build a football stadium. He needed to buy time, give Haley an opportunity to get the cops. That thought kicked his confidence's ass. Ratson was powerful, and the governor wouldn't allow Feddi or anyone else to scream into Ratson's cove. If there was a response, it would be slow, and he'd find out just how much more he was worth than Scar.

Dimitri ordered his men to take Drake away, and they led him back out into the night and into another building. Though the structure looked the same as the lab building on the outside, the interior was much different. Half the building was storage, the rest closed doors that Drake assumed were offices or small research labs. Beard Boy pulled open a door marked Janitorial, and tossed him into darkness.

Drake hit the concrete floor hard, and the knee of the biohazard suit he wore ripped. "Shit," he said.

"Howdy."

Drake jumped out of his skin, pain running down his spine as he ass-walked backward toward the door, which slammed shut. A click and buzz as the electronic lock fell into place with a finality Drake didn't like. He felt like the dumbest stump in the yard. "Who's there?" he said, trying to keep the tremor from his voice.

"Drake?" The dark figure inched closer.

"Scar!" Drake was so happy he surged forward in the darkness and threw his arms around his friend, who winced. He had a thick bloody bandage on his right shoulder. "I thought you were dead."

"Me too. Turns out they just shot my old ass and fished me from the drink."

"You smell three days dead," Drake said.

"Thanks."

"What happened? I found pieces of your boat. We all thought…"

Scar sighed. "More important, what the hell are you doing here?"

"We came to rescue you," Drake said. Locked in a supply closet, weaponless, the idea sounded preposterous.

"Rescue me?" Who the hell are you? Luke Skywalker?"

"The cops aren't doing anything, and we just couldn't... couldn't let Ratson get away with it."

"How's that going?"

Drake said nothing.

"Who's with you?"

"Haley is offshore on the Sand Dollar, Helen and Kendra are on the Mary Queen, and Trevor and John are lurking around out there in the sub. Julian and Marley were taken. I don't know where they are, and Julian—"

"They're fine. I overheard Ratson order his men to dump them in Simpson Bay," Scar said.

Air moved through the vent on the ceiling, water dripped into the slop sink, and Drake's suit squeaked when he moved.

"You were saying about Julian?"

"Yeah, he's here on the island. I pulled the plug and hopefully the cavalry will be here soon," Drake said.

Scar chuckled. "Wouldn't count on it, Captain."

Drake said nothing, the blackness pressing in on him, the faint scent of cleaning fluids tickling his nose.

"How'd they get you?"

"I used a code that got me inside the lab building, but it must've been an unauthorized entry or some shit. They had me in two minutes."

"Oh, do tell. Find anything interesting?"

"Saw some stuff I didn't understand," Drake said. "That was until Ratson showed. He mentioned nano, and I saw a strange schematic of a creature that looked half machine, half alive."

"Nanobots?" Scar fell back against the wall with a thud. "That's bad news. Very bad news."

"He said if they got out, he'd order them to eat the guy who released them."

"Like he could control them?"

Drake said, "Sure sounded like it. He had a meeting or something, then he plans to give me... and probably you, a live... interactive... demonstration."

"You mean feed us to the horde?"

Drake said nothing, his mind spinning through the possibilities, and they all ended in his gruesome death.

"Anything else?"

"Not really... except, the swarm is docile at dusk and dawn."

"Could be useful," Scar said.

"My guess is we'll get our demonstration at sunup when he moves a new group of specimens into the cove cages before they're released into the Caribbean," Drake said.

"Saw those, did you?"

Drake nodded in the darkness. "Why is he doing this? What purpose could controlling a swarm of zombie Barracuda serve?"

Scar laughed, and when he stopped, he was breathing hard. "Yeah, can't think that way. This guy Ratson is a nut. He doesn't ask if he should do something, all he asks is if he can, and there's many reasons why he's trying to control the sea. Ocean temps are rising everywhere, but there are sections where the water is becoming colder, which means more oxygen and more life. That's why the warm and shallow Caribbean Sea has little in the way of sea floor vegetation, while the dark, colder sea has abundant ocean flora. If he could control these areas."

"So? Tell me something I don't already know."

"Red tide, algae blooms, all kinds of naturally reoccurring dangers threaten the sea, the coral reefs, and a staggering amount of the world's food comes from the oceans. Not to mention that most cargo is transported on ships. Earth's surface is seventy-one percent water. Control the sea and control the planet."

"That's mad."

"James Bond mastermind level insane," Scar said. "Consider all the companies he owns that would profit. Seventy-five tons of fish are caught in the world's oceans each year, and thirty of that is for human consumption. The health of the sea is essential to human survival. The oceans are a major source of food, medicine, and jobs. Fish from the ocean currently are the primary source of protein for one in six people on Earth, and things like algae and kelp are used in making peanut butter, beer, soymilk and frozen foods."

Drake said nothing.

"The very air we breathe," Scar added.

It was crazy, but it all made sense, and his doubts started slipping away.

"So, what was your plan?" Scar said.

"Basically, hair on fire."

Scar chuckled in the darkness. "Ah, one of my favorites."

"I just wanted to look around. See if there was any sign of you," Drake said. "Clearly I underestimated the situation."

"Well," Scar said, "I guess we should get some rest. We've got a couple of hours until dawn breaks."

Two hours to stew and worry. Maybe Julian would find them? Doubtful. The kid was most likely watching from the mangroves as he was instructed. Drake leaned his head against the cold cinderblock wall and closed his eyes, but sleep wouldn't come.

21

A gray dawn leaked across the compound as Drake and Scar were herded toward the lab building, Beard Boy leading. A bruised sky hung above the eastern horizon, orange spots of sunlight piercing the rolling cloud cover. The air smelled of low tide and rotten fish, but also carried the sweet scent of hibiscus. Men stood in the shadows, their faces hidden by the early morning gloom, but Drake saw the glint of guns, heard moans of frustration and grunts of anger. He figured the sentries had gotten a reaming after he'd infiltrated the lab, and every guard on the island probably wanted to put a hole in him.

Drake scanned the mangroves, water reeds, and beach grass surrounding the buildings, searching for Julian, but he didn't see him. He knew that meant nothing. The kid could be five yards away in the bushes, but something needled him, a moment of dread that seeped through him like a virus. He had a horrible feeling that Julian had been killed.

The guards holding Drake jerked him to a stop as Dimitri typed in his security code and the door lock snapped open with a buzz and click.

Harsh fluorescent light stung his eyes, and Drake tried not to squint, but failed. As he was pushed into the building and guided down the steps, the steel mesh covering the specimen pool clinked and clanged as the beasts surged and fought, stretching and pulling the metal.

"Ah, I see you've found your friend," Ratson said. He sat behind the control console, working switches, tapping monitoring screens. "Splendid."

The guards forced Scar and Drake into seats and secured their ankles and wrists. Scar moaned as his hands were tied, the guard jerking his arm, the gunshot wound in his shoulder bleeding through its bandage.

When Drake didn't respond to the taunt, Ratson said, "That is why you came here, right? To find Mr. Scar here?"

Drake said nothing. He was doing his best to keep his heart from jumping from his chest and his nerves from shaking him apart like a speeding car with a bent axel.

"I will ask one more time, because I'm a fair man," Ratson said. "Why are you here?"

"Piss off," Scar said.

Dimitri punched Scar hard, an explosive blow that snapped his head back. Blood splattered the floor, and a tooth dinged off a stainless-steel specimen container.

Scar spat at the man.

Dimitri smiled as he wiped the blood and spittle from his face, but when he went to grab Scar by the neck, Ratson waved him off.

"I've got something fun planned," Ratson said.

Beard Boy didn't look appeased, but he stepped back.

Ratson looked at his watch. "Sunup in fifteen. Positions everyone. Activate filtering system. I'll bring the bots online." Data scrolled across Ratson's screens so fast Drake couldn't follow it.

A hiss rose above ringing metal as gauges were tweaked, water composition tested and adjusted. For a short time, it was as if Ratson and the others had forgotten about them. Scar's eyes darted about, following every move and every action.

Ratson tapped a screen and leaned back in his chair, hands behind his head.

"All systems are go," said one of Ratson's men, a husky guy with curly blonde hair and vacant eyes.

Ratson nodded and got up. "So, guys, this is where you'd normally get a last meal, but, you know," Ratson said, and shrugged.

"An asshole to the end. Not surprising," Drake said.

Ratson chuckled, then punched Drake in the gut. He doubled over, but it was half act.

Ratson said, "Terry, get ready to move the A specimens into the sluiceway. Notify outside personnel."

"Yes, sir."

"So, your nasty little guppies don't like half-light?" Scar said.

Ratson spoke with the confidence of a man who knew his audience would be impressed, and soon eliminated. "Guppies," he chuckled. They were just friends talking. Tied up friends. "The beasts don't mind the dark at all, or the light. It's that uncertainty of dusk and dawn that seems to vex them. No matter. It's convenient, actually. Adds another layer of control."

"Control? How could you possibly control the swarm?" Drake said.

"Ah, yes, control. The old trickster." Ratson said, "Initiate SeaFree." Ratson leered as he spoke, staring at Drake like he was a piece of chocolate cake.

The rabid Barracuda became docile as the red sparkling ooze was dumped into the pool from one of the yellow fifty-gallon drums. The substance thinned, like a drop of blood in clear water, and the Barracuda swam through it, sucking the nano into their gills.

"Specimen group A got their first dose last night. It takes two. That's one of the reasons why there's always two control groups," Ratson said.

"So, I still don't understand," Scar said.

Ratson punched him in the chest, and Scar wheezed as the air was pushed from his lungs. "Of course you don't. You're a simple-minded fool. A thief."

Drake rolled his shoulders. Here it comes. Ratson was about to spill, he just couldn't help himself. He had to show Drake and Scar how brilliant he was. "So what? The robots control the fish?" Drake urged.

Ratson laughed. "Way more complicated than that."

Scar stammered, "They're nanobots?"

"Micronic robots, to be precise," Ratson said. "They're the size of a dust mite. The bots, which I control, disperse the drug, SeaFree, which induces… communal and violent tendencies in the Barracuda that I can turn on and off like a light switch."

"So you did try and kill me!" Scar yelled.

"I was just protecting my island. Nothing personal."

"But you tried to murder me."

"Tom-ato, tomato."

Scar jerked against his bonds and winced. The crimson stains on the bandages wrapped around his shoulder were soaked through with blood.

"Why Barracuda? Why not sharks? Orca?" Drake said.

"So far, the treatment only works on Barracuda. Some complicated bullshit concerning prions," Ratson said.

Drake looked at Scar, who hiked his shoulders.

"Prions are mis-folded proteins. They cause chronic wasting disease, and my techs are determined to find the key to other predatory species."

"And for what?" Scar said. "So you can get a bigger yacht?"

"Maybe. I was thinking more of a submarine." Ratson glanced at Drake, a smirk peeling over his face.

Barracuda roiled and surged into the metal mesh covering the pool, and it clinked and rang. Red rimmed eyes stared up through the pink clouded water, needle-like curved teeth glinting in the fluorescent light.

"How is it nobody has seen your little horde of robots and zombie fish?" Drake said. "The U.S. government can see what color underwear I'm wearing from space."

"Barracuda hide... a natural tendency... just below the surface, and you said it yourself. The nano looks like red tide, something most people avoid. Thermal images show odd radiation, but nothing that would cause any real concern. So no, there's nothing to see unless you're very close, and then... well, you know what happens then."

"The swarm kills everything in its path."

"If I desire it."

"What kind of sick mind comes up with such a thing?" Drake asked.

Ratson laughed again. "It was an accident, just like LSD and X-rays."

Scar and Drake looked at one another again.

"Like Dr. Hofmann, who, while researching lysergic acid derivatives in his Swiss lab accidentally swallowed LSD while researching its properties and had the first acid trip in history. Or, like eccentric physicist Wilhem Roentgen, who was investigating the properties of cathodic ray tubes when he discovered X-rays, my researchers stumbled on the formula for SeaFree. I own one of the world's largest shipping fleets, as well as many commercial fishing enterprises, and my tech company has been working on nano for years."

"You're going to be like a modern-day pirate? Manipulate world markets and control the food supply from the sea?" Drake said.

"It's all about money. As always," Scar said.

"And power, sure," Ratson said with a smile.

Rage built in Drake, the anger that drives one person to hurt another. A hatred that made Drake want to gouge-out the man's eyes, blow his brains across the pool and let his fish eat him. His vision went red at the edges, and he strained against his bonds, pain knifing through him.

"6:19AM, sir," said one of the techs.

Ratson nodded to Dimitri, who sat uninterested next to a fish tank with sloshing water. He put away his phone and got to his feet, cracking his knuckles and smiling. He waved over three other guards, and they lifted Drake and Scar, and tossed them into the dry sluiceway.

Scar moaned when his injured shoulder hit the cold metal.

In that instant Drake realized he was going to die. Every bad decision he'd ever made ran through his head like a parade, mocking him, reminding him how stupid he'd been to think he could come to Kraken Island. Take on the captain of his ship. It was the same. Always him making the wrong call.

"Dimitri, unbind their hands."

Beard Boy looked at his boss, brow knitting.

"It'll be more fun."

Dimitri sighed.

"Otherwise, we could just throw them in the pool," the boss said. Then he laughed, looked at Drake, and said, "So hard to find help that can see your vision. No appreciation of the gothic." He turned his cold stare back on Beard Boy. "Or, you can deal with disposal, etc.... You think you can do a better job than my swarm, Dimitri?"

Beard Boy pulled his dive knife from its sheath on his leg, and cut the ties securing Drake and Scar's wrists. He left the ties binding their ankles.

"So, it was a pleasure to meet you, Mr. Drake. I am sorry things had to go this way, but when you stick your nose where it doesn't belong, it often gets cut off," Ratson said.

"I'm gonna kill you," Drake said, but his threat was in vain and Ratson knew it.

Ratson laughed, loud and hard. Then he waved a hand, and the technicians began feverously tapping their screens.

Metal scraped on metal as both sets of sluiceway doors inched open, pink water leaking into the steel channel from the holding pool. Teeth and red-rimmed eyes fought and pushed to get through the growing gap, and Ratson laughed.

Hollow booms echoed through the space as Scar undulated and wormed his way toward the far end of the sluiceway. An inch of pink water covered the bottom of the channel, and in seconds the newest additions to the Barracuda swarm would push through the opening and it would be over.

Drake closed his eyes. "What in the hell and all that is holy are you doing?" It was his dead mother's voice. Drake tried to push it away, but she screamed and ranted, and Drake moved. Slow at first, then like an inchworm, lifting his ass and clawing forward, face just above the nano infested water.

Scar squeezed through the door at the end of the sluiceway, and Drake looked back. Barracuda flopped and slithered through the shallow water, eyes bulging, mouths puffing as the fish fought to swim and breathe in the shallow water.

Ratson cackled.

Drake doubled his efforts, eyes locked on the exit which was only ten feet away now. Pain knifed through him as a fish snipped at his foot. He kicked it away with his bound legs, driving the creature back, but five others surged ahead.

Water poured into the sluiceway as the holding tank emptied, and the current washed Drake through the far door.

Whitewater. Coughing. Chaos. Like an out-of-control water slide, Drake plummeted down the sluiceway and crashed into Deep Hollow Cove, the cold water jolting him as he went under. For a brief instant of peace he floated there, shock numbing his extremities. At least he'd die in the sea as he was meant to. He'd always known that.

A hand grabbed him and jerked him to the surface.

Scar knelt at the end of the sluiceway, holding him by the collar, eyes red, face straining with pain as he pulled at Drake with his good arm, his other hanging limply by his side.

Gunshots rang out and bullets pinged and ricocheted off the sluiceway.

Scar disappeared in whitewater.

Drake was washed back into the cove like a piece of garbage caught in a current.

The surging water forced Drake forward and he realized he was in one of the metal holding rings he'd seen. Barracuda poured from the sluiceway, a mound of raging teeth, red rimmed eyes, and scales coming at him like a buzz saw. There was no way out, and mom was silent.

"Climb! Shit, man. Climb!" Scar's voice came as if from a dream, muffled and strange. Metal clanged as the torrent of water spilled from the sluiceway and forced him into the side of the containment ring.

Drake spun in the water like a mermaid, using his legs as one, the tie binding his ankles digging into his flesh like a knife. He stroked hard with his arms, and his face bounced off the steel cage. Then his fingers were through holes, pulling and dragging himself up, using the momentum of the water, fear growing in him and driving him on with one last rush of adrenaline.

He heaved himself over the lip of the containment ring and splashed into the cove beyond.

Barracuda surged and pressed against the sides of the barrier, red rimmed eyes peering through the clear water. The horde twisted and fought, pressing on the steel netting, scales glinting, mouths puckering, gills flaring, teeth exposed.

Drake let out some of his air and stayed submerged. He stared up at the surface and the dull blanket of gray light beyond, but there was no sunray from Heaven, no hand reaching down to pull him out this time. He pushed away from the cage and swam hard, his tied legs dragging behind him as he put as much space as he could between himself and the zombie Barracuda.

His lungs burned, tiny white sparkles blooming across his vision, muscles aching, stomach yelling, eyes stinging. He rolled onto his back and stopped, letting his head float above the surface. He took a deep gasp of air and looked around.

Commotion churned up the cove, and waves broke and shifted as yelling and screaming and gunfire echoed over the island like fireworks.

Scar thrashed and tossed in the water. He was still in the cage. The rabid Barracuda attacked as one, a mound of roiling scales and teeth. Scar screamed as he fought to pull himself out of the water, and onto the sluiceway, only to be dragged back into the sea. He kicked and struggled, the Barracuda swarm covering him like ants on a fallen lollipop. The narrow fish slithered and swam down the metal channel into the cove, and when Scar was almost out of the water another wave of Barracuda surged into him, and he fell back into Deep Hollow Cove.

A knot of whitewater rose above the containment ring as the swarm climbed and mounded on one another, biting and driving into Scar. A strangled scream pierced the morning, a thin ray of sunshine slicing through the thickening cloud cover marking the start of a new day. The turbulent pink water eased, blood bubbles popping on the surface, small pieces of fat, skin and gristle drifting in the water like leaves.

22

Drake floated in the cove, waves breaking over his face, muscles cramping. Sorrow washed through him. He'd come so far, found Scar alive, only for him to be taken by the swarm. Fire burned his stomach, tears leaking from his eyes. It had all been for nothing.

"Not if you get the hell out of here. Bring back the cops," his dead mother's voice boomed.

The channel leading into Deep Hollow Cove was clogged with boats. So much for the rescue plan. Conning towers swayed in the early morning sun, engines grumbled, and the scent of fuel pervaded the air. The gunshots had ceased, and guards were fanning out around the edge of the cove.

The containment rings holding the rabid Barracuda horde clinked and clanged as the fish fought to free themselves, a giant mass of teeth and scales. The lip of the containment ring was lowering and Barracuda were mounding over it into the bay.

Drake pushed all the air from his lungs and sank back into the cove. Stray beams of sunlight cut through the clear water, sediment and sand dancing and twisting like shooting stars. When he was down five feet he flipped over and stroked hard, his bound legs weighing him down like an anchor.

As he swam, Drake searched his memory for details about Deep Hollow Cove. Water reeds ran around the western edge, but the northern and eastern sides were more open and there was no place to hide. To the south, the blocked channel provided no options, so Drake angled southwest, aiming for an outcrop of reeds that ran off a thin sandspit that stuck into the cove.

His lungs burned, and he strained to see what was happening above on the surface, but there was nothing but cloud-filled sky. It was hard to judge, but Drake thought he had at least another fifty yards before he got to shore, and there was no way he'd make it without going up for a breath.

He pushed hard with his arms, driving up, the surface rushing at him. He gasped when his head inched from the water.

Gunshots plunked into the bay around him, tiny waterspouts shooting in the air. Guards ran along the northern edge of the cove, trying to cut him off. Gunpowder snapped and popped as it expanded, bullets whizzing and plopping.

The screech of metal rolling over metal ceased, and a mound of whitewater rose from the cove.

Drake dove again, driving hard, a trickle of air escaping his lips. Lines of whitewater streamed past him, bullets streaking through the water, losing their momentum and power.

He swam hard, arms giving out, muscles tightening and cramping, his dead weight legs dragging through the water behind him like a useless tail. The sea floor rose to meet him and when there was only three feet of water left Drake stopped swimming and crab walked on his hands and knees toward the cover of the water reeds.

"Hold up, partner."

Drake didn't stop. He pushed through the water, the sound of splashing rising above his panting.

A gunshot rang out and hit the water directly before Drake and he stopped, water bubbling and surging around him.

Two guards stood on the shore fifty feet away, their pistols aimed at him.

Drake put his hands in the air.

The crack of a gun firing.

One guard went down, gripping his leg. The other spun around, searching the mangroves and water reeds.

Another gunshot.

The second guard jerked back, his gun falling from his hand as he fell to the ground, blood spouting from a shoulder wound.

Drake waded from the reeds, getting low. Screaming and stray gunshots echoed across the cove as he came across the path he'd used the prior night.

"Pssst," came a snake-like voice from a thicket of mangroves. "Drake?"

"Julian?"

"Here," Julian said. He appeared next to Drake like a ghost.

Drake jumped. "Shit."

"This way." Julian led Drake into a large patch of maze-like scrub pine. "Man, you see what happened to Scar? These bastards. I'm gonna—"

"Stop. Not now," Drake said. "Have you heard from anyone?"

Julian shook his head no. "You saw the cove entrance is blocked, and Ratson sent patrol boats to circle the island. Anyone who tries to come to the island will be greeted long before they find us."

Drake nodded. Sweat dripped down his face and back, the early morning humidity stifling. "Thanks for back there," he said. "Nice shooting. How the hell did you learn to do that?"

"Helen taught me."

"Ah, yes, our Rambo crossing guard."

Julian chuckled. "You hurt?"

"Just my ego."

Surf rumbled and the wash of the day's first jet taking off from Tetu International Airport thundered across the sky.

"We can't stay here," Drake said.

"What do you think Haley and the others will do? Wait for the cops?"

Drake shook his head no. Haley wouldn't wait, but what would she do? If she couldn't get into the cove, she'd figure Drake would go to the drop off point, which was their backup pickup spot. It wasn't far from the shoals where Marley and Jillian had made their fire, but there were issues. That end of the island was exposed and there weren't many places to hide, but at least she'd see them. Would Ratson's men gun them down in daylight as they ran along the beach? He didn't think so, not with so many people with cell phones waiting to get their fifteen minutes of fame. If there were any pleasure crafts floating in the vicinity it would be a help, but it was early.

The voices searching for them were getting louder, so Drake eased through the pines, walking on patches of dead bronze-colored needles when he could, hiding his footprints. Wind gusted, a warm breeze that could cook bacon. It felt good, the heat feeding his tired body. Bacon. His stomach gurgled, his mouth so dry his lips cracked.

Julian came up beside Drake and held out the Glock.

Drake reached out to take it, but held back. "Looks like you're a better shot. Why don't you hold onto it. Plus…"

Julian made fish lips and frowned.

"I don't know if I'll be able to show the same… restraint," Drake said.

Julian rolled his eyes.

"What?"

Julian looked away. "It's just… shooting someone is a little different than picking off tin cans in Helen's backyard while drinking beers. What if I…"

"Hey," Drake said. He tugged Julian's arm until they were hidden within a tall patch of beach grass. "Don't beat yourself up. You did exactly the right thing. You took them down, but not with death blows."

Julian nodded.

"And I'll add," Drake said. "Those guards would've shot you without hesitation. Without thought or remorse."

"Kill or be killed?"

"You proved there's a third option."

The voices of their pursuers floated on the breeze, but they didn't sound close. Drake had lived in the Caribbean long enough to know that could be an illusion. Caribbean Sea breezes had a way of switching things up, making close sounds appear far away, and vise-versa.

Drake put a finger over his mouth.

A man's voice rose above the breeze and background static of rolling waves. "I saw them go that way. Send men to the shoreline."

"We can't cover the entire shore, Dimitri. I think maybe they hide in the scrub pine, no?"

Dimitri's voice was muffled, but Drake heard, "Stupid," and "don't care if they hide."

Of course, Beard Boy didn't care if they hid. At least they weren't running around the island in the daylight trying to signal their friends. "That's it!" Drake said so loudly Julian's eyes grew wide and Drake covered his mouth with his hand.

He waited, Julian's eyes darting around, waiting for a gun toting guard to push through the thick grass. But no guard came, and the whisper of the beach grass, the crack and pop of the mangroves, and the distant rumble of the surf filled the silence.

"We can start a signal fire," Drake said. Two seconds after he made the suggestion, he realized what a bad idea it was. Light a fire and guards would come like moths to a flame.

"That might bring some unwanted attention," Julian said.

Drake frowned.

"How would we do that, anyway? Unless you've got a Bic handy."

He hadn't thought of that, either.

"The signal idea is a good one, though. How can we signal them without letting Ratson's goons know where we are?"

Drake pondered this. "When you updated Helen, did she say where Trevor was at?"

"As far as I know he's cruising around the island, just like Haley on the Sand Dollar and Helen and Kendra on the Mary Queen."

"Wish we'd brought our cell phones," Drake said.

Julian shook his head. "Why, so we can be out two $1,000 iPhones? You know they block the signal here."

The kid was right, but anger bubbled in Drake's stomach. He wasn't thinking rationally.

The voices of their pursuers got louder.

Drake pointed, and the duo headed north, cutting through the beach grass and entering a copse of low scrub pine dotted with thickets of mangroves and bushes with small yellow leaves and stiletto-sized thorns.

The voices faded, and Drake's nerves stopped tap dancing on his spine, and guilt seeped through him like a fever. Julian was safe, Marley and Jillian probably were. Despite this, shame washed over him. Scar was dead, and Drake's lack of empathy made him sick.

Branches clawed at Drake as he squeezed through a dense patch of saw palmetto, their pointy leaves scraping and scratching, Julian in tow. The rolling surf got louder, the sound of shells and rocks tumbling in the undertow like a million cockroaches scuttling over glass. The breeze picked up, clouds filling the sky as the front edge of the storm moved in.

The patch of saw palmetto gave way to mangroves that bordered the thin beach that ran along Kraken Island's northern shore. Drake peered from the shadows, searching the beach in both directions, but there was nothing but seagulls, cyclones of gnats, and balls of seaweed rolling down the pristine beach.

"Do you still have your penlight?" Drake asked.

"Sure, but what—" Julian smiled and dug in his bag. "Do you think it's strong enough?"

"Maybe, if they're searching the shore. If the light doesn't work, I'll remove the lens, maybe use that to refract light."

"Like how you spot a sniper by the glint of his scope," Julian said.

Drake turned and looked at Julian, doing his best WTF face.

"What? You've never seen that movie Sniper? Pretty good. Those guys are nuts. Did you—"

Drake put a finger to his lips.

Julian nodded and handed Drake the light.

"How close do you think we are to where we were dropped?" Drake couldn't see the shoals off the western tip of the island where Marley and Jillian had made their fire, which told him they were still too far east.

"Not even close, mate," Julian said.

"Let's head west a ways before I try," Drake said.

Julian nodded. The young man was looking haggard; his face smudged with dirt, dark bags beneath his eyes, black sweatpants and t-shirt wet and filthy.

The duo stayed in the shadows as they worked their way along the shoreline. They were forced to hide when a guard came around the bend, jogging east along the beach, head on a swivel, AK47 held out before him like a lance.

Drake and Julian watched the man go past, and Drake wondered if the AK47 was loaded. The one he'd taken off the guard hadn't been. AK's took some weird type of ammo, and maybe Ratson's goons were out, but he couldn't make any assumptions.

The vegetation grew sparse, and Drake moved slower, using any cover he could, but the mangroves were now nothing more than low patches of scrub, and the beach grass thinned as the shoals stretched into the Caribbean like a long shadowy finger. Drake saw the dark stain on the white sand that had been Marley and Julian's small fire, and a twang of guilt rolled through him, but he pushed it down. There'd be time enough for second guessing when they were drinking martinis at Dugan's and toasting their friend. Now his only goal was to get Julian to safety.

White sand stretched into crystal clear water, tiny fish jumping and twisting from the sea, their scales glistening. Drake chose the last patch of beach grass and lay on his stomach between two tufts, Julian next to him.

There was no periscope sticking from the sea, but the whine of an outboard motor echoed over the Caribbean. Drake flashed his light, timing and counting his bursts, attempting to use Morse code to send a Mayday.

A blue boat zipped around the tip of the shoals, avoiding the shallow water that lapped over the unspoiled sand, tiny waves crashing on the spit, whitewater bubbling and gurgling as it was pulled back into the ocean.

Drake didn't know how long they lay there. At one-point, Julian fell asleep, but Drake had to wake him when he started snoring. Three guards came around the point, but didn't venture out into the shoals. Drake breathed a sigh of relief. The tufts of beach grass had been enough.

Julian let out a long breath when the Sand Dollar appeared, Haley at the controls. The boat was moving slow, maybe fifteen knots, the twenty-six-foot Zodiac Nautic's inflatable gunnels pushing through the growing surf like a brick.

Drake flashed the light, giving up on Morse code. The Sand Dollar rolled past. He repeated this process three more times. Once when the Mary Queen went by—the bigger boat was further offshore, and two more times when the Sand Dollar came around, but his friends didn't see Drake signaling. No more guards appeared, and Drake was thinking it was time to make a run for it.

"Swim out into open sea? Or go for the point?" Julian said, reading Drake's mind.

Drake ran the scenario through his metal logistics filter. Once Haley saw them, she'd beach the Sand Dollar as fast as she could. The best spot would be the tip of the sandspit where the currents kept the water deep. To get to her, Drake and Julian would have to run two hundred yards through foot-deep water, then wade through fifty yards of deeper water to get to the sandspit's tip. How long would that take? As soon as Haley pointed the Sand Dollar toward shore, guards would come running, and with Ratson's boats buzzing around the island like flies, they wouldn't have much time.

Drake said, "You up for a run? In the water we're manatee. I don't think they'll shoot. Not with Haley as a witness. For all they know, she could have a camera going."

"Never stopped them before," Julian said.

"Good point. What do you say?"

"Since I don't have a better idea, yeah."

The minutes ticked past as they waited, and when the Sand Dollar appeared off the western tip of Kraken Island, Drake pressed himself to his feet and ran.

23

Water splashed as Drake dug in, powering forward in an awkward gait, legs aching, the shallow water tugging at his ankles, feet sinking into wet sand. His heart pounded in his ears, and he heard only his labored breathing as he and Julian ran across the shoals, eyes locked on the Sand Dollar, which hadn't turned toward shore. Drake waved his arms and yelled, but he couldn't hear himself. Pain lanced through him, the water getting deeper, each step more effort than the one before. Schools of tiny fish streaked through the shallow water, darting away like he was a Great White, moving as one, like smoke being sucked into a fan. Crabs scurried away, and Drake looked over a shoulder.

Julian was twenty yards back, splashing through the shoals.

Two hundred yards offshore and coming on fast, a field of dimpled whitewater rose from the Caribbean, mounds of churning scales and teeth.

The Sand Dollar's outboard screamed, and the boat arced sharply to port, heading for the shoals. Haley had seen them.

Gunshots rang out, and Drake dove, hitting the shallow water hard, his face planting itself firmly in the soft sand. He scrambled forward, sucking in water, coughing and spitting, chaos and confusion sending waves of pain through him like an electrical shock. More gunshots, but there was no plunk and splash as the bullets hit the water, no pain.

Four guards ran along the beach, firing into the sky.

The Sand Dollar's outboard whined, and the vessel bucked and heaved as it came to a stop, the bow scraping onto the sandspit. Haley stood behind the command console, hair blowing in the breeze, the boat a hundred yards away. He plunged forward into the narrow tidal channel that split the shoals in half. The water was only a couple of feet deep, but it was like running through quicksand.

The gunfire stopped.

Julian yelled.

Drake looked over his shoulder and saw his partner go down. Julian struggled in the shallow water, fighting to get to his feet, wet sand sucking him down. A roiling knot of whitewater rose behind him, the swarm piling and slithering over one another.

Drake started back, but then Julian was back on his feet, running through the water, eyes forward.

The guards had paused in their pursuit, and stood watching, letting the horde do its job.

Two of Ratson's patrol boats screamed around the bend and came to a stop to the south of the shoals, listing and rolling in the surf. Men carrying guns filled the boats, but they held their fire. Drake had the sickening feeling that was because the men felt he and Julian had no chance.

Julian pounded through the shallow water and Drake stopped running, even though he was still seventy-five yards away from the Sand Dollar. Haley screamed, but he stood frozen, more than loose sand holding his feet in place.

Like anyone who's lived more than ten years, Drake had made a series of decisions that molded his life, and in that instant of panic when he looked back on it all, he didn't like what he saw. Despite doing what he'd felt was right, he'd betrayed his captain, had no wife, no children, and the idea of him dying alone, nobody there to comfort him, made him go cold, and he shivered in the oppressive Caribbean heat. He couldn't leave Julian behind.

Haley screeched as Drake started back, wading through the watery quicksand toward Julian, who pushed across the tidal channel, the swarm a hurricane of teeth and scales as it pushed through the water, coming at him from behind, and from the north and south.

The kid was struggling, and Drake realized with horror that he wasn't going to make it.

Julian spun around, bringing up the Glock he still clutched in his right hand. He screamed as he fired into the horde of Barracuda, the gun spitting bullets, the empty cartridges glinting as they dropped into the water.

Barracuda surged from the sea, a stream of fish wriggling as one, like a giant eel working its way through shallow water.

The Glock stopped firing, and whitewater engulfed Julian as he was overcome by the roiling mass of teeth and scales. He screamed. A sharp cry that would wake Drake from deep sleep for years to come. Like ants on a soda spill, the rabid Barracuda struggled and fought through the shoals. There were thousands of them, and a useless thought raced through Drake's head as he watched; are there Barracuda from today's batch in this horde? Was there more than one swarm?

The scream died away and Drake stopped like a child who's realized he was running toward the monster that had escaped from under his bed, not away from it. Red rimmed eyes stood out in the whitewater, streaks of pink knifing through the white. The fish were in a frenzy, and they churned and bubbled across the surface like a crashing wave as Julian was sucked under. The scent of rot and decay washed over the shoals, and the turbulence lessened as the swarm thinned, and a blood slick coated the clear sea, pink bubbles popping and snapping.

The swarm writhed and twisted, coming at him.

Haley's voice broke through the static of panic, anger and sorrow. He'd lost Julian. Scar was an old man who'd known what he was doing, the risks, and had chosen to do what he'd done. Julian had only been on this ridiculous mission because of Drake. Now he was dead, and the day wasn't over.

Maybe it was best if he died right here, now. Explaining what had happened to Feddi, Jillian, the rest of the gang, seemed like an impossible task, and Drake had the overwhelming urge to sit down in the shallow water and let the horde have him. At least it would be fast.

"Drake! Run! Run!" The Sand Dollar's outboards screamed as Haley backed the boat off the sandspit, spinning the wheel and pointing the boat out to sea.

Drake pushed through the water, which was getting shallower as he approached the tip of the shoals.

The Barracuda swarm spread out, dimpled whitewater surrounding the western tip of Kraken Island. The horde closed in around the Sand Dollar, shifting and slithering, the fish mounding atop one another as they struggled and fought. Flashing scales, gray pencil bodies, curved needle-like teeth, red rimmed eyes, puckering lips. Tailfins swayed with an unreal urgency, pushing the fish forward in their frenzy, their ravenous hatred of all things not Barracuda.

The four guards on the beach still waited, watching Drake's flight like a horse race they'd bet on. One of the patrol boats was moving in, trying to block the Sand Dollar's path should

Haley decide to make a run for it. But she hadn't, at least not yet. She stood staring at him over the transom, small waves rippling and gurgling against the inflatable pontoons. She was yelling, her arms moving in wide circles as she urged him on, but he couldn't hear her.

The Zodiac bobbed and listed before him, like an opening at the end of a long tunnel that appeared in reach, but never came. Drake threw himself forward, lungs burning, pain jolting to the tips of his fingers and toes. Then he was there, jumping from the shoals, clutching at the Sand Dollar's slick rubber gunnels, using the black handholds as the tourists did, pulling himself up. He hung there, struggling, the swarm bubbling from the water, thousands of red rimmed eyes peering out from a swirling tangle of silver and gray.

He flopped over the gunnel onto the deck.

Haley dropped the hammer, and the Sand Dollar jumped from the sea as though it didn't like the feel of saltwater on its hull. The twin Yamahas screamed, their props clawing at the water, spitting fifteen-foot rooster tails, pushing away the surging Barracuda swarm as it closed in.

The bow lifted and Drake slid down the deck like a dropped piece of bait, slamming into the transom, his legs getting tangled in the wires that ran to the command console. Sea spray arced over the boat, whitewater rising around the Sand Dollar. Red rimmed eyes stared, thousands of mouths chomping, tails working back and forth in a blur. The stench was overpowering, and Drake gagged as he disentangled himself and pushed his back to the boat's gunnel.

Ratson's goons were on a collision course, both patrol boats in motion and coming at the Sand Dollar from the north and south, cutting off their escape route.

Haley worked the wheel like she was driving through a dense patch of seaweed, snaking through the sea, the Zodiac's ragged course hard to follow.

It wasn't working. Each time she changed course, the two patrol boats adjusted, the trap closing, the swarm a roiling knot behind them.

The boat screaming in from the south came to a stop like it had hit an invisible barrier. All four men standing in the bow flew from the boat, arms cartwheeling, guns flying. The vessel listed and swayed as the surf pushed it around, a thin tendril of black smoke snaking from the craft's engine compartment.

The glint of a periscope stuck from the sea like a giant metal single finger salute.

Haley whooped, and arced the Sand Dollar south, cutting past the stopped boat as the Barracuda came at them.

Drake sat with his back to the inflatable gunnel, static filling his ears, mind spinning. He looked around in a daze, his unbelieving eyes squinting, stomach churning. His thoughts strayed, the pain taking over, shock settling in and making itself comfortable.

The Sand Dollar skipped over the sea, a fist of water rising before them. Haley waited until the last possible moment, until the mountain of whitewater filled with red rimmed eyes and glinting teeth stood before them like a breaking wave. She spun the wheel, cutting to starboard, the wave of Barracuda breaking off the port bow.

The move bought Haley several critical seconds as she maneuvered the boat through the thickening sea of fish. Barracuda arced through the air, jaws flexing, using each other to push and surge forward and up. Whitewater frothed over the gunnels as Haley turned the boat hard, zigzagging through the sea, the outboards sputtering and coughing as the props diced Barracuda into sushi. Scales, bones, white flesh, and blood splattered the Sand Dollar's deck, pieces of Barracuda raining down on Drake.

A horn sounded.

The Mary Queen chugged offshore, white smoke pouring from its single stack, but there was nothing Helen and Kendra could do to help. The Sand Dollar's fight would be over before the large trawler could reach them, which it probably couldn't because of the depth of the water. The large blue digital numbers on the depth finder slowly crawled upward, and though Drake saw the exposed barren sand bottom of the Caribbean in the boat's wake, the boat was in six feet of water.

The sharp scent of gasoline filled the air, pushing away the salty rot. Barracuda fought and struggled to get over the Sand Dollar's gunnels, but Haley kept jerking the wheel, slicing through the horde.

Drake got up, the deck bouncing and rolling beneath his feet. He grabbed a boat pole from its rubber clamps, holding it like an elongated bat, searching for fish to pound.

Ratson's second patrol boat was coming in from the north, but it wasn't moving as fast as the first boat, which was still halted and bobbing in the sea like a children's toy in a bathtub. The Caribbean was a churning mass of whitewater and teeth. Haley pulled back on the control arm, and the engine whine fell, the bow dipping.

Unease and worry massaged Drake's neck and back, the cold fingers of death creeping over him like a chill. What the hell was Haley doing?

Barracuda surged against the boat, the rubber gunnels squeaking and farting.

Haley turned the wheel as far as she could, the twin outboards rotating on their mounts, angling to port as far as they could go. She slammed the control lever down, spinning up the motors, and the Yamahas wailed, spitting whitewater as the boat spun in a tight circle, tearing up fish like a blender.

Drake gripped the gunnel, sea spray filled with blood, bone shards, and fish chunks pelting him.

Haley hooted, letting the wheel slip through her fingers as the boat came out of its circle and broke through a mound of Barracuda, the bow arcing north.

The scent of death hung in the air, blood spraying the Sand Dollar's gunnels, pieces of fish splattering the deck like gelatinous hail.

Drake stared at Kraken Island through the mist lifting from the Sand Dollar's wake.

Ratson's men had peeled off, and no boats pursued them, but the field of whitewater rolling over the crystal-clear Caribbean Sea sent a jolt of nausea through Drake. Scar's face, red with blood as he was dragged under by the swarm, and Julian's final scream filled his head as the island receded into the distance. Scar's blood might not be on his hands, but Julian's certainly was, and the thought of facing Jillian replaced the nausea with savage chest pains.

This was all Ratson's fault. His quest for more power and money. The way he used people like disposable napkins. Drake recalled telling the crew he was going to burn Ratson's operation down. He'd meant if figuratively, but now the thought of literally burning the island to blackened silicon and charred coral seemed like the only logical course of action. If the authorities wouldn't do anything, he would. To that, the rational side of Drake's brain reminded him that two people were dead, and that would be hard for even Feddi to ignore.

Haley set course for Simpson Bay and pushed the throttle arm down as far as it would go, the outboards wailing, bow lifting as the Zodiac skipped across the water.

The field of dimpled whitewater trailed behind.

24

Midday heat rolled across the Caribbean in invisible waves as the Sand Dollar's engines sang, thick mist lifting from the boat's wake as its bow sliced through the rough sea, throwing spray. Haley looked comfortable behind the vessel's command console, one hand on the wheel, the other messing with various controls and monitoring screens, making adjustments, changing settings. Her dirty-blonde hair was pulled back in a ponytail bound together with a purple scrunchie. Her right foot tapped the deck, a sign she was nervous. Drake had only seen her do it a couple of times.

Every few moments Haley glanced aft.

The swarm had gone deep, but they were still there. The turbulent sea stretched out behind the boat, extending well beyond the boat's wake. Like a school of shiners zipping through the shoals, every few moments a Barracuda would arc from the sea, scales and curved needle teeth glinting in the half light. Drake wasn't an expert, but he knew Barracuda didn't jump. They hid in depressions, between rocks and in small caves, waiting to ambush anything stupid enough to venture near, but not these fish. He needed to keep that firmly planted in his frontal lobe. Whatever he thought he knew about Barracuda, no longer applied.

"You O.K.?" Haley yelled over the hum of the engines.

Drake nodded, his mind still spinning. Pain inched through him as the adrenaline drained away, his lower back and neck pulsing like someone stabbed him with an icepick. He gripped the handrail, his knees on the verge of coming unhinged. His legs didn't notice the difference between land and sea unless the ocean was being particularly nasty, but his body was starting to give up the ghost. He felt like he hadn't had food or water in weeks, and despite being drenched to the bone, his mouth was as dry as flour, his lips cracking and stinging, salt sucking the moisture from his skin.

Concern slid across Haley's face, her eyes sliding back to the sea, shoulders slumping.

"I'm fine," he said and gave her a thumbs up.

The smile Drake had been expecting didn't come. Haley stared aft.

A knot of Barracuda swam in the boat's wake, launching themselves off waves, red rimmed eyes locked on their target like guided missiles with mouths full of teeth. The horde had closed the gap, and Drake estimated it was only a hundred yards back and closing.

"Hold on, I'm going to try some evasive action," she said.

Drake moved behind Haley, gripping the handhold on the side of the center console with his right hand, and holding the back of her seat with his left.

Haley spun the wheel, and the outboards whined as they sucked for the water needed to cool the engine's powerheads. Like a car stalling as it powered through deep water, the motors sputtered and coughed, but as Haley brought the vessel out of its sharp turn the motors evened out, their steady hum echoing over the Caribbean.

The swarm shifted like a flock of birds being blown around by a sea breeze, tiny whitecaps rising from the water as the horde surfaced. The slithering mass of fish arced north, then west as it tracked the Sand Dollar, like some god was working a joystick.

Drake looked around, expecting to see Ratson floating above the sea on one of those fancy water propelled jetpacks, holding the controller to his most ambitious game. But there was no Ratson. There was nothing but the churning sea and mist hanging in the air like smoke in the Sand Dollar's wake.

Haley repeated her erratic moves several times, Drake holding on like a child on a roller coaster, Haley letting go of the wheel, letting the momentum of the engines turn the craft.

It wasn't helping.

Barracuda arced from the sea, their red rimmed eyes locked on the Sand Dollar, hungry jaws chomping and snapping. The swarm was coming together, scales, teeth and eyes becoming one like an explosion in reverse. A fist of whitewater tumbled in their wake, lifting twenty feet from the water, Barracuda slithering and surging over one another, a massive buzz saw of white teeth and flashes of silver.

Static burst from the UHF, then Helen's voice blared from the radio. "Drake? Do you copy? Drake?" Helen was always calm and cool, tough as bamboo roots and slick as a politician running for re-election. She never raised her voice or yelled. The squeaky, scared voice that thundered from the radio made Drake roll his shoulders in an attempt to drive away the angst that seeped through him. He failed.

He leaned around Haley, pulled the handset from its cradle, and opened a channel. "We're here, Helen." He looked back at the swarm, rabid Barracuda leaping from the sea and arcing over the boat's rooster tail. "Don't know for how much longer, though."

Static, then, "Is there anything—" Static. "...you?"

The Mary Queen was a fishing trawler designed with power in mind, not speed. Drake did a fast position check and saw the thin line of white smoke trailing into the sky from the Mary Queen's single stack to the southwest. Drake couldn't see the vessel, which told him the Sand Dollar would be on the bottom and he and Haley would be fish food long before the Mary Queen could reach them, and what the hell could they do when they got here, anyway?

Helen didn't wait for Drake's reply—perhaps knowing the answer—and she said, "I got through to the cops. Spoke with Feddi myself. They're sending out a boat. Should be on scene within ten minutes, though they said that fifteen minutes ago."

Drake craned his neck and peered north toward Simpson Bay. No boat streaked over the sea, lights flashing. Fishing boats and pleasure craft swayed and bobbed in the gentle surf, but no police boat.

"10-4," Drake said. "Have you heard from Trevor?"

"Yes," Helen said. "He had to head in. The collision with Ratson's boys did some damage to the sub and he was taking on water. Nothing serious, but he had to bow out."

"O.K. Keep eyes on us if you can. Over," Drake said.

"Got it. Mary Queen out."

The radio fell silent, the buzz of the engines, and the static of water being thrown on water filling the silence as the Sand Dollar made a final push.

The sea surged on all sides now, Barracuda mounding on each other like maggots, slithering and jerking as one. Seawater bubbled over the gunnel and the bilge pump snapped on, sending a giant-sized pee stream shooting from the side of the boat.

Haley trimmed the motors up, making one last attempt to drive away the swarm. She jerked the wheel, the Yamahas screaming and coughing, the bow bouncing and tossing over its own wake as Haley pulled the craft into a tight circle.

The current tugged on the Sand Dollar as it knifed through the deep water that ran between Tetu and Kraken Islands. The white line of Two Mile Beach stretched out to the east, and Drake saw people walking at ease, tiny black specs moving slowly along. Dark clouds puffed over the eastern horizon, like a teddy bear's stuffing bursting through a rip. Thin bolts of yellow lightning streaked across the sky, a dark veil of rain filling the gap between the clouds and the surface of the sea.

"Look!" Haley yelled. There was hope in her voice.

Drake's head snapped up and he scanned the horizon.

A boat tore from Simpson Bay's main channel, a single red light rotating atop the aluminum pilot's cabin.

An instant of relief flooded through Drake, and a sharp pain in his right leg brought him to his knees as he screamed. A Barracuda had pushed over the gunnel, whitewater filling the Sand Dollar, and the beast had clamped down on Drake's thigh, thin streams of blood leaking from the creature's mouth as it thrashed and pulled in an attempt to take Drake's leg off.

Barracuda are only a couple of feet long, but their powerful jaws are like a vice, and the fish didn't let go as Drake kicked at it. He scooped up the boat pole he'd dropped to the deck, and swung it, letting loose all his fury, all the anger, the frustration, and the loss. The blow connected with a hollow twang and the Barracuda sailed over the gunnel, face smashed. The fish took chunks of Drake's leg with it, and blood poured from the wound. He grew lightheaded, his vision getting dull and cloudy, like soapy water covered his eyeballs.

The Sand Dollar bounced and swayed, and a shrill klaxon rang out in the chaos, an angry pulsing beat that knifed through Drake's head.

"Not now!" Haley screamed.

The braying electronic beep was the overheat alarm. A thin stream of black smoke escaped from the port engine. He worked his way to the back of the boat, hands out before him like an old man, the boat swaying and lifting, whitewater frothing, Barracuda fighting to get inside the swamped boat.

The Sand Dollar's outboards had been cutting through a field of fish, and guts, bones, and skin clogged the intake ports at the bottom of both motors' lower units that supplied water to their cooling systems. Without water being sucked into the machines, the engine's water pumps would burn out and the motors would seize.

The black smoke leaking from the port motor's engine compartment got thicker and darker, and the left engine belched clouds of smoke out its water exhaust port. The sound of metal on metal resounded over the sea, the motors sputtered, cried out, metal melding together, the heat in the cylinders rising to catastrophic levels. As if they had consulted each other, both Yamahas screamed one last time, then fell still. The Sand Dollar came to a stop in the turbulent sea, bobbing and swaying as it got pushed around by the swarm.

Zodiac boats are heralded as unsinkable, and usually that was the case. The inflatable gunnels are broken into multiple zones, and sections of the sidewalls can be damaged and uninflated, and the craft will still function. Only one gunnel compartment needed to be inflated to keep the vessel from flipping, and if every section of the inflatable gunnel went flat, the foam packed into the hull would keep the vessel afloat, even if it flipped over.

Drake's leg wound ached, blood dripping down his leg, the top of his foot slick with blood.

The swarm knifed into the Sand Dollar, teeth ripping into the vessel as it sat motionless, unable to move, thick clouds of black smoke pouring from the outboards, which would require complete rebuilds to be saved. The crazy stuff you think of in those final moments. Drake was cheap, but damn, worrying about money as his boat went down, that was too much.

The police boat was coming on fast, its light spinning, its bow throwing spray. It wasn't going to make it in time, and there'd be nothing left but the remains of the Sand Dollar, and a blood slick.

The horde surged into the boat from every direction, fish fighting to get over the gunnel. Those who made it were booted, smacked, or poled from the deck, but Drake and Haley were losing the battle, and the water in the boat was getting deeper as the gunnels were popped and sliced. Air escaped the Zodiac with a psssshhhh and large bubbles rose from the sea as the sidewalls fell flat, the boat dropping in the water, the sea pouring into the vessel and carrying the swarm with it.

The police siren carried on the breeze, and everything stopped, like some cosmic gamer somewhere had seen enough, and had decided to pause the game and pick it up again tomorrow. The insane image of Drake as a boy crowded its way into his grief stricken and panic addled mind. He loved the game Monopoly as a boy, and he would cheat when he was winning to help other players just so the game wouldn't end.

The horde gave up. Just put their marbles down and swam away.

Whitewater flattened, and the swarm dove, silver scales disappearing into the depths.

When Drake hit the water, it was almost a relief. Though he saw the swarm moving away, he still hadn't processed what that meant as his mind struggled to put his thoughts in order and catalog all the events of the last hour.

He slipped under the water, his thoughts drifting to Haley, and he asked himself why he'd never told her how he felt. Opportunities lost. A life lost.

The patrol boat screamed to a stop, and a yellow life ring hit the water next to Drake.

He grabbed it in a daze, blue sky filling his vision as he was dragged through the sea. His thoughts drifted back to Haley and he realized with a sickening dread he didn't know where she was. He twisted in the life preserver, his face hitting the water. He coughed and spat as he fought to see.

Haley stood on the patrol boat, staring down at him as the rope attached to the life ring went taught and Drake was lifted from the sea. He saw stars, those tiny pinpricks that told you a change to your personal situation was on the way.

Two officers helped him over the side of the police boat, and Haley ran to him, throwing her arms around him as the police asked Drake questions he couldn't hear. He rolled on his side and coughed up water, his chest muscles aching, heart headbanging to heavy metal. The police boat rocked, the Caribbean Sea a torn-up field of wind torn whitecaps.

The Barracuda swarm was gone.

25

The sun started its descent to the horizon, whitecaps breaking in the shoals off Boot Tip Point to the north. The thin line of sand that was Two Mile Beach stretched into the distance to the east, and Kraken Island was a dark mound fading into grayness in the southwest. The police boat skipped over the rough sea, throwing spray that dimpled the clear water. Drake shivered and hugged himself. It was eighty-three degrees with seventy percent humidity, yet he felt chilled.

Feddi worked the controls in the pilot house, three other officers standing behind him like soldiers. After he'd been plucked from the sea, they'd headed back to port and Feddi had listened intently to Drake's story as a medic bandaged his leg, Haley watching, worry and pain carved into her smooth creamy skin. After hearing the entire tale, Feddi had sighed, slapped his leg, and said, "Enough is enough. If you're lying…"

"Let me prove it to you," Drake had said, and so he, Feddi, and the officers that had fished him out of the drink were heading to Kraken Island, where Drake was to show the police what he'd seen. Haley gave him some shit when she was told she had to stay behind, but she relented when Helen, Marley, and Jillian were told the same. He hadn't seen Jillian, and part of him was thankful for that. Haley had agreed to tell the girl of her brother's death, and though it made him feel like a coward, he was thankful for it. There would be time later to mourn, to comfort, but all he wanted to do now was get his hands around Ratson's neck, though he knew he couldn't do that. He'd have to settle for putting his balls in a sling, and his businesses being under investigation.

The police SAFE boat cut through the straits, the water running fast and deep, spray arcing over the bow. Drake ducked, and the water missed him, and he smiled. Had to take the small pleasures when they came. As if reading his thoughts, two dolphins leapt from the sea, squeaking and taunting the police boat, trying to play. Feddi ignored them and adjusted the vessel's course slightly, his gaze never shifting from the sea ahead.

Kraken Island loomed to the west, and Feddi let the ship's wheel slip through his fingers as the boat turned toward the entrance to Deep Hollow Cove. A line of fishing boats, tour charters, and pleasure craft lined the strait as they headed north toward Simpson Bay like a parade of ants.

Feddi eased up on the throttle as the SAFE boat flew past the buoy that marked the channel. It had been a little less than twenty-four hours since he and Marley had buzzed into the cove and been chased off. This time he had the law with him.

The boat slowed to a crawl, tiny waves snapping and cracking against the blue inflatable gunnels. Feddi waved Drake into the pilothouse.

"You are to say nothing," the officer said, worry lines running over his black face, eyes red as cinders. "You're an observer only. We can talk after. Do you understand?"

Drake nodded. He'd put Feddi in a tight spot, and he was surprised when the cop said he could come, but he was the only witness. Pain and sorrow washed through him, Scar and Julian's faces mocking him. "Yes, you sure are the only witness. Thanks for the help," those haunted memories said.

The SAFE boat's Johnson purred as the vessel slipped into the water reeds that ran along both sides of the channel that led to Deep Hollow Cove. Drake's brow wrinkled. No boats blocked the entrance as they had just hours prior. Drake's body felt like a rubber band, one that had been stretched too many times. He'd gotten an hour of sleep in his closet holding cell, but other than that, he'd been going for thirty-six hours and he couldn't keep it up much longer.

The reeds fell away, revealing Deep Hollow Cove. Only two boats were moored at its center, research vessels that hadn't been there the prior day. The patrol boats were gone, and no conning towers or flying bridges rocked in the gentle breeze.

The two steel holding rings that had been set in the water were gone.

Drake traced the metal sluiceway from the nearest building, but when it reached the cove, it simply plunged into the inky water. He glanced at Feddi, who was looking at him. The cold fingers of doubt poked him, the shard of ice in his stomach growing to a brick.

A floating dock jutted out into the cove and Drake noted it hadn't been there just hours before. Ratson stood at the end of the floating pier, waving and smiling.

Feddi frowned, and said, "Didn't you say there were holding nets in the water?" He made no attempt to hide his skepticism.

Drake said nothing as he gazed over the mangroves, going over the morning's events in his mind. Julian had died out there, and he looked to the sluiceway again and he saw none of Scar's blood splattered on the gleaming metal, no sign anything had happened at all.

Feddi pulled the SAFE boat in along the dock and shut down the engine. An officer scurried to the bow, one aft, and they tied-off the boat.

"Welcome," Ratson said. He smiled, eyes gleaming, no signs of anger or malice. "How may I help you today?"

Drake exited the pilothouse and mounted the gunnel, preparing to jump onto the dock, but Feddi put a hand on his shoulder. No words were needed, and Drake fell back.

"Afternoon, Mr. Ratson. I'm Officer Feddi."

Ratson nodded, but said nothing.

"Do you know Mr. Drake here?" Feddi motioned toward Drake, the SAFE boat shifting slightly beneath his feet.

Ratson's eyes squirmed, like maggots fought and crawled there. He said, "I'm afraid I don't. Pleased to meet you." The man held his hand over the gap between the dock and boat.

Anger surged in Drake, and it took every bit of control he could dredge up from the boiling inferno that was his chest, but he managed to say nothing, because if he started… If he started, he didn't know how things would end. Most likely with him in jail, not Ratson. Drake didn't take the man's hand.

Feddi sighed. "Sir, I don't mean to bother or inconvenience you, but Mr. Drake has made some startling accusations and others have supported his story."

For the briefest of instants anger flashed across Ratson's tanned face, but he pushed it down fast, a creepy smile inching back over his face. "Story? What story?"

"He said you're breeding rabid Barracuda in your labs here, and that the horde killed two people. You don't know anything about that?"

"I'm sure I don't," Ratson said, doing his best to look stressed.

"So, you don't mind showing me your labs? Letting me take a look around?" Feddi said.

"Not at all," Ratson said. Then he turned his withering stare on Drake and said, "He, however, isn't welcome. People who make crazy unwarranted accusations don't get guided tours of my property."

"You don't own the sea," Drake said, and sucked his teeth.

Feddi shot him a look and Drake looked at the deck. The officer stepped over the gunnel on the shifting dock. "Bramston, you're with me."

Drake stepped up onto the dock.

"I'm going to need you to stay he—"

"I'm coming," Drake said as he planted his feet on the listing dock. With five grown men standing on the dock, it shifted under the weight.

Whether it was the look on Drake's face, or the fact that Feddi realized Drake was right, the officer said, "Mr. Ratson, right now Mr. Drake is my witness. I'm going to need him to show me what he claims he saw. If as you've said there's nothing to see, then let us take our look and we'll be on our way. No harm, no foul."

Ratson waved a dismissive hand. "Fine. Fine. Come with me."

The dock swayed and shifted as they made their way to the nearest building, which Drake had identified as the main lab building. His leg wound shrieked as the party made their way to the lab's entrance. Ratson typed in his code, and the door snapped open with a familiar beep and click.

The lights were on, and Drake could tell immediately something wasn't right. Metal netting no longer covered the pool, and there were no yellow drums stacked along the far wall. The tidal tanks still swept and pushed water around, and two people sat at the command console, talking and working the controls. The sluiceway was dry.

The metal steps clinked as Drake and the others made their way down to the main level. He felt Feddi's eyes on him. Nothing looked the way Drake had described it. Drake went to the pool and stared down at the fish squirming within. They weren't Barracuda, and they didn't have red rimmed eyes.

Drake knelt and ran his fingers over the ring where the tank's metal covering had been secured.

"These are Bermuda chub fish. We're studying how their chemical composition affects the reefs they live in. We hope to come up with a way to help restore the world's reefs. Did you—"

Drake couldn't contain himself any longer. "Bullshit!" He felt his face growing red hot, eyes stinging, his back throbbing with pain. "What did you do with everything?" Drake turned to Feddi, "You're not believing this crap, are you?"

Feddi's eyes showed sympathy, but he said, "Mr. Drake, I think it's time we left."

"Indeed," said Ratson. His face was a red contorted tangle of anger, all pretense of hospitality gone. At least Drake had gotten the man's blood pressure up.

Drake stepped forward and Feddi put out an arm. "This isn't over, Ratson. You'll pay for Scar and Julian. Bank on it."

Ratson only smiled and rolled his eyes. Eyes Drake wanted to gouge out with his fingers, feel the man's blood trickling down his arm.

"Let's go. Now." Feddi pulled Drake away, but Ratson and Drake locked eyes, and the billionaire chuckled.

***

The throb of Drake's wound faded with each martini. Reggae music floated through Dugan's, a gentle breeze pushing around the beach grass, thin beams of moonlight streaming through the thick cloud cover blotting out the stars. Helen sat on one side of Drake, Haley the other. Jillian and Marley sat across from him. Kendra had yet to arrive. The group was somber, and every few minutes Jillian would squeal and cry, tears streaking her makeup. She said she didn't blame Drake, but the way she looked at him, her face a mask of barely contained anger, and the way she spoke to him in short sentences, told Drake she did hold him accountable for her brother's death. Why shouldn't she? If it wasn't for Drake and his stupid plan, Julian would still be alive. Nobody mentioned Scar, and Drake didn't raise the topic. He knew the man had no family, no relatives that he knew of. There was nobody to call, no body for a service. The plan was to honor him at Julian's ceremony, which would be two days hence. Jillian planned to spread her brother's ashes across Boot Tip Point, and Drake liked the idea.

Haley slammed the table. "And Feddi bought that whale shit? What does he think? You made the whole thing up?"

Drake downed the rest of his drink and held up the empty glass. Chance was there in an instant with a fresh martini, taking away the empty like a magician. "Says he doesn't know what to believe, but he'll err on the side of covering his ass, I'm sure of that," Drake said.

"What does that mean?" Jillian said between sobs.

Drake hiked his shoulders. "He'll tell the captain, but it's not what he says, but how he says it." He sighed, fighting back sorrow. "You know how that goes. If Feddi tells the story with skepticism in his voice, leads the captain down the path of 'nothing to see here', that's the way the captain will go. If he's truly worried, which I think he is now, he'll be honest, and the captain will go to the governor, who will in turn cover his ass. The question is, who will St. Croix send? And when? What type of support will they have?"

Nobody spoke. Reggae music, the crackle of the beach grass rustling in the breeze, and the faint static of small waves rolling onto a rock beach filled the silence. The deck out back of Dugan's was only half full, and no other patrons sat around the crew's regular table.

Kendra arrived and sat without a word. She'd heard the entire story from Helen, so what was there to say? Two more people had fallen prey to the swarm the same way her husband had. She ordered a rum and coke, took a long pull, then said, "I think I've got some good news."

All eyes turned to her like wolves who'd seen a baby lamb.

"St. Croix said they're sending a boat to investigate," she said.

Drake leaned forward in his seat. "You believe them? Or were they trying to get you off the phone? They say who they're sending?"

Kendra finished her drink, looked at the table, and shrugged, but said nothing.

If Drake knew anything, he knew there were no certainties in this life, or any other.

The night deepened, and Dugan's closed. Chance brought fresh drinks and sat at the table. "You guys hear the latest?"

Drake cracked his neck and looked at Haley, who was on her ninth beer and looked like someone had let the air out of her.

"A fisherman was just killed in Teapot Cove," Chance said.

"How?" Jillian said as she wiped away tears.

Chance said nothing and stared down at the table. They all knew what had killed the fisherman, but none of them wanted to say it for fear of making it real.

A horn sounded, a large vessel entering the channel to Simpson Bay.

Drake got up and walked to the railing, peering through the darkness, trying to make out what type of ship it was.

Haley joined him. "Finally," she said. "Looks like St. Croix was true to their word."

She handed Drake a small set of night binoculars she'd produced from a pocket; they looked like the old school kind that folded up to look like a cigarette case.

There were three ships chugging slowly into Simpson Bay; a large police boat with a tall conning tower and floodlights pointing in every direction, making the vessel look like a launchpad. Flanking the ship on either side were police SAFE boats, tiny red lights spinning atop the pilothouses.

Drake heard Jillian sob and cry and heat built in him, rising from his stomach to his head until he felt like he was being barbequed.

"Looks like the cavalry has arrived," Haley said.

"We'll see about that," Drake said. "We'll see."

26

Classroom 119 was on the ground floor of the school that housed most of Tetu's K-12 children. Rain lashed the island, and a stiff wind rattled the windowpanes. The governor had decided not to have the status update at Town Hall because the front steps were filled with fishermen and concerned citizens. The death of Rando Keel in Teapot Cove the prior day had wiped away any doubts that there was something dangerous prowling the shallows around the island, though there was no shortage of opinions as to what that dangerous thing might be. Drake's unofficial count had a Great White well ahead of the second-place fish, bull sharks. There were no votes for a rabid Barracuda swarm.

As the main witness, Drake had been invited to the meeting to repeat his tale. Present were Markus Debenou, Chief of Police, Governor Kip Trainer, Lieutenant Yesmire Krinkle from St. Croix, and her four support officers, who sat in the back of the room and hadn't said a word. Feddi was in attendance, Prof. Wexford, as well as representatives from the US and British consulates, and Jarred Abonya, head of Tetu's marine bureau, which consisted of himself, one other patrolman, and the old SAFE boat that had assisted Feddi when he'd plucked Drake from the Caribbean.

Drake's leg wound shrieked. He'd gotten preliminary medical attention, but before his head had hit the rack he'd gone to the hospital, where the docs gave him eighteen stitches, and a bottle of antibiotics to ward off any antibacterial infections, which had been on the rise in the calm, warm, Caribbean Sea.

Governor Trainer sat at the front of the room with Chief Debenou, and nobody had said a word since Drake finished his story. Trainer looked tense, foot tapping, eyes shifting to his chief of police every few moments. Kip Trainer was a transplant from Chicago, where he'd served as deputy mayor for two full terms. He wore standard island business attire: khaki slacks with a white golf shirt and blue blazer with big gold buttons. His face was sunburned, his nose peeling, and as he cleared his throat, jowls jiggling, he made eye contact with Drake. "Well, that's some story," he said.

"I mean no offense, Mr. Drake, but what proof do you have to present?" Debenou said.

"Guess you don't read your email," Drake said. "You've gotten numerous pictures and video clips over the last twenty-four hours."

Here the rep from St. Croix piped-up. "I've seen them," said Officer Krinkle. She wore a squared away uniform with a crisp white shirt that complemented her brown skin, her black hair wound in a tight knot atop her head. She had piercing blue eyes, the kind of eyes you could lose yourself in forever. "They're quite disturbing and appear to show a school of Barracuda attacking Mr. Drake's boat."

Governor Trainer waved a hand. "That's impossible, Lieutenant, and you know it. Barracuda don't travel in schools."

"They're antisocial," Debenou added.

"Yeah, well, I know what I saw." She looked sidelong at Drake and threw him a smile. Did he have an ally? "The question as I see it," Krinkle said, "isn't what is killing people, but when and how? If it's a shark, they don't normally hunt people. The sharks in these parts get plenty of food when they want it, and rarely do they wander close to shore." She shook her head. "And it doesn't matter. Whatever took down Mr. Drake's boat, and presumably killed the others, was definitely more than one fish. Watch the video."

"What do you propose we do?" Trainer said.

"Have you questioned this guy Ratson?" Krinkle asked.

Rain lashed the windows, dark clouds rolling over the island like smoke.

"So…." Krinkle said.

Debenou sighed. "We've checked out the island," he said as he looked at Drake. "But we didn't find anything."

Drake slapped his thighs and Governor Trainer jumped in his seat a little. "Feddi went on a guided tour. Only looked at what Ratson showed him." Drake threw up his hands. "I told you," he said. "They must have moved everything. They had plenty of time."

"And these… zombie Barracuda? What did he do with them?" Debenou asked.

"He put them in the sea and ordered them to kill me! Where the hell have you all been? You've seen the report from Dr.

Weston and Dr. Piper from the University of Miami. These things have nanobots in them. It's undisputable."

Prof. Wexford grunted, but said nothing.

"What is disputable…," said the governor, who'd gotten more than half of his campaign funds, and many of his votes, thanks to Ratson, "… is that it was Mr. Ratson who created the bots. Or that he was involved at all."

Prof. Wexford cleared his throat.

"Yes, Professor, you have something to add?" the governor said.

"I think, perhaps, you don't understand what a technical marvel these nanobots are. A handful of labs in the entire world can design and manufacture the bots in these fish. I've never seen anything like them, and they're definitely coded and locked up tight."

A spark zapped Drake's brain, and he blurted, "Can they be hacked?"

Professor Weston shook his head. "I don't know, but I doubt it. To make a fundamental change to the bots, one must first get inside them, and that will take an expertise far beyond mine, beyond anyone I know."

"How do you think he's controlling them? A radio frequency?" Drake said.

"Maybe, but even if the fish aren't programmed to do anything specific, there's still a swarm of rabid Barracuda around, looking to eat. If Ratson—"

"That's enough!" Governor Trainer interrupted. "I will not allow you to assume Mr. Ratson did this. Until I have proof, I—"

"What?" Drake said, a bit too loudly. "I'm lying about everything? That he destroyed Scar's skiff, took him hostage, and then killed him? Just like he tried to do to me? And why wasn't Haley Right asked to come to this meeting? She saw, very clearly, the horde take down Julian, and Mrs. Longly saw her husband killed by the swarm. Why isn't she here?"

Debenou said, "Without any proof, any bodies, nothing, what do you want us to do?"

Drake pushed to his feet, leg wound protesting. "Something. That's what. Do something."

"We could try and find the creatures," Krinkle said. "Take them out before they do any more damage?"

Drake shook his head. "How would we do that? It would be like trying to catch smoke; the things are fast and move as one."

"Wish you would have gotten us an actual sample of one of them," Trainer said.

Drake had to grudgingly admit he'd screwed up there. There'd been numerous opportunities for him to snag a dead specimen, but in his panicked flight from Kraken Island it hadn't occurred to him.

"What if we trapped them?" It was the first time Feddi had spoken and everyone turned to him. "I responded with Abonya to the scene in Teapot Cove yesterday. Gave me a thought. Perhaps we could trap them in the bay."

"What? Lure them in with a chum slick or something?" Debenou said.

"Exactly."

"One hitch," Drake said. "These things are being controlled. Ratson won't take the bait."

"What if the bait was you?" Krinkle said. Drake didn't know if he wanted to kiss her, or punch her in the jaw.

"What are you suggesting, Officer Krinkle?" Trainer said. "That I authorize you and Mr. Drake here to harass one of the island's most important people?"

Drake had had enough. His bullshit filter was full, two of his friends were dead, and this dipshit was worrying about protecting someone that not only didn't need his help, but didn't deserve it. He got to his feet and walked to the front of the room.

Trainer stared up at him, his face indignant.

Drake put his palms on the table and leaned in close, so his face was a foot from Trainer's. "Now you listen up, you little pissant." Trainer started to protest. "Shut up!"

Rain. Wind. Air moving through a vent.

"This is the real deal, and whether you believe my story or not, it's true. You want to go down for this? That's what's going to happen if you ignore this, put your head in the sand. For what? So Ratson can contribute to your next campaign?"

Debenou said, "You're out of line, Dra—"

Drake slammed his fists on the table. "Out of line? Four people are dead, and you're worried about saving Ratson? I will make it my mission in life to make sure every person on the face of this planet knows you let this happen. You will go down, and Ratson will simply pick a new lap dog."

Debenou appeared next to Drake and put a hand on his arm. "Come on, Drake, take it easy."

Drake shook the man off and looked him in the eye. "What happened to you? You used to be an upstanding cop. When did you go dirty?"

Debenou's face went red and he balled his fists, but said nothing.

"O.K.," said Krinkle. "That's enough."

Everyone looked at her, the governor's mouth twisting and Debenou's eyes going wide. Drake smiled.

"Mr. Drake, are you willing to go on patrol with us—as an observer only—show us the spots?" Krinkle asked.

Drake nodded.

"Can you get a chum together?" Krinkle asked.

"No, but I know someone who can," Drake said.

"Good. Debenou, put out an all-points bulletin. No boats are to leave the island in the next twenty-four hours, and nobody is to go in the water."

Trainer said, "That's not possible. Do you know what it costs to come here? Thousands of dollars for a week in paradise, and you want me to tell them they can't snorkel and go fishing? They'll hang me by my toes from the Town Hall flagpole."

"Do I look like I care?" Krinkle said. "My job is to protect the public. Drake is right. Go ahead, don't follow my orders. St. Croix will love it when we make the news up north and it comes out you didn't listen to the pros they sent in. They love that shit."

"How do you plan to keep them in the bay if you manage to trap them? It sounds insane even saying it," Trainer said.

"Working on that part," Krinkle said.

"Let's say you manage to trap them. Then what?" Debenou said.

"We kill them," Drake said.

For the next hour the group debated methods for killing the swarm without sending a noxious cloud through the Caribbean Sea.

"Perhaps we can change the composition of the water? Use poison?" Trainer said.

Dr. Wexford said, "I had a colleague, Dr. Sun Wah Lee. She died out at the drop off when Tranquility Base was destroyed. She did all kinds of studies on water composition, trying to determine what was causing the die off out there."

"Do you know what really happened?" Debenou asked. "I heard the storm wasn't the only thing that took the place down."

"Quite right," Wexford said. "They were overrun by mutant sea creatures. Rabid sea spiders."

The room fell still, and Drake heard Trainer's heavy breathing in the stillness, rain pounding the island, thunder booming and rattling windows.

"Any possible connection?" Drake asked.

"None that I can see. Based on the data, scientists believe the mutation that occurred at the drop off was a derivation of zombie deer disease."

"How the hell did it get all the way out there?" Trainer asked.

Wexford hiked his shoulders. "Nobody knows, but there was no mention of nanobots, or a drug called SeaFree."

There it was. The proverbial elephant in the room.

"So, why did you bring it up?" Trainer said.

"Because, Sun Wah's research on the toxicity of sea water could help us kill these things. Maybe come up with a poison that's specific to Barracuda," Wexford said.

Drake had been paying close attention, but now he thought Wexford had gone off the rails and judging by all the frowns and shaking heads, he wasn't alone in his disappointment.

"There's no time for that," Krinkle said.

"Electricity?" Debenou ventured.

"Possible," Krinkle said. "Might kill them and wouldn't leave residue in the water."

"There are people who fish with explosives," Feddi said.

Everyone looked his way again. "Sounds crazy, I know, but explosives and the ensuing shock waves created by carefully placed charges could be enough."

"And explosives we've got," Debenou said. Blasting coral to build roads and house foundations was standard practice, and it wasn't uncommon for the peace on Two Mile Beach to be disturbed by the crack and pop of dynamite breaking away centuries of hardened coral.

"Let's prepare for multiple options," Krinkle said, taking control again. Drake marveled at the ease with which the woman commanded the room and took all the wind out of the governor's sails. He liked the woman, maybe like wasn't the right word. "Drake and my crew will head out and search for the swarm. Debenou, get the bulletin out, then gather all the big boats you can, preferably metal. You know, ferries and the like. Bring them to the mouth of Simpson Bay and await my orders." She looked around at the rest of the group and zeroed in on Feddi. "Officer Feddi, prepare to execute your fishing by bomb plan, and Dr. Wexford, give me something better than bombs."

The Prof. nodded vigorously and got to his feet.

"I'll report back to St. Croix, let them know how helpful you're all being." Krinkle looked at Trainer and smiled.

The governor looked down at the table, tapping his fingers like he had somewhere more important to be.

With preliminary plans laid, and the island's inhabitants cared for, Drake's mind drifted to Haley and his crew. Scar... Julian. The eggs he had for breakfast sat in his stomach like a spoiled piece of fish, bile inching up from his stomach and burning his throat. He rolled his shoulders as he got up, pain running through his sore muscles. He'd gotten little sleep the prior night, the sound of Scar's screaming and Julian going under in a mound of red tinged whitewater filling his head. There would be a reckoning, he'd see to that, and his friends would be remembered. Avenged. Anger and frustration nibbled and gnawed, and all he could think of was the Barracuda swarm, and how Ratson would look as he was torn to ribbons by his own creation.

27

"Thank you for back there," Drake said. "For believing me." Drake and Krinkle walked down main dock, her support team following behind. A thin mist hung in the air as the storm moved out and sunrays broke through the cloud cover like spotlights from Heaven. It was low tide, and the air smelled of rot and decay, but beneath it, Drake caught the scent of Krinkle's perfume, a deep floral scent he recognized, but couldn't name. Beach something. A steady offshore wind pushed around the boats in the harbor, providing another, more palatable reason for keeping the charters and swimmers in for the day.

"Not to worry," Krinkle said. "I'm having trouble finding your motive for lying. The governor, however…" She rolled her eyes.

"So, the folks on St. Croix know how things go here, huh?"

"Of course. We pay more attention than most folks think, and we keep in constant contact with the Brits, share information, so it's like Tetu has two police forces."

Drake nodded. He hated dealing with the British police. They were so damn formal and polite, even on the speck of coral and sand that was Tetu.

"You should know that Tetu isn't much different from all the other small islands. Most folks up north don't know Tetu even exists. Never heard of it, so politics on these rocks tend to get incestuous, personal, and dirty."

They arrived at the large gray police boat, its floodlights dark. The boat didn't shift or sway in the gentle surf. Haley stood in the vessel's shadow next to the gangway that led up to the police boat's main deck, a white sealed bucket stained with age and fish guts next to her.

"Lieutenant Krinkle, I'd like you to meet Ms. Haley Right."

Krinkle held out her hand and smiled.

Haley took the woman's hand, an awkward grin spreading over her face. A smile that said, "What is this hot woman in uniform doing hanging out with my man?" The thought made Drake smile inwardly, his face expressionless.

"That our magic sauce?" Krinkle said.

Haley's brow knitted, then she nodded vigorously. "There's rotten fish, some oil and alcohol to break it down, a dead cat, and several fish heads and pints of tuna blood I got from Chance. It's been percolating for a few hours. Don't open the bucket until you're ready to use the stuff, then ladle it into the sea slowly. You don't need much." She handed them both cloth facemasks.

"That bad?" Drake said.

Haley nodded. "Any chance you've changed your mind about letting me come with you?"

Drake said, "No way. We need you at Salt Lick anyway." Dr. Wexford was working on a chemical that they hoped would kill the fish, but he'd been concerned the compounds might do permanent damage to Teapot Cove so the decision was made to move the containment attempt to Salt Lick Cove, a tiny coral bay surrounded by crumbling coral cliffs that looked like salt.

Haley nodded. "See you over there?"

"You bet," Drake said. Haley was taking the Mary Queen around with Helen. Jillian, Kendra, and Marley were to remain on land as backup, but Drake didn't believe for a second the kids and the widow would stay behind. No, they'd be on the Mary Queen with Haley, and Drake couldn't blame them. The swarm had taken Jillian's brother, and the crew was all Marley had in the world.

Haley walked away and a surge of sorrow ran through Drake, a feeling of loss and worry so strong he almost ran to her side and pulled her into his arms. Instead he stood watching her, a feeling that he was never going to see her again burrowing into him like a worm, setting up camp and burning his nerves for kindling, pain stabbing his back like someone was massaging him with a saw blade.

Krinkle stopped halfway up the gangway and turned back to Drake. "You coming?"

Haley disappeared between two boats and Drake went cold. "Yeah," he said. He rolled his shoulders and cracked his neck, trying to chase away the angst, and failing. He tore his eyes away from where Haley had been and started up the gangway. "You hear from Feddi?" he asked, just to make conversation. He knew what Feddi was doing and where he was.

Krinkle continued up to main deck. "Yeah. He's got some dynamite with blasting caps, and two generators with a few extension cords." She shook her head. "I've got to admit, though I'm not an electrician, the electricity idea sounds loco. Won't the generator blow up if he drops live cords in salt water?"

Drake shook his head no. "While I agree the electricity option should only be used as an extreme last resort, it might work. Salt greatly enhances the conductivity of water, and unless the power arcs back, the current should run endlessly into the Caribbean with no backlash. Theoretically."

She pursed her lips and opened the door to the bridge.

"Like you said, we're no electricians. Let's hope the doc comes up with something better," Drake said.

"Worst comes to worst, we nuke Salt Lick," she said.

Drake nodded. If only it was that simple.

The sun arced past noon as Krinkle piloted the police boat from Simpson Bay, the two SAFE boats flanking her on either side. The Mary Queen, two ferries, and several other large fishing boats trailed behind the police boats, as backup, and would clog the entrance to Salt Lick Cove when the order was given. In the meantime, everybody would search for the swarm.

When the police boats were cutting across the strait between Kraken and Tetu Islands, Drake gave Krinkle a mask. She eyed it suspiciously and didn't take her hands off the ship's wheel. Drake knew the modern vessel could be piloted by computer, but Krinkle preferred the old school approach.

Drake nudged the mask toward her.

"I'm staying in here. Don't need it," she said.

Drake raised an eyebrow and she frowned.

"On second thought," she said as she took the mask and slipped it on.

Out on deck, Drake peeled open the chum bucket like it was filled with nuclear waste. He'd smelled Haley's special sauce before, and it never failed to make him gag, mask or not. He felt the contents of his breakfast fighting for daylight, but he breathed deep and pushed it back down as he scooped some of the chum into a small container. He spilled the concoction slowly into the sea as Krinkle moved the boat out of the strait. The chum slick would be carried for miles in the current. Small fish were already knifing through the nasty oil that coated the surface, chunks of rancid fish meat and cat floating in the undulating water.

A couple of bull sharks swam through the slick, some dolphins, a school of porgy, but no Barracuda. Drake was getting a headache staring through the binoculars, the rolling sea twisting and churning his stomach, the scent of the chum nauseating.

Half the chum was gone, and the sun was long past noon when Feddi came tearing up in Tetu's police SAFE boat.

Feddi stepped from the pilothouse as the SAFE boat bumped into the St. Croix police boat, inflatable gunnels squeaking. "Ahoy," he yelled.

Krinkle looked at Drake and shook her head.

Drake yelled down at the officer. "Yo, any luck?"

Feddi shook his head. "Nothing. You have any chum left? I'll hit the western side of Kraken Island. They wo…"

Won't mess with me, Drake thought and smiled. Feddi was coming around. "Yeah, I've got some left. Hang on." Drake got a length of line, tied one end to the bucket's metal handle, and lowered it down to Feddi.

"Where are the other two police boats?" Feddi asked as he received the chum.

"Patrolling," Drake said. They were probably sunning themselves on Boot Tip Point. Hell, that's what he'd be doing if all he had to go on was some dude's crazy story.

"10-4. I'll be in touch," Feddi said. He spun the motors and the SAFE boat leapt from the sea, the roar of the engine fading as the boat arced west.

Drake checked in with Haley, who'd seen nothing. She was drifting along Two Mile Beach, keeping an eye on the entrance to Teapot Cove. When she reached the entrance to Salt Lick Cove, she'd start the engines, head north, and start the process again.

The sun had started its descent to the horizon, a bruised sky giving way to dark clouds, when Krinkle said, "We need to be more mobile." She called in one of the SAFE boats and she and Drake replaced the officers, who would man the large boat. "Call us if you see anything," she said, as she dropped the throttle arm, the engine screaming.

Krinkle piloted the SAFE boat around Kraken Island, letting up on the throttle so Drake could scan the shoreline with binoculars. Nothing moved along the shore except guards and the entrance to Deep Hollow Cove was blocked with boats pretending to do research.

"I guess this guy Ratson is a bit more patient than we gave him credit for," Krinkle said. "He doesn't appear to be taking the bait." She pushed the throttle all the way down and peeled east, cutting across a rough line of breakers, the SAFE boat bouncing and listing.

Drake gripped the handhold on the command console, the boat jumping and skipping through the surf, throwing thick spray. His mind wandered as he watched Krinkle, a thin sheen of moisture forming on her mirrored sunglasses, her dark skin slick with sweat. She looked tough, yet still managed to look feminine, but Drake felt none of the normal urges. He was attracted to her, but something held him back. He knew what it was, but didn't want to admit it. He kept going back to that feeling he'd had when Haley left him earlier. That sick, deepening dread that made him want to puke. The thought of losing her...

"You alright there, cowboy?" Krinkle said.

Drake chuckled. "Cowboy? Far from it."

It was her turn to laugh. "No, mon, you don't see. All you buffalo soldiers are cowboys." She turned and smiled at him, and Drake knew she was pulling his chain.

"Fair enough," Drake said. "Having tourists trashing your home must be hard to see on a daily basis. I lived on an island when I was a kid, and every Summer people would come out from the city. Rude, entitled assholes would crowd my surf spots, my hangouts, and get pissed when they had to wait for five minutes."

"You go," Krinkle said.

"Just saying I get you," he said. "I used to hate tourists."

"Until you became one?"

He said nothing.

The radio crackled and ended the awkward break in the conversation.

"Krinkle here," she said.

"This is the Mary Queen, over."

Drake took the handset. "We hear you, Haley. What's up?"

"Fish finder showing crazy activity and it looks like we've got a fairly large field of whitewater advancing on a pod of dolphin playing off Two Mile Beach. There's a crowd on shore taking pictures."

"I'll notify Feddi and the others," Drake said. "On our way. Out."

Before Drake could close the channel, Krinkle was spinning the ship's wheel, arcing the boat in the tight turn that would take them back east, engine wailing.

"I see them," Drake said. He had the binoculars pressed to his face, the eye scopes jamming into his eye sockets every time the SAFE boat bounced or jumped. A thin trail of dissipating white smoke marked the Mary Queen's position off the port bow.

Feddi's SAFE boat circled in from the north and was almost to the Mary Queen.

Drake scanned the surface of the sea, but saw only undulating inky water. The seconds flew by, the SAFE boat skipping and hopping, Krinkle's eyes locked on the Mary Queen.

"Drake!" Haley's voice trumpeted from the radio.

Drake grabbed the handset, and said, "We're almost to you. What's wrong?"

"It's here," she said. "The swarm."

"Hang on. They can't get to you. Don't panic. We're almost there," Drake said.

A hollow boom reverberated over the Caribbean. Then another, like faint mortar fire.

"What's happening?" Drake yelled into the radio.

"Feddi's dropping explosives in the water," Haley yelled.

Krinkle drew back the throttle as the SAFE boat screamed onto the scene.

The swarm surrounded the Mary Queen, a roiling mass of scales, teeth, and driving tailfins. Whitewater frothed along the Mary Queen's gunnels, but the surging horde was still well below main deck, and the Mary Queen was made of steel.

Feddi's SAFE boat, however, like Krinkle's, had inflatable gunnels. Feddi's boat circled the swarm, the boat jumping its own wake, Feddi hanging over the transom dropping dynamite.

With each explosion a spout of seawater would spout from the sea, a spiraling swirl of dead Barracuda and blood, but it didn't look like he was even making a dent in the horde. Hundreds of rabid Barracuda still pushed and surged forward, fighting to get at Feddi, whose SAFE boat peeled off and made a wide turn, preparing for another attack run.

The swarm came at the boats from all angles, some attacking as others circled. They didn't appear to be working together, and some of the fish weren't doing anything, just floating still, gills flaring, red rimmed eyes staring up through the clear water.

Krinkle didn't ask for advice, or Drake's opinion. She didn't even look his way as she pressed the throttle arm down as far as it would go and knifed through the swarm.

The engine coughed and sputtered like the boat was cutting through seaweed, blood, bone, white flesh, and Barracuda entrails splattering the gunnels and deck as Krinkle powered through the horde, wiggling the SAFE boat's wheel to maximize the damage.

Suddenly the swarm moved as one, the cloud of Barracuda pulling together and coming at Krinkle and Drake.

The lieutenant arced the SAFE boat north, pulling the vessel out of its turn, fish guts and blood shooting from the engine's exhaust ports.

The swarm followed.

28

"Incoming!" Drake yelled into the handset. The SAFE boat surged through the growing surf, throwing spray thirty feet out, the hull bouncing and listing. Sunlight cut through the clouds, the scent of sea rot filling his nostrils.

A field of dimpled whitewater trailed behind, Barracuda cutting in and out of the boat wake.

"We're not ready, Drake!" Haley boomed over the radio.

Drake shook his head.

"The professor just arrived with his concoction and it will take a few minutes for us to get to Salt Lick." Static snapped and popped.

"How long do you need?" Drake asked. He looked over his shoulder and saw the field of whitewater gaining, his gaze shifting back to the narrow opening that led to Salt Lick Cove. Several vessels, minus the Mary Queen, bobbed in the surf on both sides of the narrow channel.

"Five minutes," Haley said.

"Fine, I'll tell the others to block the entrance as soon as the swarm enters the cove," Drake said. Sweat dripped down his back, worry gnawing at him like a cancer. The channel that led into Salt Lick Cove was shallow, but still eight feet in places. "You hear back from your buddies?"

"Affirmative," Haley said. "I've got a bunch of nets, and two with the reinforced Kevlar strands."

"Great, you think they'll hold?"

"Hopefully they won't need to. Kill them, Drake. Don't mess around."

"Make sure those nets are doubled, and pack the boats into the entrance as tight as you can." Drake had wanted to blow-up the cliffs and seal the channel, but his crew didn't think it would work and was too dangerous.

Krinkle made a slight course adjustment, giving the cluster of boats on both sides of the channel a wide birth. The swarm adjusted course and followed as the SAFE boat zipped through the narrow channel into Salt Lick Cove, Feddi falling in behind.

Salt Lick Cove was usually a tourist attraction and normally there was a string of boats from one end of the small bay to the other. All types of fish enjoyed the calm, sheltered water, even sharks and dolphins. On this day the cove was free of boats, the bad weather and mandate from St. Croix holding sway.

Tall, white, crumbling coral cliffs lined all sides of the cove, a thin crushed shell beach running around the entire bay. The Caribbean looked even more blue against the walls of white. Tiny fish leapt from the water, and the dorsal fins of dolphins slashed through the calm sea.

A fist of whitewater rose from the sea and rolled into Salt Lick Cove like a tidal wave, breaking over the surface and spreading out like an avalanche.

Feddi arced his boat right, and Krinkle broke left, trying to split the swarm, but the horde stayed locked on Drake's boat.

"Drake, we're ready." Haley's voice sounded steady.

Drake got close to Krinkle so she could hear him, and the intoxicating scent of her perfume tickled his nose. "They're ready with the poison. How do—"

A roar of a generator starting rose above the outboards. The zap and buzz of electricity arced over the cove, spider thin fingers of power reaching into the sea.

Fish leapt from the water, scales darkened, eyes black.

The SAFE boat's outboard sputtered, belched black smoke, and stalled. "Shit. Shit. Shit," Krinkle yelled as she spun the motor.

Drake gripped the handhold on the command console and peered through the binoculars.

One of Feddi's men piloted their boat, turning in a wide zigzagging circle that was bringing him back in Drake's direction. The officer was still feeding extension cord into the water. "He's trying to fry them," Drake said.

It was working, but not well enough.

The swarm pressed on, surging into Feddi's boat as he fed extension cord into the sea. Barracuda bubbled to the surface, red eyes bloody, bloated swim bladders keeping the dead creatures on the surface.

Metal screeched on metal as the SAFE boat's engine's flywheels spun, Krinkle urging the motor on, willing it to start.

Drake had just enough time to wonder if the electricity in the water had done permanent damage to the motor, when to his surprise the engine rumbled to life with a wheeze that settled into a steady murmur.

Krinkle eased the boat up on plane, the swarm boiling from the cove, a knot of whitewater lifting over the bow like a cresting wave. She tugged hard on the ship's wheel, driving the bow to port. The boat bucked and whined, but didn't stall.

The shriek of a dying machine echoed over the cove, and the generator Feddi had been using puffed white smoke and caught fire. He and another officer threw it overboard, but in the ten seconds it took the officers to regain their positions, the horde was upon them.

The Barracuda swarm drove from the water in a massive, coordinated torrent of teeth and scales. Whitewater bubbled over Feddi's boat, its inflatable gunnels going flat, the pilothouse sinking into the turbulent sea.

"Drake!"

The shriek from the radio made Drake remember Haley. "Here," he screamed into the handset.

"I'm coming in on a tender with the poison," Haley said.

"No!" The fierceness with which he yelled made Krinkle look in his direction, but he couldn't see her eyes behind her mirrored shades. Realizing he'd been… overzealous in his response, AKA an asshole, Drake attempted a quick recovery. "We're on our way. Stay put."

"No we're not," Krinkle said. She'd set course for Feddi's sinking vessel.

"Haley! Haley!" No response. Drake thrust the handset back into its cradle.

Krinkle didn't take her eyes off the sea as she pointed the boat's bow toward the cove entrance.

"Son of an onion," Drake said.

A center console eased through the blockade, pushing through the sea, Haley at the controls.

So many thoughts rammed their way into Drake's head he couldn't put them in order. Feddi was going down, the swarm was attacking, and the woman he loved was sailing into it like she was on a fishing charter. A zap of pain marched down his spine and planted an icepick in his lower back.

The woman he loved?

Drake had never had an epiphany before. He'd never fallen in love at first sight. Never gotten a glimpse of his future in a dream, or a flash of clarity. So when it hit him, finally struck home, it felt so obvious and right he didn't understand how he'd never seen it before. He loved Haley, or thought he might, or could. He jerked the handset from the UHF.

"Haley," he called. "Head back now. Do you understand? Haley? Pick up. Please."

Drake was about to yell at Krinkle, but his words caught in his throat.

An explosion rocked the day, a massive concussion that echoed off the cliffs like a Bose speaker. A fountain of water shot into the sky, Barracuda, pieces of Feddi's boat, and presumably Feddi and his crew, shooting into the sky like a bloody firework display.

In his final moments Feddi had ignited his explosives. Fish bubbled to the surface, dead Barracuda floating in the turbulent water.

The rest of the swarm didn't even slow down.

The mound of whitewater flattened, tiny whitecaps spreading over the surface, the horde shifting like oil, moving as one as it turned and re-engaged.

Krinkle eased up on the throttle and arced the SAFE boat toward the approaching center console. "You have any idea how they plan to…" she searched for the right words. "…administer the poison?"

Drake had no clue. He'd assumed they'd just dump the stuff in the water, but that sounded too simplistic. He said, "Not sure, but I'm thinking we create a slick like we did with the chum. The tide is coming in, right?"

She nodded. The tides on Tetu were minimal, but coves felt the change in water depth more than the shorelines, and the steady stream of seawater pushing into the bay would help contain the poison. In addition, the boats blocking the channel would use their motors and the driving force of their props to send a torrent of water into the cove. Not long-term solutions, and cleanup might be needed, but Drake and his team hadn't been thinking beyond sunset.

The casualness with which Drake considered his own death startled him. He'd always been a worrier, but suddenly he didn't care about anything except getting to Haley and making sure she was safe. What happened after that, happened.

A waterspout rose from behind the crowd of boats at the cove entrance, and Drake couldn't help but smile. A whale was swimming past the chaos, investigating what all the commotion was about.

It hit Drake like the realization he loved Haley. "Krinkle, I've got an idea."

The marine officer looked over her shoulder and saw the swarm surging toward the boat, and said, "I'm all ears."

The sight of the whale spout brought an image up from the basement of Drake's mind. His ship had been heading for Boston, and was cruising past the mouth of Cape Cod Bay when Drake and his crew were treated to a rare sight.

Whales were feeding, the big boys going in circles, spiraling downward, containing a school of minnows, the other whales in the pod knifing through the trapped fish, feasting.

Drake called into the radio, "Pick up, Haley."

A male voice Drake didn't recognize boomed from the comm. Pain poked his stomach, the fire of jealousy licking his throat. Drake didn't know who the guy was, and they were minutes from possible death, and Drake felt jealous. If that didn't confirm his feelings for Haley, he didn't know what did.

"Drake, what is it? Haley is occupied."

Drake contained the frustration that threatened to release his surging anger and explained his plan.

The swarm bubbled from the cove, and Krinkle took evasive action, jerking the wheel back and forth, the outboard whining.

Across the cove, Haley's center console turned in a wide arc, spiraling inward.

Krinkle piloted the SAFE boat in the opposite direction, also spiraling inward.

The swarm followed, Barracuda breaching from the sea in the boat's wake, red rimmed eyes focused, jaws flexing. The roiling knot of fish rose above the surface, the Barracuda mounding and pushing over one another, surging from the sea.

Haley was two hundred yards away, her circles getting tighter as she got closer.

Krinkle tightened her turn, the swarm shifting and writhing as it followed.

Precious seconds ticked away as the two boats circled inward, each pass bringing them tighter, the swarm rising in the SAFE boat's wake.

Haley guided her boat to the outside of the spiral, Drake and Krinkle circling inside her radius, the swarm in the spinning whirlpool created by the two vessels.

"Now. Come on," Drake said, willing Haley on, sending mental vibes Drake hoped she'd receive. It was insane, but when you've got next to nothing, you hold on to what you do have.

On Haley's boat, two men worked on a stainless-steel cylinder that looked like it had contained pressurized gas at one point.

Krinkle whooped.

Like a giant bug spray applicator, one of the men held a black hose, liquid shooting from its end. The guy arced the spray back and forth like he was working a flame thrower, the dark poison spreading across the cove like sewage in clear water.

An earsplitting, high-pitched wail echoed over Salt Lick Cove as the Barracuda sucked the poison into their gills, their insides turning to jelly.

The horde gathered itself and writhed in the water, then split into two swarms, one surging toward Drake's SAFE boat.

"Oh shit," Krinkle said.

The second wave of teeth and scales rolled toward Haley, whitewater bubbling, the field of whitecaps growing in size. Fish screamed as they died, piercing wails that sounded like cockroaches being cooked alive.

Krinkle cycled up the engine and the boat jumped from the water, outboard wailing.

All the poison was in the drink, and the two men who'd been working with the sprayer backed away from the gunnel, the sea fizzing as Salt Lick Cove boiled.

Haley's center console launched from the water, rising twenty feet in the air as the swarm came together in a torrent of scales and teeth, driving the vessel from the sea, whitewater frothing over the boat's gunnels. The vessel's engine sputtered and died, and Haley, along with her two helpers, were tossed from the boat as the vessel splashed down with a thunderous crash.

The swarm mounded over the sinking boat like bees on a honeycomb and the white fiberglass hull disappeared under the surging sea.

Krinkle jammed her hand down on the SAFE boat's throttle control arm, but the engine was already maxed and pushing 4000RPM.

The knot of whitewater was dissipating, the swarm spreading out, looking for a new target. Haley's center console broke the surface, its Bimini top shredded, its deck swamped. Like the SAFE boat, many vessels had Styrofoam between the outer and inner hulls, allowing the boat to stay afloat even after it was filled with water.

Haley swam for her boat.

"Yes, that's it," Krinkle yelled. They were almost to her, and Krinkle's SAFE boat had begun to slice through Barracuda, the engines coughing and sputtering as the propellor diced fish to chum.

One of Haley's crew, the guy who'd been working the spray nozzle, appeared next to her, swimming hard as he put himself between Haley and the dying swarm, trying to protect Haley's blindside.

The swarm shifted like oil that's been poured in vinegar. It gathered itself, the mound of fish building, dark eyes locked on Haley and her rescuer.

Drake didn't know the man's name, but Haley owed her life to the guy.

With prey in their path the swarm didn't shift or deviate. With a scream of pain that sounded like the man's skin was being torn from his body, Haley's savior went under in a bloody knot of whitewater and didn't come back up.

Fifty yards away, Haley's second crew member was dragged under, his cries for help strangled as his mouth filled with water.

Krinkle pulled back on the throttle and jammed it in reverse. The outboard bucked and wailed, but the SAFE boat came to a rocking stop beside Haley's sinking center console.

Drake grabbed Haley under her arms and pulled her aboard.

Krinkle pushed the throttle arm down, and the SAFE boat tore across the field of dimpled whitewater, chewing through what was left of the swarm. She went in circles, the horde chasing the SAFE boat, and each time the rabid Barracuda sliced through the cloud of poison at the center of the cove, more fish floated to the surface, bloated and dead, red rimmed eyes dark and glassy.

Drake helped Haley to her feet and hugged her so tight she squealed.

"You O.K., Drake?"

"I am now. I am now."

The hum of the outboard lessened as Krinkle eased up on the throttle. The SAFE boat came to a halting stop, bobbing in its wake.

The clear bathtub that had been Salt Lick Cove was shrouded in a crimson cloud of blood, and hundreds of dead Barracuda clogged the surface, their swim bladders full, eyes dead, fins still. The scales glistened in the sunlight, the scent of chemicals and fish floating on the breeze.

29

Drake and Haley sat in beach chairs at the end of Boot Tip Point, their feet in the Caribbean, the sweet scent of hibiscus carrying on the breeze. Seagulls squawked, the gentle static of crashing waves and the distant hum of an outboard filling the silence. The midday sun glared down, but the warmth felt good. Haley reached across the gap between them and put her hand on Drake's arm. They were going slow, but it felt so right Drake didn't know how long he'd be able to keep his engine at idle.

The Mary Queen was moored offshore, the small Zodiac they'd used to get to shore pulled onto the beach. Marley and Helen fished, knee-deep in the sea, their long black surfcasting poles dipping and jerking as they worked their reels. Jillian sat up the beach with Kendra. The two women had found solace in each other, having both lost someone close.

A plastic cooler sat between Drake and Haley's chairs, a beer and a rum and coke sitting on its top and sweating in the heat. A tablet was propped up on its case, and a football game in progress—Drake still thought of the sport as soccer, but when in Rome—a coach wailing about some perceived slight. Tetu's team wasn't very good and got beat badly by the other island teams on a regular basis, but that didn't stop the island from supporting their lads. Football games on the island were an event, and the Tetu team could be losing by ten goals and still people would stay until the end.

Drake took a pull of his rum, the sweet burn familiar and gratifying. He closed his eyes, his vision going pink as sunlight fought its way through his eyelids. He rolled his shoulders and took a deep breath, the air like perfume.

"Here it comes," Haley said as she reached forward and turned up the volume on the tablet.

The football game shifted to a lower corner of the screen, everyone standing around during a timeout. The main screen filled with a native woman with dark skin, long curly hair, wearing a blue floral pattern dress. She stood at the end of main dock in Simpson Harbor, people streaming past in the background.

"This is Yolanda Carbenal and I'm here to bring you the latest on the rash of deaths that have devastated our small community."

The news lady paused for effect and Drake rolled his eyes at Haley, who lifted her eyebrows.

"KGtv has learned that a rabid school of Barracuda, what the authorities are calling zombie fish, were responsible for the attacks and Tetu Island Police assure me the threat has been dealt with."

The picture shifted to a long shot of Salt Lick Cove. The camera zoomed in, focusing on the thick covering of dead Barracuda undulating and bobbing on the surface like a bloated silver carpet.

Then the fiction started to flow. "Despite Barracuda not typically traveling in schools, authorities theorize that the fish were somehow infected with a virus that caused their aggressive tendencies to be heightened. As you can see by the pictures we're showing now, the swarm has been terminated, and it's safe to go back in the water."

Drake's gaze shifted to Helen and Marley where they stood in the surf fishing, his nerves never fully at ease.

"In a related story, US federal agents from the Department of Homeland Security raided Kraken Island and though specifics have yet to be released due to the ongoing investigation, a warrant has been issued for the arrest of billionaire shipping magnet Sir Javier Ratson. Mr. Ratson wasn't on the island at the time of the raid, and is believed to have fled the area. More on this breaking story as new details become available."

The last few lines of her report was a voiceover as the picture went back to the football game in progress.

"I need a walk," Drake said. He got up, kissed Haley on the forehead, and headed down the beach away from his friends.

The Caribbean stretched out before him and he knew there was no place he'd rather be.

Something white floated in the sea and he waded into the water to see what it was.

A hibiscus flower floated in the current. One of the flowers from the remembrance ceremony they'd attended earlier in the day for all those lost. Drake picked the flower up, caressing it and rolling it in his palm. It wasn't his fault Scar, Julian, Feddi, and the others had died. He hadn't created the swarm, set it free on the world. But he did miss his friends, and he'd make sure no one ever forgot them.

A flash in the clear water caught his attention.

The sleek pencil-like shape of a Barracuda knifed through the sea. When it saw Drake it turned, its curved teeth glinting in the sunlight. The fish didn't have red rimmed eyes. At least Drake didn't think it did.

The End

Other Severed Press novels by Edward J. McFadden III: The Cryptid Club, Dinosaur Red, Drop Off, Jurassic Ark, Keepers of the Flame, Throwback, Sea Tremors, Primeval Valley, Shadow of the Abyss (#1 Amazon Bestseller), Awake, and The Breach (#1 Amazon Bestseller, Amazon #1 Hot New Audio Release). His other novels include Quick Sands – A Theo Ramage Thriller, Dogs Get Ten Lives, The Black Death of Babylon and HOAXERS. Ed is also the author/editor of: Anywhere But Here, Lucky 13, Jigsaw Nation, Deconstructing Tolkien: A Fundamental Analysis of The Lord of the Rings (re-released in eBook format Fall 2012 – Amazon Bestseller), Time Capsule, Epitaphs (W/ Tom Piccirilli), The Second Coming, Thoughts of Christmas, and The Best of Pirate Writings. His short stories have appeared in over 75 magazines and anthologies. He lives on Long Island with his wife Dawn, and their daughter Samantha.

Check out other great

Sea Monster Novels!

Edward J. McFadden III

SHADOW OF THE ABYSS

Out of the past comes an immense horror. An ancient creature that must feed its voracious hunger. A massive landslide on Grand Bahama Bank sends a thirty-foot wave traveling at 150MPH toward the east coast of Florida, and the tsunami drags in something horrible from the depths of the Mid-Atlantic Ridge rift valley. Now a monster roams Florida's east coast and its shallows, searching for prey. Matthew "Splinter" Woods lives in Sailfish Haven. He's a washed-out Navy SEAL who lives off the grid on his dilapidated boat and has withdrawn from society rather than face his demons. But when his ex-girlfriend, charter boat captain Lenah Brisbee, comes to him for help, Splinter gets drawn into a battle that pits him against the strongest enemy he's ever faced as he races against time to find the monster before it turns the waters he loves blood red.

Eric S. Brown

PIRANHA

The rains came, flooding the sleepy, little town of Sylva. Sheriff Hanson never thought that he would be fighting a battle to survive against real life monsters. . .but with the waters came flesh eating, hungry creatures that swept through Sylva's streets like locusts, devouring everyone in their path.

Check out other great

Sea Monster Novels!

Robert J. Stava

NEPTUNES RECKONING

At the easternmost end of Long Island lies a seaside town known as Montauk. Ground Zero on the Eastern seaboard for all manner of conspiracy theories involving it's hidden Cold War military base, rumors of time-travel experiments and alien visitors... For renowned Naval historian William Vanek it's the where his grandfather's ship went down on a Top Secret mission during WWII code-named "Neptune's Reckoning". Together with Marine Biologist Daniel Cheung and disgraced French underwater explorer Arnaud Navarre, he's about to discover the truth behind the urban legends: a nightmare from beyond space and time that has been reawakened by global warming and toxic dumping, a nightmare the government tried to keep submerged. Neptune's Reckoning. Terror knows no depth

Bestselling collection

DEAD BAIT

A husband hell-bent on revenge hunts a Wereshark... A Russian mail order bride with a fishy secret... Crabs with a collective consciousness... A vampire who transforms into a Candiru... Zombie piranha...Bait that will have you crawling out of your skin and more. Drawing on horror, humor with a helping of dark fantasy and a touch of deviance, these 19 contemporary stories pay homage to the monsters that lurk in the murky waters of our imaginations. If you thought it was safe to go back in the water... Think Again!

Check out other great
Sea Monster Novels!

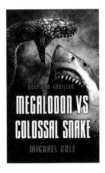

Michael Cole

MEGALODON VS COLOSSAL SNAKE

Brought to life by the miracle of DNA cloning, a 93-foot Megalodon shark has escaped captivity. With an insatiable appetite and unmatched aggression, it travels west for the Georgia coast, leaving a path of destruction in its wake. Bullets and harpoons can't penetrate it, steel nets can't hold it, and it's only a matter of time before the whole world finds out about it. In a race to stop the beast, the organization responsible recruit a marine biologist and a herpetologist to develop a plan to catch it. To do it, they must unleash the company's other genetically modified experiment—a 150-foot snake, resurrected from the DNA of the mighty Titanoboa. The pursuit leads to inevitable combat, and the scientists are forced to witness the deadly realities of genetic tampering. As the battle escalates, it is clear nobody is safe...and that nature never intended for these beasts to return. As the destruction mounts, and the death toll climbs, the true loser of Megalodon vs. Colossal Snake is humanity.

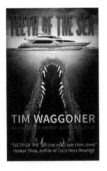

Tim Waggoner

TEETH OF THE SEA

They glide through dark waters, sleek and silent as death itself. Ancient predators with only two desires – to feed and reproduce. They've traveled to the resort island of Las Dagas to do both, and the guests make tempting meals. The humans are on land, though, out of reach. But the resort's main feature is an intricate canal system . . . . . . and it's starting to rain.

Printed in Great Britain
by Amazon